Mixed Feelings

A Gwen Arthur Novel

Olivia R. Burton

Second Edition. Mixed Feelings was previously published by Candlemark &
Gleam, November 2014, edited by Kate Sullivan.

Contributing Editor: Marika Gerow Verheijen

ISBN: 978-0-9976333-2-0

Peacock Deceiving a Suitcase
www.PeacockDeceivingASuitcase.com

OTHER TITLES

Gwen Arthur Series
Mixed Feelings
Business With Pleasure
Cold Feet
Hollow Back Girl
Change of Heart

~

Bone to Pick
Flesh and Blood
The Writer's Overnighter
Gut Feeling
Suckered In
Split Second

The Preternatural PNW
Rattle
Metal
Knell

~

Throb
Murmur

COLLABORATIONS
Passage Through Moonlight
The Godfather's Naughty Daughter
Song of the Argyle Goddess
Belladonna Clasped
Cash Grab

OLIVIA R. BURTON

CONTENTS

OLIVIA R. BURTON

DEDICATIONS

In no specific order, I'd like to give a shout out to my various friends and family who have had some sort of a hand in allowing me to create Gwen in all her cupcake-craving glory. So many thanks to Margaret Bishop: Plot Hunter for helping me work through the early versions of this series, and for helping me really understand my own characters.

My mom once gave me a copy of a magazine that celebrated history's most influential women and said I'd be one of them. I don't know if I quite believe her on that specifically, but if it wasn't for the confidence she helped me develop, I can't say you'd be reading this book.

Jenny Myers is and always will be (I hope!) my number one fan. She's stuck by every crappy version of every story I've given her to read, and begged me shamelessly for more.

Naomi Clark forever has my gratitude for answering my stupid publishing questions, passing on advice she earned through hard knocks, and for letting me meet her grizzled, food-crazed cat Fergus. R.I.P Fergus, the dribblingest cat there ever was.

Last—and, if you were to ask him, least—I need to thank my ex-husband Ryan Burton for never being bothered when I'd hide in my office writing for hours only to emerge and babble incoherently about my plans or frustrations. He always had it in him to make real encouraging sounds and hand gestures and sometimes that's all you really need.

OLIVIA R. BURTON

One

The best part of being an adult is being able to eat half a dozen cupcakes for dinner. The worst part of being an adult is the awareness of the fact that eating half a dozen cupcakes for dinner is bad for you. I decided to focus on the positives in life and go for it. You only turn twenty-nine once, and these birthday cupcakes weren't gonna eat themselves. Or, if they were, I was damn well going to beat them to it.

It was one week past my birthday and, quite frankly, I was surprised I had any cupcakes left. Yes, even considering the fact that my baby brother, my best friend, and a werewolf I hated had each sent me enough baked goods to feed ten children's birthday parties. After all, I'm aces at taking down pastry in ways that would shame a lesser woman. The only reason I'm not bigger than my house is that my best friend-slash-assistant Chloe forces me to work most of it off at the gym several times a week.

My mother had begged me to come home to Montana for my birthday but, as I do nearly every year, I had given my reasons for why I couldn't. This year, my reasons were entirely valid, which wasn't always the case. I love my family, but it's safer for my father and me if we stay a few states apart.

At the moment, though, I was counseling a woman in the middle of a divorce, and taking time off to eat cake and blow out candles seemed unfair to Loraine. Any therapist worth her salt feels for her clients, but I've got an edge that allows me to literally experience what they're going through when they sit in my office and pour out their hearts.

Sensing Loraine's sloshing, thick sadness fill the room twice a week was more than enough to make me feel guilty at the thought of missing even one appointment for birthday festivities. While all my clients matter to me, I felt a little something extra for her, considering her circumstances. So, rather than flying home to be squeezed and coddled by my mother, I was on the couch in frumpy pajamas watching reality TV. Family party or not, though, I was going to put my all into enjoying my birthday treats.

I felt Chloe at the door just as I was taking my third and final bite of a chocolate cupcake and panic seized me. She didn't know anyone else had sent me fattening food. If she caught wind that I was eating more than my fair share—hell, more than President Taft's fair share—of cupcakes, she'd double or triple her efforts to keep me healthy. I'd be eating kale and broccoli and whatever else is green for weeks.

"Coming," I said around a mouthful of contraband as I scrambled to hide the evidence. Panic jumped in my throat again as I felt the smoky edge of suspicion puff through her contentment.

I scooped up the box of cupcakes and made it to the kitchen before Chloe realized she didn't have to wait for me and walked right in.

"What are you eating?" she asked, a note of knowing accusation in her voice. The suspicion had grown, no longer a wispy leak but a full-blown torrent. I might have let out a terrified squeak.

"Nothing!" I protested, tossing a dish towel over the box as if that would do any good.

"Gwen," she said as she leaned through the kitchen doorway. I winced as her suspicion solidified enough to be an ooze of disappointment. I whipped around to grin innocently at her, but found myself immediately distracted.

"You have chocolate on your teeth," she said. I ignored the fact that she had a valid point and looked her up and down.

"Why are you dressed up?" I asked.

"I'm not, really," Chloe replied, looking down at her outfit. Chloe is small, sleekly muscled in a way that I'm always jealous of when we hit the gym. Her hair is a light blond, cut boy-short around the back and sides but left long in the front. Her bangs were swept across her forehead, pinned to the side with little clips that held shiny red baubles. They matched the four piercings in each of her ears and the skinny scarf-necklace draped around her neck. The red managed to bring out the blue in her eyes.

She'd pulled leggings in the same deep red over her short legs and had somehow managed to walk gracefully across my living room despite the fact that she was wearing shoes with heels so long and sharp I was sure the TSA would have tackled her to the ground had she entered an airport. The cable-knit baby pink sweater she wore over it all draped heavily down to mid-thigh, but didn't manage to hide the fact that she's in great shape. I pointed.

"You look… not fancy, but nice."

"I always look nice," she said, slipping past me to lift the towel and peer into the box at my illicit sugar. She didn't say anything, just twisted expertly on her heels to smile my way and wag her brows. "Come on, let's go out."

"But… cupcakes." I pointed at the box, then figured I might as well just reach a little bit further and grab a treat. She blocked me before I could get what I was aiming for, pulling my arm until I had no choice but to move as she wanted. The next thing I knew, my back was pressed against her chest, my forearm over my belly like we were dancing.

"No more cupcakes, Gwen. We haven't been out in awhile. Let's get you dressed. Come on!"

"I don't—" I started to argue but realized it was fruitless. She was already shuffling me out of the kitchen, around the corner, and down the hall to my bedroom. I probably *could* have argued if I was really invested in the idea of staying home, but I couldn't think of a reason not to let her have her way. While my empathy means I don't do so well in crowds—all those emotions zinging around like Nerf darts shot at my face by caffeinated children—Chloe knows what I can handle. Sometimes I think she knows me better than I know myself, which is how she always picks out more flattering outfits than I can pull together. I let her fuss over me, putting on what she handed me and making small talk as she gussied me up.

As Chloe stood in front of me next to the mirror and started working her makeup magic, I considered my reflection. I'm pretty cute, though not in the same way Chloe is. I'm a smidge below average height with dark hair I keep ruler-straight at my chin and across my brows. Chloe's exercise regimen can only do so much, so while I'm not straining to get through any doorways, I *am* a bit pudgy. On the plus side, I've got a great rack.

"I don't even remember buying these jeans," I mused. "They make my ass look pretty good, though."

"That's why you bought them," she sighed. "You don't remember because you bought ice cream right after and froze your brain cells. Now look at me or you'll end up with eyeliner on your ear."

I did as commanded and Chloe got back to doing something that made my green eyes look big and innocent. It wasn't long before I was all dolled up and Chloe was handing me a pair of heels and doing an excited little hip wiggle.

"This is gonna be fun!"

"Where are you taking me? You know I don't do clubs or discothèques, or whatever places you crazy kids are hanging out at these days."

"Kids? I'm three years younger than you."

"Don't change the subject."

"I promise you'll enjoy it. I'll buy you a cocktail, something with sugar on the rim."

"But I have sugar in the—"

"No arguments. We're leaving and you're going to have fun. Have I ever steered you wrong?"

I racked my brain for some example that would allow me to finish my cupcakes, but nothing was coming to mind. Chloe doesn't back down when she wants something and it might do me good to work on my shielding some. Maybe I'd be able to enjoy being around hordes of angry miscreants by my thirtieth birthday if I tried hard enough.

Chloe and I were draped across a white couch in the corner of Mettle, a vegetarian lounge in the Fremont neighborhood of Seattle. True to her word, she'd bought me a sweet, baby blue cocktail with matching sugar on the rim. I sipped it slowly because, as good as it tasted, alcohol and my empathy don't mix. If I get more than a bit buzzed around others, every emotion is amplified to excruciating levels. Eternally smarter than I am, Chloe had a mocktail version of the same thing, though she'd opted for no sugar on the rim. Jerking her chin towards someone behind me, she winked.

"Go say hi. He looks like your type."

I glanced over my shoulder and spotted a man in nice jeans and a slate grey vest leaning up against the bar. He *was* pretty cute, but it seemed like too much effort to get up and go over to him.

"Eh," I grunted, turning back to Chloe.

"He's cute!"

"Then you date him."

"I need to leave someone for you," she teased. "It's been a few months since you've been on a date."

"I've got Sonny," I said, taking a sip. "I'm fine."

"He's a bird. He can't fulfill every one of your needs."

"Yes, but he's adorable and he doesn't complain when I eat cupcakes for dinner."

"Speaking of rotting your insides, how many other sweets do you have hidden around your place?"

I cleared my throat delicately, then took another long sip in an attempt to avoid answering. Chloe's not an empath like me, but she *is* a body language polyglot. No matter what your body is saying, she can understand it. Fiddling with my drink was the only safe response.

"I know you got a dozen from your family and I know I sent you a half-dozen. Those were neither of those batches." She nudged me with her knee. "Did Madeline send them?"

I wanted to lie, since it was totally plausible that I'd gotten the cupcakes from the café that takes up nearly the entire bottom floor of our office building. I'm at The Internets almost every day and Madeline, the owner, had indeed given me free birthday sweets, though it had just been a Chestburster—a spicy Mexican hot cocoa—and a slice of cake.

Chloe's smugness was rooting around in my brain and I could tell without looking that she already knew the answer to her own question.

"Oh fine. Mel sent them," I admitted.

"I knew it!" She laughed, clapping her hands together around the stem of her martini glass. "So naturally you're going to thank him with sex."

"Gross," I whined, rolling my gaze down to look at the last of the liquid in my glass. Talk of sex with our attractive but insufferable work neighbor had made me lose my appetite. "Why do you hate me?"

"Gwen, honey, I love you. That's why I think you should give him a shot. Believe me, he's worth it."

"I really don't want to hear it." I thought for a second before morbid curiosity got the better of me. "When did you sleep with him?"

"Maybe a year ago? It was right after you hired me, before we opened. I ran into him at The Internets and he seduced me with his cheesy pick-up lines."

"That's just disgusting."

She laughed, her whole body shaking with it. She was happy as a clam to tease me about Mel Somerset. Despite my desire to remain grouchy due to the subject, I felt her glee bubbling against me, fizzing into my brain pleasantly. Being an empath has its upsides. After a few seconds, she shook her head. "You'll fall prey at least once. I don't know why you've resisted this long. You've seen him shirtless; it's awesome. Besides, after you sleep with him, he kind of lays off."

"Doesn't look that way to me."

"Eh, he's all talk now." She lowered her voice, accounting for the fact that most of the population has no idea that the supernatural side of the world even exists. Hell, I'm technically part of that world and I barely know the extent of it, though that's mostly by choice. "I think it's a werewolf thing. Don't get me wrong; if I showed up at his office with no panties on, he'd sweep everything off the desk and we'd go at it like bunnies, but that train has left the station, you know?"

"I really don't. He's all over you all the time."

"Not as much as he's all over *you*. Next time he comes by, watch how he acts with you and then with me. It's a whole different ball game."

"I thought it was a train."

"Maybe there's a ball game going on *in* the train."

I took the last swig of my drink and set it down on the end table next to me. "Let's just get out of here. I'm getting a headache from being around all these people."

"No, you're not, but we can leave." Chloe pushed to her feet, took my hand, and yanked me up. "I need to stop by the office before I take you home, though."

"It can't wait until morning? It's late."

"It's nine-thirty, Grandma. You can handle it. I'll be quick. Come on."

Chloe slipped an arm around my shoulder and led me toward the door before pausing. "Oh! One second. I forgot to tip."

"You gave her five when she brought us the drinks."

Disapproval bumped out of Chloe and jabbed me like an elbow and she shook her head. I should have been used to her tipping habits, and it wasn't like I resented them, but I know what I pay her and it probably isn't enough to be as generous as she likes to be.

Though, she does all the books for me so maybe I've given her a few raises I'm unaware of. Considering that, I watched as she hopped energetically—and somehow safely, despite the skyscraper heels—back to where we'd been sitting. She pulled a bill—probably a twenty—out of her bra, moved her glass over near mine, and tucked the cash under the bottom. Catching our waitress's eye, she pointed at the glasses and then bounced back to escort me out of the club.

We work in an office building in the Wallingford neighborhood of Seattle. I'm a therapist by trade; back in high school, I figured that my empathy made hearing about people's problems and discussing their feelings a natural vocational choice, and I haven't looked back. I'm pretty successful, thanks in large part to Chloe, the best assistant ever. When I've got a particularly hard case in the waiting room, she makes sure to let me know to put my mental shields up. Shielding, for me, is kind of like plugging your ears at a really loud concert. It doesn't block everything out, but it's a mental muscle flex that helps me concentrate without collapsing in a bloody-eyed heap.

The best part of having Chloe for an assistant, though, is that she can organize absolutely anything and has no qualms about dealing with insurance companies. She's nearly as good at double-speak as they are and it's pretty impressive what she can get out of them when she uses her Serious Voice.

It was late, but we still had to park down the street and walk up to the building. The Internets was jumping, despite the fact that it was nearly ten on a Sunday night. Even though the emotions inside were the mental equivalent of static on an old TV turned up to full volume, I veered toward the café, my eyes on the pastry case clearly visible through the window.

Still determined to deny me any chance at sweets, Chloe yanked me off to the left and held my wrist as she unlocked the door that led into the narrow lobby. I looked through the windows between the lobby and the café and spied three besuited gentlemen and a girl in a stiff dress with bronze-colored mounds in perfect rows down the skirt. She was holding what looked like a tiny plunger. I realized it was *Doctor Who* theme night.

I really wanted a mug of TARDIS-blue hot cocoa but Chloe kept a firm grip on my arm all the way to the elevator, refusing to let me indulge my addiction. I let out a sad sigh as the doors shut, which Chloe chose to ignore.

"I'll be quick," Chloe said once we were in the waiting room. She moved to her desk to grab whatever she'd come for and I went into my office, trying to make it look casual so she wouldn't suspect anything. Chloe does her best to keep me healthy but I still manage to smuggle in the occasional king-sized candy bar. That very afternoon, in fact, I'd been forced to hide half of one in the desk lest she find me eating it and take it away. As much as I loved her and appreciated the effort she'd been putting into watching what I ate, there was a limit to my willpower, and passing up cupcakes and my favorite café had exceeded it.

I was two bites into nougaty chocolate and caramel when I felt the slap of Chloe's shock against me. Worry wriggled about inside my gut and I stepped around my desk, realizing that we weren't alone.

A cold, desperate hunger crackled through the office, and only concern for Chloe sent me walking toward it. I wanted to turn and fling myself through my window, despite the fact that I was three stories up. My heart leapt into my throat and I pressed my hand over it, wanting to feel small and protected. I felt sweat break out over my torso as I started shivering. Something was there; I was terrified that I knew what it was and that this time it wouldn't leave me in peace.

Two

My first official notice that there was a world beyond the one humans know (and that *it* was aware of *me*) came when I was four years old. I was out in the backyard when I felt emotions different than any I had ever come across. Human emotions, I learned then, have a very specific pattern to them. While describing it to someone who's never felt someone else's emotions has always been tough, I *can* say that what I felt was curiosity and, even stronger, hunger. Whatever was coming toward me wanted to learn more about me, and it liked how tasty I smelled.

Before I could scramble to my feet and run inside to get my mommy, two beings appeared in front of me. From my seat on the grass, they both looked distressingly tall, but only one of them resembled something human. The other had a furry body like a grizzly bear, broad in a way that looked natural rather than as a result of one too many servings of Hansel and Gretel. It had a wide face with tusks protruding downward from under its upper lip, hands the size of scooter tires, and the arms to support them. It was not the one that wanted to eat me; in fact, I could feel nothing coming from that being at all.

The other was stark white and black, like someone had turned up the saturation on an old movie. There wasn't a single shade of gray that I could see anywhere on him. His lips, fingernails, eyelashes, and teeth were shiny black like vinyl, while the rest of him was flat white. Under his open black trenchcoat and white outfit, his body was painfully skinny, like a skeleton with an eating disorder. It made his head look too big, despite it being narrow like the rest of him.

We stared at each other in silence for what felt like ages. Even at four, I could tell you what emotions I liked and which ones I shied away from.

9

Usually amusement made me happy and I wanted to hug the person feeling it so I could take it into myself and laugh along with them. This was much different, the opposite of when I did something silly and it made my mother giggle. This seemed like I was being laughed at and it made me feel bad.

At some point, I let out a whimper and the skinny one smiled at me, dropping to the grass. His arms and legs bent outward, bony limbs squeezing into impossible angles, leaving his chest close to the ground. When he paused on my left, closing in, I shied away from his face. In that moment I had been convinced I would feel sharp jaws take a chunk out of my arm, but nothing came. I risked a glance just as he slithered a snake's tongue out to inspect me. I showed remarkable restraint in not peeing my pants.

"It is not useful."

The skinny one looked up as the other monster spoke and nodded. "No. It is not a threat."

The tongue darted out again and a hand followed it toward my face. I made a scared squealing sound, still convinced I was about to become something's breakfast. The hand hovered near my face. I felt the curiosity come at me harder, wrapping around my upper body like a hug from my smelly, bony great-grandmother. The only thing in the world, at that moment, was the bleached white of his tentacular fingers twitching just above my skin. I couldn't even feel the river of tears soaking my face and shirt.

"A level three, at best." The skinny one shifted, standing up to his full height once again, and stared down at me. I whimpered.

"Child, have you been told what we are?"

I shook my head. The bigger being lumbered forward and held out a hand. I flinched away but he didn't try to get any closer. He held his hand there above my head, as if offering to pull me to my feet, but I had no desire to reach for it. The skinny one laughed and it reminded me of a crow's call. Finally, the furry one spoke again.

"You are being watched."

I didn't see them again for twenty-five years.

While my childhood nightmares were a lot shorter than I remembered, I was still shivering, trying my best to control my bladder as I stared at them from just inside my office doorway. Skinny turned, lifting a brow as he regarded me. Chloe was quiet, nervous energy thrumming through her, hitting me like standing too close to a subwoofer. We were all still and silent, the furry creature staring at Chloe expressionlessly while the other watched me. Furry was still a void to my empathy, but Skinny was predatorily amused at my fear, just like when I'd been small and helpless.

Some tiny, contrary part of me was instantly irritated by the fact that he was enjoying my terror. It shoved back the fear, making me take stock of the situation. These creatures, whoever or whatever they were, had just appeared in my waiting room without a word. They hadn't yet offered us any harm, despite the fact that Skinny's stomach seemed to think we were dinner. I forced myself to rationalize that, had they wanted to hurt us, they would have done so already. The tusks on Furry alone could have gored me half to death.

Swallowing my panic, I pushed forward, held out a hand, and spoke, my voice only slightly squeakier than usual.

"Laurel and Hardy, I presume?"

Surprise blossomed in Chloe like a tiny mushroom cloud as she let out a laugh made of pure, nervous shock. I wasn't sure if she got the reference to the visually mismatched comedic duo, or if she figured I actually knew these two by name. I didn't really think it was the time to explain, so I let the nicknames stand. The room was quiet again after that, Skinny staring down at my hand like I'd offered him a jar of baby vomit. Confusion had rumbled into his psyche like a storm and it somehow pulled some measure of calm to life inside me. If he was confused too, then maybe I could use that to get some kind of upper hand. When neither monster seemed interested in shaking, I dropped my arm and turned to meet Chloe's eyes. She shook her head minutely; she had no idea what was going on, either.

"We're here for your assistance," Hardy said, his bulk brushing Laurel's coat as he stepped around his skinny partner toward Chloe. She hopped back, holding her hands up.

"Not me," she said quickly. Laurel turned to her, baring his black teeth in frustration. Before he could protest, Chloe pointed at me, panic making her psyche spark like fireworks. "She's the one with the superpower. I'm just the assistant."

Both creatures turned to me and I flinched at the painful jab of irate disbelief that arced out of Laurel. I rubbed my face where it felt like I'd been hit and threw a glare at Chloe. Normally she had my back in anything, but stand her in front of two terrifying monsters and she shoves me under the bus. Sheesh.

Still trying to keep my composure, I swallowed, shifting my weight.

"I think you have the wrong place, fellas. I'm a therapist. Unless you've got daddy issues or—are you married? Is there trouble in paradise?" They simply blinked at me, no sign that they got the joke. "So you're not here to blame your mother for all your troubles with women?"

"We are here for assistance," Hardy said, addressing Chloe again. A spike of panic shot from her into my ribcage and it awoke some protective instinct in me I hadn't realized I had. I waved my arm, trying to get his attention.

"Hey, buddy. Over here! Leave her alone. Like she said, I'm the one with the powers. What do you want?" Hardy shuffled to face me and it made the floor creak beneath his feet. I eyed the carpet nervously, hoped the building had been constructed with monsters the size of adolescent elephants in mind. "If you're waiting for us to offer you some sort of refreshments, you might as well leave. We don't make coffee this late."

"You are the one we seek?" Hardy asked. He was gentle as he nudged Laurel aside to approach me, but Laurel seemed to take being moved as an insult. Something else was thrumming within him and, though it was different than the crackling of his other feelings, I didn't like it any better.

"In an ideal world, no, but you're obviously here for a reason. What is it? And make it quick," I said with a sniff. Maybe if I feigned disinterested confidence they'd just give up and go. It had worked for me with bad blind dates, after all. They glanced at each other and Laurel shifted. The emotion that was making me jittery snapped into focus; it felt like having a tuning fork pressed against my rib cage and I realized in an instant that he was *nervous*.

"We have heard that you serve your mistress well," Laurel began, making my eyebrows shoot up. I had a mistress? "We are mere scouts, here with a request for one as powerful as yourself."

"Scouts? Like Girl Scouts? Are you selling cookies?" Hardy blinked, his shoulders slumping slightly like I'd said something that offended him. I tried again. "Talent scouts? If you're here about Monster Star Search, you're out of luck. I haven't got a single talent."

"As scouts," Hardy said, something in his tone making me think he appreciated my humor about as much as my parents had when I was thirteen. "We are under orders to visit human children to determine their importance to Fairy. When they are weak, useless, we leave them be. If they are powerful, we take them."

"Take them? Where?" I asked, the memory of my first meeting with these two suddenly flashing like a spike of lightning through my consciousness. It got harder to keep calm as I realized that, had my power not been simple empathy, I might not have grown up in my happy home with two parents and two siblings.

Hardy's brow furrowed and, even without his emotions to back it up, I got the feeling my question confused him. He didn't answer, but kept after his mission.

"The last three children we were to inspect had been taken before we arrived."

"Was it some sort of mix-up?" I asked. Laurel narrowed his eyes, getting unhappier with me every time I spoke up. I pressed on, even though sensing his disapproval was starting to feel like having hives on top of a sunburn. "I mean, maybe there was a double-booking and some coworkers got to the kids before you?"

"Coworkers," Laurel said as if tasting the word. "What is coworkers?"

"I mean, some other ... What *are* you?" They'd claimed to be scouts but I didn't see any merit badges or cookies tucked in the pockets of Laurel's coat. I doubted they'd have been accepted into any troop looking like they did, anyway.

Laurel's head snapped back, his offense hitting me like a truck. I grunted against the force of it, feeling for a second like I might lose my balance. Hardy stepped slightly forward, taking the lead while Laurel continued to bristle.

"We are simple scouts without a singular bloodline and we understand we have no right to even stand in front of you, that you are being so gracious as to not punish us for the audacity of asking. Your reputation for leniency reaches far and your deeds are celebrated. For these reasons, we ask that you lend us your resources and aid us in finding these children. Had they made their way to the queen, we would have been alerted. Should we not locate them and their powers prove too much to keep the balance, we shall be punished. We can offer you payment."

I couldn't imagine what sort of payment they meant, but the idea didn't appeal to me regardless.

"I don't ... uh ..." I trailed off, trying to decide what would be the best thing to say. These two had come to me when I was a child, menacing me and making snide comments about my "power level," but judging me harmless and leaving me with a warning. Now here they were asking for my help. I needed to know more about why the tables had been turned. "Are you absolutely sure they were kidnapped? Maybe someone just got wise to your gig and hid them from you. I mean, if I knew you were coming when I was little, I would have holed up in a crawlspace until you went on your way. It can't be on anyone's bucket list to let you near their babies."

Another snap of frustration whipped out of Laurel to cut into my cheek, but there was a muddy edge of disgust in it. I straightened slightly, bitter at his reaction, and turned toward him, frowning. It took him only a moment to notice my expression and the nervous thrumming in him boomed like thunder as Hardy spoke.

"They were taken, not hidden. We found chaos, panic, crying humans, but no trace of the children."

I squirmed slightly at the picture he painted. Crying humans and chaos meant missing kids to me. I had enough experience with parental panic to imagine how bad it could have been. My mother had nearly had a meltdown once when my brother Thomas had hidden too thoroughly in a hall closet. Three sets of parents finding out their children had been kidnapped would have been a million times worse.

"Okay," I said after a few moments, still stuck in the memory of my own mother's anxiety. Pity for the missing children and their distraught parents was sloshing in my belly like I'd sucked down a gallon of olive oil; I was feeling more than a little sick.

"We were assured you would be of help!" Laurel said when my silence stretched on. "Are you helping? Why do you not answer?"

I looked his way as Hardy mumbled something I couldn't understand and Laurel quieted. Begrudgingly, he lowered his head slightly as if he'd been chastised. His humiliation wasn't any more pleasant to experience than any of his other emotions.

I turned to Chloe, realizing the feeling of her was nearly lost against the riot of Laurel's revolving psyche. She was watching me intently, fascinated and impressed, all worry over the appearance of our guests gone from her mind. I liked the way she was looking at me, actually. It was rare to surprise her, especially in such a positive way.

I was pretty impressed with myself, come to think of it. Not ten minutes ago I'd wanted to pee my pants and hide under my desk. Now here I was being given the respect of two beasts that had haunted my nightmares since childhood. I latched onto her awe, using it to muffle the greasy pity and Laurel's painful remorse.

I took a deep breath, focusing on Chloe and on the fact that I'd been asked to help reunite three families. I considered my own fear as a child when I'd been confronted by these so-called scouts, and how awful it had to be for three kids who were taken from their families before they'd even been given a chance at being judged harmless and left in a sandbox.

What if whatever had taken them was worse than these two? I might've been the only hope these kids had. I couldn't turn my back on them, not if there was anything at all I could do.

"I'll help," I announced. I wasn't sure how, or what, but something had to be done and I knew I wouldn't be able to live with myself if I didn't at least try. Maybe I'd impress Chloe again and think of something brilliant that would save the day. These two certainly thought I had it in me; maybe they were right and I'd have the little ones home by the end of the week.

"You are most gracious," Hardy said, bowing low. Laurel followed suit, though I could feel how much he disliked doing so. "Your mistress has chosen wisely."

There was that mistress again. Did they mean Chloe? We weren't dating, but maybe they had assumed differently. As if she knew I was thinking about her, Chloe spoke up.

"What can you tell us about these kids? Names? Ages? Can you tell us what powers they have? We're going to need something to go on besides the fact that they're children." She made a good point and I felt shame creep in to needle my pride until it started to deflate. I hadn't even thought that far. So much for having a snap of brilliance that would save the day.

Laurel tensed as if he might stand up but both he and Hardy remained bowed down like they were expecting me to behead them. Chloe gave it a beat before exasperation fizzed through her and she gestured at me to speak.

"Uh, stand, answer her," I said, at a loss as to what exactly they needed to hear. This time, they didn't hesitate, focusing on me even though Chloe had been the one to ask the question.

"We are told where to locate the children, but this time we found there were none present," Hardy explained. "This has happened in the past, but three times in such a short span is not right. The balance between our world and the human world may be in danger. We have been unable to track the children and do not know how to make sure it is done, and discreet."

"And you were told I could do better?"

"Your resources are vast. Your mistress passed along a list of your accomplishments when sending word we were to meet you."

"You spoke with my mistress?" I guess they didn't mean Chloe after all. She likes messing with me sometimes, but there was no way she'd been in on this beforehand.

Laurel's eyes bugged out so hard I thought they'd burst and get carried away on the ocean of panic that washed over him. As Laurel sputtered and began to shake as if he'd explode, Hardy clarified.

"An emissary was sent to us. We dare not waste your mistress's time with our presence. She called upon us. Please understand we did not mean to imply we have sway with her."

"No," I shook my head, desperate to flush out Laurel's tumultuous fear as it flapped through my chest like a bickering murder of crows. "I didn't mean it like that, jeez."

Hardy's square face pulled tight as he looked between us and I wondered if he was catching on to how unpleasant I found it to be near his partner.

"We are sorry we could not be of more assistance, but surely you have connections and means that we can only dream of. If there is nothing else you require of us, we will take our leave."

I liked that idea. "Yeah, you can go. I just need to know how to contact you if I find anything."

Hardy winced, his massive shoulders hunching up around his neck. "You need not waste your breath. We will come when you need us."

"It's that simple?" I asked. It couldn't be that easy. I glanced at Chloe and then back. They weren't there. "What the hell?"

I did a quick turn, sweeping my gaze around the office, trying to figure out where they'd gone. The door hadn't opened, the only window in the room was too small for even Chloe to get through, and I was pretty sure we didn't have any trap doors under the rug. They couldn't just be *gone*. Surely they'd blown up or been reduced to a puddle of some sort? When blinking and leaning forward to swipe my hand through the empty air where they'd been didn't tell me anything, I turned to Chloe.

"Where did they go? What the hell just happened?"

She had a question of her own. "You have a *mistress?*"

Three

I hustled Chloe out of the office, shushing her when she tried to speak. I didn't want to risk Laurel and Hardy coming back with more questions or the realization that I wasn't who they thought I was. They seemed pretty scared of me, but if they figured out they'd just bowed and groveled before a lowly level three human who didn't have a scary mistress, that would likely change. Laurel had already seemed halfway set on taking me out. I didn't want to risk Hardy and his dangerous tusks feeling the same way. I didn't relax until we were buckled into Chloe's little sedan.

"Do you have a second job I don't know about?" Chloe demanded as she started the car.

I shook my head rapidly. "No! I'm way too lazy, you know that! They clearly thought I was someone else."

"Obviously," Chloe said, back to being her unflappable self. Meanwhile, I was practically vibrating, eager to get as far away from the dark office as possible. "I mean, they looked at little old human me first."

"*I'm* human!" I insisted. "They shouldn't have been looking at either one of us!"

"Yes, but you're human-plus. Human with benefits. I don't know if I'd call you *super*-human, but—"

"Okay, stop. I get it. And hey! You pointed them straight at me. What if they were there to hurt me—or hurt whoever they think I am?"

"I panicked!" she admitted. "Believe me. If things had been different, I wouldn't have put you in that position." There was a trace of disappointment in her and it was clinging like a slug to the greasy edge of her guilt. "I'm so sorry."

I knew she was sorry. I could feel it, though I didn't want to—not just

17

because it was an unpleasant experience, but because none of this was her fault.

"It's okay," I soothed, wishing I could project feelings, not just receive them. "It was … um, I don't know what that was, but they weren't there to hurt me. They seemed to be scared of me, actually. I don't think anyone's ever been scared of me before."

"Except the pizza boy when he's late with your dinner."

"Well, he's asking for it," I agreed, shaking my fist as comically as I could manage. As I'd hoped, Chloe laughed and we both went quiet for a few minutes, basking in the glow of not feeling terror or worry. Finally, I piped up.

"Did I really just agree to help them? Me? Why would I do that? I don't know the first thing about finding kidnapped children. I've lost two cell phones in the last year. What was I thinking, agreeing to handle this?"

"I think you were thinking that two scary monsters were standing in front of you, telling you that they'd found parents in distress over their missing offspring. Not even you could turn your back on that."

"Not even me?" I rolled my gaze her way and caught the slight smile on her lips. She was teasing me. Instead of giving in to her ribbing, I pushed ahead with the matter at hand. "We should look into that before anything else. If families have just gotten wise and found some way of hiding their kids from these … things, then there may not be a problem at all."

"You could ask Mel to help!" Chloe suggested. Cheer tap-danced out of her psyche and all over mine. I ground my teeth, trying my best to figure out a reason why I would not—*could not*—ask Mel Somerset for help. Sure, he's a successful private investigator, but he's also *Mel*.

"Fine!" I huffed after my brain failed to offer me an out. "You can call him tomorrow morning and ask if he's willing. I don't want to ask him for anything. He might take it as an invitation to take his pants off."

"You should invite him to take his pants off anyway," Chloe said, her optimism fluttering against my grumpiness and threatening to suffocate it. "Not now, of course. Wait until he's helped find the kids and then pay him in sex."

"I hate you both."

"You love me," she said, patting my thigh. It reminded me of my sister, which wasn't surprising, since Chloe is practically family. In fact, they both have the frustrating habit of trying to get me to take proper care of myself and laughing at me when I fight them on it. God help me if they ever teamed up.

"Fine," I said again, calmer this time. I wanted to hold onto my grouchiness, as it had conveniently taken over for the fear I'd felt around Laurel and Hardy, but I knew Chloe wasn't going to let me. Just being this close to her, I could feel myself cheering up, absorbing her giddiness through my pores. "I love you, but not Mel. Never Mel."

"Okay," Chloe said, though I could tell she wasn't really agreeing.

Midnight ticked past and I let out a groan, rolling onto my back in hopes the ceiling might drop onto my head and forcibly knock me unconscious. I wouldn't be getting any sleep without outside help. My brain was racing, going over the night's events in a nervous, spastic, rambling way. I couldn't make my thoughts line up coherently, so they jumped from moment to moment.

One second I was seeing the face of the man at the bar, the next Laurel's expression when I'd tried to shake his hand. After that, I had moved on to trying to make a list of groceries to buy. Two items in (honey and sugar) and my brain hopped back to the dark office and the look on Chloe's face when I'd addressed our strange visitors so flippantly.

I wasn't sure how much Chloe knew about the magical world around us, but I was guessing it was probably less than me. And I barely knew anything. My general knowledge is kind of hazy, and my personal knowledge pretty much stops at Mel the werewolf gumshoe and the fact that both my siblings have powers like mine.

Of the three of us, I definitely got the rawest deal. My brother Thomas is preternaturally lucky. The day he'd turned eighteen, he bought a lotto ticket and won. That isn't even the best thing that's happened to him in his short life, either. The kid manages to avoid nearly every bad situation that might come his way. I can't even tell you how many times I've seen him pause, weave, or duck for seemingly no reason, only to watch bird poop drop right into the spot where he'd previously been.

My older sister Robin has a form of very minor mind control that's activated by touch. She can't make you fling yourself off a building or stick your tongue to a frozen metal pole, but if you're ambivalent about doing the dishes and she gets her paws on you, you'll be elbow-deep in dishwater before you know it.

Then there's me, the empath stuck working in the same building as a werewolf who thinks it's hilarious to show up and rub his stupid emotions all over the place. I know my mom is just a plain, Chloe-level human, but I've long suspected my father has something extra going for him. The fact that he's with my mom—a woman way out of his league if you ask any of us kids—is enough to convince me. But there hasn't been a second of my life past age twelve where my father and I have been able to communicate maturely. Three words into any conversation and we devolve into a screaming match that is only won when one of us storms off screaming nonsensical insults.

I've never had the guts to ask about any abilities he may have because doing so would require I talk either to or about him. Neither prospect is appealing.

Other than the first time I'd seen Laurel and Hardy as a child, I'd mostly managed to avoid the magical world. Sure, Madeline at the café was a creature of some sort and Mel was around more than I would prefer, but I'd never run afoul of a leprechaun or discovered a sword of plus-five dexterity. I couldn't even tell you if those things existed. If I'd had my way, my first interaction with Laurel and Hardy would have been the last scary, magical thing I'd ever dealt with. Even spending the evening talking with them like we were all people and none of us were horrifying hadn't entirely quelled my fear. If *they* were out there, who knew what else there was?

No, I had no interest in stumbling on something with tentacles in place of eyeballs or a taste for empath kidneys. Once these kids were safe and sound, it was back to blissful ignorance for me. Although, if I could get Hardy to pay me by taking Mel off my hands, it might actually turn out to be worth running into them again.

Rubbing my hands over my face, I wondered if I had any cold medicine I could chug to knock me out. The idea of anything alcoholic magnifying my empathy even temporarily wasn't appealing—there's a gopher in my backyard that's perpetually grumpy, though I don't mind when I catch wind of squirrel emotions—so I fumbled around on my dresser and grabbed my mobile phone. I chose the most relaxing music I had to play and settled in to give sleep one last shot.

Wishing I had my sister there to order me to catch some Z's, I curled up on my side and decided to count sheep. Thoughts of farm animals made me wonder if Mel had ever blown a house down around a were-pig. Strangely, that put me right out.

My night was anything but peaceful, my restlessness due mainly to strange, walrus-and-bear-filled dreams. I finally gave up on my bed at just after five-thirty, shuffling like a zombie out to Sonny's cage. The second my pet sun conure heard my footsteps dragging along the floor, he started calling to me, welcoming me to the new day as loudly as he could. I grumbled back but my puffy face and lack of enthusiasm didn't deter him. In fact, he started ringing his bells at me the closer I got, as if he was aware of my empathy and hoped to infuse cheer straight through my pores.

The loud greetings continued as I unlatched his cage and reached in to rub his bright yellow chin. Before I could stop him, he zigzagged his colorful little body and climbed onto my hand and up my arm. I let him pick through my hair lovingly as I padded down the hall. We made idle conversation while I slowly made my way back to my room and bathroom, where Sonny hung out on a perch I'd had installed in place of a towel rack along the back wall.

Time to wake up, Gwen.

After the shower, I scooped Sonny up, dropped him back on my robed shoulder, and shuffled barefoot to the kitchen. Nothing looked out of place at first. My kitchen is long and L-shaped, with my dining table stashed around the corner. I grabbed a plastic cup off the counter next to the sink and filled it straight from the tap. As I turned toward the fridge, the cup slipped out of my hand onto the floor.

My refrigerator looked like someone had sneezed words all over it.

Someone had come into my house and opened up what looked to be all my boxes of magnetic poetry, nearly covering the fridge and freezer door with crooked, sideways, and occasionally upside-down phrases. I couldn't read them from my position, but I instantly pictured Laurel and Hardy carefully detailing some sort of magnetic manifesto about how they were going to take revenge on me for lying to them. As I closed in and read some, though, I realized that would have been ridiculous for several reasons.

Sonny squawked, curious about my sudden tension. I turned, got a bird-kiss on my lips, and set him down so he could patrol the counters. Stepping around the puddle, I walked back to the fridge.

The sentences were whole but unrelated. The diatribe started with, "*Mind the towels*" and "*Jewelry, pizza, and wine: make it happen,*" then rambled on for the entire length of my fridge. After the fourth line (*The Gavel will bang again*), I gave up reading them individually and just started scanning for a pattern. Nothing jumped out at me, though the magnets proclaiming "*Princess Mel*" gave me pause. My brain gifted me with an image of Mel in a frilly dress, tossing his hair out the window of a tall tower, and I started giggling. It was half exhaustion and at least a quarter nervous energy, but it felt good to laugh regardless. Realizing I was going to need documentation of this to prove to myself I wasn't going crazy, I fled to my office to grab my camera.

Less than a minute later, I hit the kitchen at a hop, forgetting about the water, and went sliding. My foot shot sideways, hitting the counter, and I ended up wedged awkwardly between two cabinets.

My back and foot hurt like hell, but my camera and I were otherwise unharmed. I swallowed, eyed "*Mind the towels*" suspiciously, and pushed myself up slowly, awkwardly. I set the camera down long enough to check myself for bruises and squish myself back far enough to get most of the fridge in the frame. I took a wide shot of the whole thing first, then moved in for a series of closer shots.

I took careful photos of every section of magnets, making sure that any pictures I took would be legible if printed out. As I sunk lower and lower, I read random phrases, unable to make sense of most of them.

Almost at the end, I found one phrase sticking out from others,

21

separated by blank space. It said, "*Answer the phone :) :)*"

Before I could wonder how my magnetic poetry had manifested smiley emoticons, the phone rang. I yelped, crawling away to put my back to the wall, my heart pounding away like a boxer. Whatever had filled my fridge with the magnetic equivalent to *Minority Report* had left my mobile phone within arm's reach. I hadn't even noticed it missing from my nightstand when I'd woken up. Swallowing, I grabbed it, tapped the answer icon, and pressed it to my ear.

"Hello?"

"I didn't think you'd be awake!" Chloe chirped.

I scowled at myself, realizing I'd half expected to hear some mysterious voice tell me I only had seven days to live.

"Yet you still called at this ungodly hour." I got to my feet to look over the fridge again.

"What's wrong?"

"Some... some*thing* was in my house last night. It decorated my fridge."

Chloe was silent for a beat before saying carefully, "Okay."

"I'm not joking!"

"Are you sure you're not dreaming?"

My gaze fell on six word magnets that seemed to know exactly what was going on. They spelled out, "*you took pictures you'll prove it.*" The tiny shiny rectangles had a point.

"I took pictures. I'll prove it," I said, tipping my head suspiciously at the fridge. "What do you want?"

"I got ahold of Mel. He'll meet us at The Internets for breakfast at eight-thirty. We can tell him what went down, see what he might know about these guys. Maybe he has connections in the preternatural world, someone who knows who Laurel and Hardy think you are."

"Yeah, maybe," I mumbled. My gaze jumped to another set of magnets. These instructed me to open the cereal cabinet. I started to wonder how this prophetic jerk had managed to use words that I was sure none of my sets even contained. "I'll meet you guys there."

"Eight-thirty," Chloe said, her voice slow.

"Yes, I got it."

"Repeat it back to me. I'm still convinced you're unconscious and this is all some sort of sleep-walking endeavor."

I grunted in disgust and hung up on her as she laughed at me. I stuck my phone in my robe pocket, whirling on my cabinets like they'd threatened me. It occurred to me as I grabbed the handle that maybe they *were* dangerous. Maybe whatever had been in my home had filled them with giant radioactive scorpions or possibly even the Scorpion King himself. While having The Rock in my kitchen sounded pretty pleasant, I figured it was much more likely that blindly opening my cupboards was going to get my head lopped off by snapping pincers.

"Dammit," I whined. Sonny squawked at me and I sighed, scooping him up to put him back in his cage, where I hoped he'd be safe. My next stop was back in my office, where I grabbed a wooden baseball bat from next to my desk and stepped into my slippers. They had some pretty solid rubber bottoms and would probably smash bugs well enough if it came to that.

I stood in front of my cabinets working up my courage, then took a deep breath and let out a quick battle cry, yanked open the door, and hopped back. Nothing jumped out at me, screamed threateningly, or tried to raise Anubis' army from Hell. I blinked, confused for a few moments at the fact that all I spied were my boxes of cereal, oatmeal, and—and an upturned, empty Twinkie box.

"No," I whispered, dropping the bat to the ground as I reached for what had, only two days before, been an entire case of spongy, cream-filled delights. "No!" I snatched the thing out of the cabinet and shook it, as if that would activate some secret compartment and my treats would come tumbling out. I should have known better; there were empty Twinkie wrappers littering the inside of the cabinet. The box remained barren, but I did notice a pink sticky note on the back.

I didn't recognize the handwriting but I could read it; it said, *Laurel and Hardy will be unhappy with you if you don't find those kids* followed by a sad face. Was my food threatening me? I shook the box again, knowing it was futile.

Maybe I *was* dreaming.

Slamming the cabinet shut, I eyed the rest of my kitchen. Who knew what else the Twinkie thief had taken or touched? Maybe my pastries weren't the only thing it put its hands all over. Marching to the fridge, I gave it one more scan, hoping for answers. None of the magnets had moved. The one proclaiming *"Stay away from the baby sasquatches"* still sat right next to *"Don't accept the ring!"*

Worrying slightly less about scorpions and slightly more about the state of my kitchen, I went through the cabinets. Gone. It was all gone. Not a speck of anything sugary or sweet remained anywhere, not even in my most careful emergency hiding spots. That bastard.

Seething, I took the time to go through the house, checking windows and doors, checking my valuables, checking my clothes to make sure nothing had been taken. Maybe ten minutes into my reconnaissance, I stood at the edge of my closet, torn between being disgusted at myself for the state of it and terrified that I'd actually have to open the box I kept hidden at the back.

I'd been married once, jumping into it at the tender age of eighteen with a man who had, even at the time, deserved much better than an immature sugar addict like me. I hadn't spoken to him or heard from him in ten years but that didn't stop my guilt over how things had ended. That regret had fueled a series of impulse purchases over the last six years, leaving me with a box full of milquetoast mystery novels written by my ex. I'd never read any of them, but I couldn't bring myself to get rid of them. Stanley only had four novels out, but I had somehow amassed somewhere around thirty copies of his books.

After a minute of staring at the pile of old coats that concealed the box from prying eyes, I convinced myself that my visitor hadn't found the books, that I didn't need to check to make sure they were safe. It was just good sense, you see. Not cowardice. I swear. I moved on to checking the other parts of my closet.

At the bottom of my underwear drawer, I found another sticky note.

I'm not interested in your unmentionables. Don't be weird.

Somehow, despite everything else, the note offended me the most. I wasn't the one showing up in a stranger's house, leaving notes, and stealing sugar. What was this creature playing at? Irritated, I carried the pink square to my office, grabbed a pen, and wrote in the bottom margin: *I'm not the one being weird, you freak!*

Satisfied I'd put the creature in its place as well as I could—considering the fact that I had no actual access to it—I contemplated the note. Where should I leave it? Was I actually hoping to get it back to the thief? I held it as I wandered back into the kitchen, stared at the fridge for a moment, and then stuck it to the door over the magnetic phrase, "*Werewolf puppies!!*"

Deciding there was nothing else to be done at the moment, I fed the bird and went to get dressed. I wasn't exactly looking forward to seeing Mel, but if he had answers about what had gotten into my home and what had shown up in my office, I needed them.

Four

I loosened my scarf as I stepped into the warmth of The Internets half an hour early and did my best not to make squeaky excited sounds at the sight of the pastries in the case. Madeline, the owner, greeted me with a lift of her chin and a smile before going back to the customer in front of her. The line was long, curving along the counter to fold back around toward me. I rubbed my hands together as I tried to decide which geek-themed items I felt like eating.

I'd tried everything from the butterbeer to the slice of Lie (chocolate cake with cherries on top) and, since it all had at least some sugar in it, it all looked good to me. Today the display case was filled with plenty of cakes, cookies, donuts, and even pre-wrapped sandwiches. Half the selection was vegan but it wasn't just that Madeline and Chloe were in cahoots; Seattle has a pretty good-sized vegan community and it's getting less likely to see a place within city limits that can't adequately feed someone who, like Chloe, eschews animal products. I'm not against vegan food but it seems to me that limiting oneself to a smaller section of the sweets in the world will only end in heartbreak.

I eyed the D-20 cookies, despite their lack of eggs, butter, and processed sugar and decided it was going to come down to their pink and white frosting versus the 1-UP cupcakes and their green and white fondant. In the end, I went with my old standby.

"Hey, Madeline," I said as I stepped up to the counter. She smiled at me again and I felt a curl of something velvety reach out of her and snake around me. Madeline isn't human but, as with the few other non-humans I'd met, I'd never had the guts to ask exactly what she is. The fact that she'd never offered an explanation for her strange, breezy emotions made me think she either didn't know I had a power, or she didn't want to talk about it.

I wasn't about to risk her peeling back her head like a Pez dispenser to reveal a giant mouth with teeth specifically designed for chomping into an empath, so I'd never mentioned that I could tell she was different.

"Saw you eyeing the 1-UP cupcakes, so I'll assume you want your usual," Madeline teased. Her affection for me brushed across my empathy like a soft summer breeze.

My lips tugged up in a goofy grin as I absorbed her fondness easily and reflected it back. Since Madeline had never offered me any harm and her emotions were pretty pleasant, I'd fallen out of the habit of shielding around her. Thus, I usually found myself pretty damn happy to see her once I was close enough. Sometimes, despite the fact that she's not much to look at, I was even convinced I had a crush on her.

"It's a bit early for sweets, though," she said with a wag of her finger and that was definitely playful and maybe even a little flirty. I shrugged, my usual irritation at being policed for my food choices nowhere to be found.

"I keep hoping to get a life and yet, despite eating dozens of the suckers, I'm still lacking."

Madeline chuckled. "A friend stopped by, wanted me to give you some things," she said, leaning into the case. I frowned at her through the glass as she scooped a green and white spotted cupcake and an oatmeal carrot muffin onto a plate. She pointed to the muffin I had no intention of eating. "This, and I'm also supposed to give you this …" Sliding the plate across the counter, she stuffed a hand into her massive apron and pulled out a copy of a paranormal romance book that had seen better days. I took the book from her, perplexed.

"Who was it?"

"Friend of the café, that's all I'm allowed to tell you. Said to give you the book and the health food. Did you want a drink?"

"Uh," I mumbled, still staring at the paperback. The spine was badly creased, the cover had been scrawled with red scribbles, and the pages were folded back at the tops and bottoms. I recognized the title, but this copy looked like it had gone through the wringer. I'm not always the best with books, but even I didn't torture them this much. "Ah, sure, yeah. Gimme a Chestburster."

"You got it." Madeline rang me up for my drink and cupcake, then shooed me out of the way of the next customer. I took my haul to a small round table near the front window to wait for my drink. It was a little chillier the further away from the horde of excitable nerds at the back, but that just meant I got more solitude. With a little distance between us, I could better block out the buzz of emotions from the geeks and gamers swarming around. Despite the fact that it was early, the place was jumping with the before school/work crowd.

The tables at the back were surrounded by people cramming together to take advantage of the free wireless on their laptops and tablets, while the massive couch in front of the gargantuan TV was packed with gamers watching each other take turns street fighting through the magic of pixels and button mashing. Sitting next to the front window left a few tables empty to stand guard between the cacophony and me.

The book intrigued me enough that I held off forking into my treats until I'd given it a good look-see. Nearly every page was covered in red pen, notes scrawled in the margins, between the lines, along the header, below the text in neatly printed footnotes that would have looked pre-printed if it weren't for the color and slight bleeding of ink. From the look of it, the friend of The Internets did not like the book. I flipped through, reading notes like, "Whose hand is this?", "Is this a person's chest or a chest of drawers?", and "Why does he have a Bedazzler?" before I flipped to the title page and felt my mouth drop open.

To Gwen,

Since I know you're not getting any action in real life, at least enjoy something steamy to read!

Love, Robin

Now I knew why I recognized it. My sister had given me this book as a birthday gift. It had been sitting in my home office waiting to be read for two weeks and now it was here at The Internets, covered in red pen. As I looked over the notes more carefully, I realized the handwriting looked familiar and the nonsense phrases reminded me strongly of the notes I'd found on my fridge.

"Son of a bitch," I sighed, setting the book down.

"What's up?"

I jumped. Holly, the assistant manager, set my mug down and lifted a hand to her wide hip.

"I... Who left this here?" I asked, waved the book spastically at her.

Holly shrugged and shook her head. "No idea. I didn't even know Mad had it until she handed it to you. Why?"

"This is mine. Someone stole it out of my desk at home and wrote all over it."

"Someone you know?" Holly asked, taking the book out of my hands.

"I don't think so."

"Has to be someone you know. That's your handwriting," she said, peeling a sticky note out of the middle of the book. She watched me as she handed it over and then leafed through the book. I blinked down at the little pink square I'd left on my fridge an hour before, feeling my face pull into a snarl. The creature had somehow *already* found my retort and evidently wrote all over my book as punishment for calling it a freak.

Why you gotta be calling me names? I was just being nice :(

"Probably for the best," Holly said as she set the book on the table. "It's a crappy book. Most of the notes are dead on, though I can't read the ones in French so I can't vouch for those."

"French?" I demanded, realizing I'd missed those.

Holly laughed at me and I got the feeling she thought I was joking. "I gotta get back to the counter, but I think Madeline knows French if you want her to translate."

"Yeah, maybe," I muttered, distracted.

"Everything okay otherwise?"

"Other than having an arch-nemesis that destroys my books, yeah. Sure. Why?"

"You've only got two things on your plate today. That's practically starving yourself." Holly winked and headed back to the counter. I sighed, stabbing into the crumbly carrot muffin as I stared at the cover of the book, wondering what the hell I'd done to deserve some sort of pest that stole sugar and wrote all over my reading material. I had a brief bout of panic over my books at home and told myself I'd have to check the margins of each and every one as soon as I could.

Figuring it was probably for the best that the creature was stealing sugar instead of using its red pen to stab me in the jugular, I took a sip of my super-spicy Mexican hot cocoa and tried not to obsess while I waited.

Chloe showed up a few minutes early, zipping straight over. She had only to wave a hand at Madeline to order her usual: a green tea soy latte and a Monster Carrot muffin of her own. I wondered briefly if she and the candy thief were conspiring against me; why else would it have instructed Madeline to give me something healthy?

"Sleep well?" Chloe asked as she slid into a chair next to me, unbundling herself. Her eyes dropped to the ragged book in the middle of the table. "What's that?"

"It goes with these," I sighed, reaching into my bag to pull out the prints I'd made of the pictures I'd taken that morning. "I wasn't lying. I woke up to find that something had eaten all the sugar in my place—all of it! It even downed my jars of white sugar! What am I supposed to put in my tea?"

"You could drink it plain," Chloe suggested, skimming through the book. She stopped on the sections that contained French and squinted at them. Amusement blossomed inside her, but I pressed on with my complaints.

"This is not the time for jokes. Something was *in* my *house*! It left me with these." I shoved the pictures across the table to her and she set the book down, making a giddy *ooh!* sound as she yanked them out of the envelope.

"These aren't tasteful nudes!" she joked after a few moments of fanning through them like a flipbook. Then she made a thoughtful noise. "What are they?"

"That's what I was looking at when you called. I found the fridge covered this morning. Hundreds of messages—most of them nonsense, far as I can tell—were spelled out in my magnets."

"Weird!" Chloe said, still looking the pictures over. "Was anything else touched? Did you find lipstick messages on your mirrors or threats spelled out in blood on the walls?"

"No, nothing like that. In fact, the only other change I could find was that all my sugar is gone. The magnets, fine, I can deal with that, but the asshole ate all my Twinkies and candy. It even ate my fruit pop cereal."

Chloe threw me a look that was decidedly less than sympathetic. I went quiet in an epic pout, watching her flip through the pictures. She skimmed quickly, only stopping on one or two to give them a closer look. About three-quarters of the way down the stack, she let out a loud, shocked laugh. I peered over and found her looking at one that focused on the phrase, *"The Gavel will bang again."*

I raised a brow. "What's so funny?"

"It's uh …" She trailed off and then looked up at me as if considering something. "I like it. Can I keep it?"

"I guess. I have copies at home. I saved them everywhere, just in case."

She brightened, tucked the picture in her jacket pocket, and then put the pictures back into their envelope. "Mel should be here, although he didn't sound completely conscious when I called him, either."

"Well, you called him at, what? Five in the morning? He'd probably only just gotten home from nailing hammered co-eds." Chloe snorted and I changed the subject back to my problem. "So what do you think?" I asked, gesturing to the envelope.

"About what?"

"About someone breaking into my house to eat my food and leave me weird notes? That last note, about the phone? I read it right before you called. It's like it *knew*."

"Well, it's more likely some*thing* and not some*one*," Chloe pointed out. "Your capacity for taking down sugar and cholesterol is impressive, but you're saying something managed to eat all the sugar in your house overnight?"

"I think so. There were crumbs and empty boxes, cupcake wrappers even." I huffed at the fact that I wouldn't get to enjoy my own birthday treats. "I didn't find any sign of the stuff in the garbage, but I can't imagine anyone throwing away perfectly good food like that."

I felt a puff of loving chagrin, but she didn't engage me about my stance on what constitutes good food.

"Well, then, it's *got* to be a thing and not a person. I've seen your house,

Gwen. Nothing human could eat all that in one night without ending up in a diabetic coma on your floor. You didn't find any corpses stuffed awkwardly in the couch cushions, right?"

"No, nothing like that."

"And it didn't touch you at all? It left Sonny alone?"

"I… guess it did? I mean, I didn't wake up with sticky handprints on my boobs and Sonny can get pretty loud if a stranger tries to get all up in his business. I'd've woken up."

"I'm sure it's fine, then." Chloe waved off my concern, which made me a bit grumpy.

"What if it's not? What if it's something dangerous?"

"Then I think it would have already hurt you." Chloe held her hand up as if sensing I was about to argue some more. "Gwen, you sleep like the dead, but you're not deaf. You said it yourself, if this thing had messed with Sonny, he would have let you know. I can guess it'd be the same for you. Did you hear anything? Notice anything else weird? Did you hear any glass breaking when—wait, how'd the thing get in?"

"I have no idea. I checked all the windows and doors when I was cleaning up and they were all locked. It must have beamed itself in."

"Well, then clearly it was just an ensign from the *Enterprise* using your kitchen as an away mission. I wouldn't worry."

I rolled my eyes, deciding her attitude was not helping. Despite my confusion and concern, Chloe was completely unbothered by my predicament. I could feel it in her, could tell she wasn't going to be sympathetic. Before I could dive right into a hissy fit, though, I felt Mel as he entered the café.

Mel Somerset is a good-looking guy; even I can admit that. He's got a strong, straight nose and a square chin like a cartoon superhero. There's a shallow dent in that superhero chin that isn't quite a dimple and his smile can immolate panties from thirty paces. His eyes are a clear, bright blue under thick eyebrows that lend a puckish bit of sex appeal.

That said, he's one of the most arrogant jackasses I have ever had the unfortunate luck of running across in a bar. Even his dark hair, blue eyes, and fabulous body cannot make up for the frustration and anguish I experience just being in the same room with him. Part of my aversion to him is just *Mel*. He's inappropriate and has no sense of personal boundaries. On top of that, he knows how my empathy makes it physically painful for me to be near him and yet he still insists on dropping by the office once or twice a week "just to say hi." Jerk.

Mel wagged his brows at us as he crossed the room to take a seat across from me. Immediately my skin started jumping, twinges of electric agony twisting my nerves into knots.

"Ladies," he said, leaning back in his chair as he laced his fingers behind his head and flexed conspicuously. Despite the weather outside, he was wearing only a snug sweater and pleated khakis. It made him look good, but I was in too much pain to appreciate it. He waited for one of us to speak— or perhaps to vault the table and try to tear his pants off. To listen to him talk, this is how every encounter with a single woman of legal age ends when you're Mel Somerset.

I resisted the urge to tell him where he could cram his flexing biceps.

"Gwen slept poorly; she's cranky," Chloe said with a smile.

"She's always cranky," Mel said, catching my gaze. The bottom corner of my left eye started to twitch and I let out a low sound like vomiting. The sooner we got this meeting over with, the better. "And I barely slept at all. *If* you know what I mean."

I made another vomit sound, but Chloe pressed on.

"We had an interesting night last night. We stopped by the office and got visited by some ... people?" Chloe turned to me, curiosity wafting out. "I guess that's what we're calling them?"

"They were monsters," I said, shaking my head. "Some people are monsters, but no people look like these two. I knew them, sort of."

Chloe's eyes went wide. "You did?"

"We're not, like, pen pals or anything, but I've seen them before. I don't think they remembered."

"Well, spill it!" Chloe urged. Mel was still resting in his chair like a photographer was perched outside taking candids.

"Yeah." One eyebrow went up as he paused to lick and bite his bottom lip as if inviting me to some naughty, private party. "Spill it."

My other eye started to tic and I snarled his way, "Shut up. It's bad enough I have to be in the same building with you." He chuckled and his emotions sizzled along my skin, his amusement taking on a white-hot edge. I leaned away, as if that would take me out of range of sensing him. "When I was four, these two—I don't know what to call them. Still Laurel and Hardy?"

Chloe nodded and I paused, realizing that the candy thief had somehow known the nicknames we'd chosen. It made me wonder if they were all in cahoots.

"So anyway, Laurel and Hardy showed up in my backyard when I was little. I was playing in the yard one minute, blissfully unaware that anything truly terrifying existed in the world, and then they just *appeared*. I was too scared to do anything, but they looked me over, talked to each other about how I'm not a threat, and then told me they'd be watching me. I guess they were lying, or they'd probably have known I wasn't the one with the mistress."

"Mistress?" Mel purred, lowering his arms to link his fingers on the table. The skin on my scalp started to jump with sharp jerks of pain. "Do tell."

"Shut up," I ordered again. Chloe was controlling her expression, but I could feel that she found my mistreatment of Mel funny. Pitting us against each other seems to be a sport to her. I was pretty sure I'd seen her egg him on and suggest he be ever more over-the-top sleazy each time he stopped by; she'd denied the allegations, but I know when people are lying, after all.

"After they disappeared, I think I fainted. I've never fainted since, so I don't know if it was the same, but I remember keeling over in the grass, too scared to do much else, and coming to with my mom standing over me, telling me to come inside for lunch. Until they showed up at the office, I'd convinced myself it was all a bad dream. I never mentioned it to my parents or anyone. I guess because I was too scared to think about it again." That didn't feel quite true, but I couldn't think of any other explanation, so I let it go.

"But they just happened to show up at our office last night," Chloe said. Holly brought over Chloe's drink and muffin, set down an extra-tall skinny latte in front of Mel, and winked at him.

"Your Slenderman, Mr. Somerset." Holly and Mel took a second to make eyes at each other before she broke the spell and went back to the counter. Mel looked back to us, clearly proud of himself for something I figured I would rather know nothing about.

When Holly was out of earshot, Chloe continued. "They thought Gwen was someone else, obviously. They came at me first. I guess I look more responsible than she does." She grinned my way, but I didn't argue; she doesn't just *look* more responsible than I do. "I was too nervous to do much except point to her. I mean, they were definitely *not* human, and Gwen's... got that whole superpower thing going on. Why wouldn't they think she was the boss?"

"I'd hardly call sensing emotions a *super*power," Mel said, taking a sip of his steaming latte. I winced, wondering how he could stand it so hot. "So they showed up, they were monsters—tell me more."

"They said that three kids are missing and they asked for my help finding them."

Mel snorted outrageously. "You? You have to spend fifteen minutes just trying to find your car each night."

"You're thinking of how long it took your date to find your dick last night," I spat.

Instead of engaging my rudeness, Mel just grinned at me before sipping his latte. Maybe he knew he didn't need to say anything to win the pissing contest; my skin was nearly broiling from his childish glee.

Chloe rolled her gaze between us. "You two need to get a room?"

"Only so there are no witnesses when I beat him to death with a chair."

"Now, now, children," she said, putting a hand to my wrist. "Let's focus on the actual problem, here. Once we're sure these kids are safe at home, Gwen, you can go on a murder spree."

Mel just watched me over the rim of his drink, his eyes roaming to my cheek as it jumped twice. I slapped at it as Mel set his cup down.

"Chloe, when you told me Gwen needed my help, I had assumed you meant sexually. This doesn't seem to be up my alley."

"It's definitely up your alley," she said, dipping her pinky in her cup just long enough to test the temperature. "Gwen's not exactly the best candidate for this sort of thing and I'm only her assistant. We figure you can help with the sleuthing—being a P.I. and all. We were also hoping your furry side would give you insight into exactly why they came to her."

"And what do I get out of this?" he asked.

"You help rescue *children!*" I snapped.

Mel snorted, shaking his head. "Relax, Ms. Furious, I was teasing. I'll help. Tell me everything they said, what they looked like. I don't spend much time around the world of ..." He paused, waving his hand vaguely. "—*other*, but I might recognize what you're talking about."

"Fantastic!" Chloe cooed, turning a smile my way. I didn't bother trying to return it.

Five

Chloe related everything that had happened the night before with an attention to detail that made me think she'd been hiding an eidetic memory from me all along. Thinking it might be connected, I explained my ordeal from that morning and Mel flipped through the pictures, mostly unbothered. Although when he came to the picture of the "Princess Mel" magnets, he paused long enough to glare up at me like it was my fault. He didn't need to say anything for me to feel his displeasure like it was the opened Ark of the Covenant.

"I'll do some research," he said finally, setting the pack of pictures back on the table. "I have contacts in the police department and I'll ask about any missing kids. I don't know what specifics we can find without more information, but I'll get back to you guys by this afternoon."

Mel got to his feet, gave Chloe a cheeky little salute, winked at me, and deposited his cup in the compost bin before heading out the back door that led into our building's lobby. My skin kept jumping even after I could no longer feel him.

"Our turn," Chloe said, gathering up my garbage and stacking everything together as she stood. "Come on. Bring your ruined book and your sadly not-dirty pictures." I hauled myself up, stretched out the muscle tension that I had acquired from being so close to Mel for so long, and dragged myself after her.

"Where are we headed?"

"Up to work," she said, as if it was the most natural thing in the world.

"But ... don't we have some kids to save?"

"Located them, have you?" she asked as she hit the elevator button. "You're ready to dash off at top speed, kick down a door, and carry them to

35

safety?"

"Well ..." I trailed off, unsure how to take her flippant attitude. Sensing I was confused, she softened.

"Look. We can't do anything right this minute, can we? We don't have any information to go on until Mel gets back to us. We don't know names or locations; we don't have any idea where to start. I mean, if you've done this before and you have a better idea, by all means, explain to me what we should be doing when we've got three appointments today and no idea how to help the kids."

I didn't have any answers, though I racked my brain as we rode up to our floor. Chloe let me think as we went, leaving me to yearn for some spark of brilliance, some new superhero genius Gwen produced by not falling to pieces in front of Laurel and Hardy. Nothing came, and as she draped her coat on the rack, I finally admitted it.

"Yeah, you're right."

"I know," she said, rounding the corner into the records room to fire up the kettle. I rolled my eyes after her but moved on. Chloe's competence is one of my favorite things about her and, my post-Mel mood aside, I really did find it a comfort to know that I could rely on her thinking the smart thoughts.

The second I pushed open the door to my office, I noticed something was different.

I stopped just inside, warily peering around. Flattening the door against the wall to make sure no one was hiding behind it, I eyed my things, trying to figure out exactly what was wrong. It was almost like one of those "spot the differences" puzzles, only my phone hadn't been replaced with a banana or an eggplant. The planter on my bookshelf had been twisted, its one pink flower turned outward; my pens had all been recapped and turned upside down—or perhaps having the ballpoint end down was right side up? In any case, I wouldn't be accidentally drawing on my fingertips anymore.

My scissors had been pulled out of my drawer and left hanging on a tack under an accordion cutout of hearts hung across my bulletin board. My trashcan was empty—though that might have been Chloe's doing—and, as I stepped closer, I noticed that my blotter was ruined.

"What the hell?"

I dropped my bag in the middle of the room and raced around to the back of the desk. The handle of my top middle drawer was shiny, possibly sticky, and the drawer itself was ajar. Tucking a finger under the bottom lip of the drawer to avoid the handle, I pulled it out all the way. My stash of gel pens had also been recapped and lined up in order of their proper hues. Apparently Roy G. Biv had snuck into my office, organized it and—was that honey I smelled? I kicked my chair back, dropped to my knees, and frantically started rooting through my drawers. None of the important files and such had been touched, but my stash of honey packets had been raided and drained, and the culprit hadn't been too careful about it. My middle drawer must have been assaulted after the honey thief had struck, thus explaining the shiny stickiness.

I took a slow breath, trying to calm myself, and pulled my chair forward again so I could sit and survey the damage. Chloe stepped in then, eyebrows raised.

"What's up?"

"I think whatever was at my house showed up here, too. It ate my honey packets."

"Probably for the best," she said with a smile. I grumbled at her but she wasn't deterred, pacing around my little office, looking over all the small changes that had been made sometime during the night.

My blotter, from the looks of the sometimes-illegible pink and purple scrawl all over it, would never be useable again. I lifted the pages and dropped them one by one. Every page of the blotter had been drawn and written on. I didn't understand most of it—it wasn't even entirely in English—but some of the art was cute at least. I went through it a bit slower, noticed that the bottom left corner had been made into a flipbook, and went through it faster.

A tiny flower bloomed. A tiny flower with fangs.

What the hell?

I scooped the blotter up, initially intent on throwing it away, and stood for a moment, tapping my foot. Chloe watched me silently, waiting me out as if we were in the store and I was trying to decide what flavor of fruit snacks sounded the tastiest. I tried to mimic her calm as I reviewed what it was that was bothering me so much.

Nothing valuable had been taken. The stash of change and dollar bills I kept in my top drawer hadn't been stolen, just all aligned and somehow flattened as if freshly minted. The computer wasn't on and my password was rock solid, so I was reasonably sure nothing had been touched there. I yanked on the drawers in the filing cabinet and found them still locked.

"You okay? You look like you're thinking pretty hard and it hurts," Chloe said.

I scowled at her and pointed toward the door. "If you can't think of anything nice to say, get out. Go buy me more sweets to replace the ones this jerk ate."

"I'm not buying you any sugar," she retorted, turning to stroll out to her desk. I scoffed loudly, wondering why my life had suddenly gotten so difficult.

I slid my blotter behind the file cabinet and sat back in my chair, drumming my fingers on my empty desk. The sugar thief had struck again, but the worst damage done was the honey on my desk and the nonsensical notes on my blotter. As irritated as I was by having my space invaded, I found myself curious about this creature. Clearly, it was curious about me. It wasn't acting like any predator I could think of; if it had wanted to kill me, it likely would have done so at my house and eaten my organs rather than my Twinkies.

Sighing, I shook my head, deciding to push the incidents out of my mind, and concentrated on cleaning up the mess.

Mrs. Ellen Quottrich arrives every Monday, sitting her flower-clad bony ass in my comfy client chair and going off on all the ways she's been slighted during the week. My office is laid out to give my clients a choice of where they want to sit while they ramble. I have two comfy chairs and a couch available to them. Most people choose the couch while I sit in the chair that faces them. Quottrich, however, finds the couch distasteful and prefers to sit across my desk from me, giving me the stink-eye for the entire hour.

Her life seems small and petty and I understand why her only son never visits and why her siblings and husband all had the good sense to die well before she did. She's nasty and vindictive, wishing horrible things upon everyone from the paperboy to the bagger at the supermarket. While it's not as bad as being in the same room as Mel, sitting across from the jagged edges of her ire is pretty damned uncomfortable, even when I shield my psyche as well as I'm able.

I mostly just nod politely, occasionally risk offering my perspective on things—always a mistake—and try to remind myself that I'm the only person she really has in her life, and that I should at least feign interest. I'd considered ending our professional relationship several times since I'd taken her on as a client. She's miserable to be around, both because her presence is to my empathy what feedback is to your ears and because she's just so damned ornery.

I can never quite bring myself to send her away, though. I can feel the loneliness in her, garbled up along the edges of her hate like gum stuck to the bottom of really uncomfortable shoes. It seems to jump out at me sometimes, so cold it nearly burns, reminding me that, sure she's as awful as a leering gargoyle, but she's still human.

So I put my best professional foot forward every week, grinning and bearing her presence and assuring myself that one day karma will reward me for being a good person.

Waiting for karma can only get me so far, though, so I satisfy myself in the present by refusing to offer her any of the candy in the dish on my desk. When there's candy in it, that is—the honey thief had made off with that, too. Or Chloe had hidden it; it wouldn't surprise me now that she knew how many extra birthday cupcakes I'd scarfed down.

"I know you're just waiting for me to *leave*," Mrs. Quottrich said tartly, surprising me. I glanced past her as quickly as I could to the clock above the couch and nodded, my insides leaping with joy. I had somehow lost track of time and not noticed I was nearly free of her. When I looked back to her, I found her irritation had been knocked down and kicked to the side to make way for a swampy flood of insult. I hadn't even said anything, but evidently she saw something in my face that she didn't like.

"Yes, it does look like our time is up. Would you like some help to the door?"

Mrs. Q's eyes narrowed as her lip pulled up slightly in a snarl. I ignored it, pushing to my feet and moving around my desk to help her. Stubborn resolve, or perhaps arthritis in her narrow legs, kept her sitting as I stepped toward her as slowly as possible. I could put up a front like I would help her, but we both knew it would never happen. The few times I'd tried, she'd slapped at me and insisted she didn't want me to touch her.

Watching her make her hobbling way out, I stuck my tongue out at the old lady's back. Chloe's cheery goodbye got her only a slanted look and a cross comment regarding her low-cut shirt. As the outer door slammed shut, Chloe grinned at me.

"You survived!" She clapped gleefully.

"Unfortunately, so did she," I sighed.

Chloe pressed on, refusing to let me vent the grumpy steam I'd built up spending an hour with Mrs. Quottrich.

"I was thinking about our problem—the real one," she clarified, anticipating and ignoring my forthcoming bitchiness. "We should go see Merrin."

"I hadn't even thought of that," I admitted, leaning against the desk. "It's been awhile since we've seen her, actually. I wonder how she's doing."

"Oh, I visit from time to time. I was there two weeks ago, just to get a palm reading and toss her some cash. She looked better, actually. Still not... you know, *normal*, but cleaned up."

"Hopefully that works in our favor. We're free for, what?" I held out a hand, gestured to Chloe's watch when she didn't step closer. "Two hours until the next appointment? We can bolt over, ask for help, drop some cash and maybe a few sandwiches on her, and be back in plenty of time. Even if it ends up snowing like the weatherman threatened and everyone else forgets how to drive."

"Will do, boss." Mimicking Mel's action from earlier, Chloe saluted me, turned stiffly on her heel, and headed to her desk.

I waited, still leaning against my desk as I thought about our young witch friend. When I'd first met her, I wouldn't have known to call her a witch, but she'd informed me of the label during one of her rambling, vacant-eyed speeches. I'd also learned then that if she was to travel to certain parts of Indiana, she might still be burned as such.

What the hell do you say to a thing like that?

I didn't know her exact age, but her slight, almost underfed stature and dreamy personality made me think she wasn't yet twenty. I'd stumbled on her a year or so ago and Chloe and I had sort of made her our pet project. Merrin lived in a tiny apartment at the edge of downtown, reading palms and tarot for a living. I'd offered to let her move in with me for cheaper than she paid at her crappy apartment, but she said she loved it there, that the roaches were her friends.

That's about all one needs to say about Merrin Smith.

In the hall leading to Merrin's apartment, Chloe and I could hear a mix of loud music, loud sex, and loud fights. It was typical of her building and it didn't seem to bother her, so I tried not to let it bother me. We reached her door at the end of the hall and Chloe knocked. The door flew open immediately, revealing a tall, slender, naked woman.

She had at least a full head of height on me, making her an Amazon of muscled pale skin. Her perfect brows matched her vibrant electric-blue hair. My eyes traveled the length of her body before I could tell them they were being rude and, without my permission, they lingered on her breasts. The tips were a pale almost-blue, reminding me of a glacier. In fact, just looking at them I could almost hear the dry, frigid cracking associated with overwhelming amounts of solid ice.

Noticing I was staring, Chloe stepped forward, holding out a hand.

"Hi, we're here for Merrin?" She made it a question, curiosity pumping off of her. I wondered suddenly if Merrin had moved since Chloe had seen her and we were in the wrong place. The woman continued to watch me watching her and I noticed then that she wasn't human. The hair and the skin should have given it away immediately, but I'd been more preoccupied by the way she looked than the way she felt. I swallowed hard, shooting a sidelong look at Chloe. My assistant was still smiling pleasantly, waiting for an answer or a handshake.

The woman's interest in us waned, washing off of me like the tide receding from a frozen shore. She stalked back into the apartment, leaving the door open. Chloe looked at me, gave a half-shrug, and strolled in boldly.

Everything in the apartment looked basically the same but with a few small changes; blue and black throw pillows had been added to the sagging couch and piled on the floor. Stylish, sharply-angled chairs that looked to be the seating equivalent to runway high-fashion faced the couch like an audience. Things looked cleaner, too, as if Merrin had dusted. This struck me as odd, since the girl barely remembered to brush her hair.

I took a breath, feeling out the apartment to see where she was. Excitement, nervousness, and concentration pulsed from the pantry. I glanced at Chloe and we headed into the tiny kitchen. I pulled open the pantry door and found it empty except for Merrin, who was hunched on the floor below the barren shelves, hands fluttering between a bunch of cards set out in a deliberate pattern. I squatted down and put my hand on her shoulder. She didn't notice me.

"Merrin?" I asked. She mumbled and leaned forward. Her auburn hair fell over her shoulder, trailing to the floor. Her locks looked brushed and conditioned, instead of frizzy and unkempt like usual. Merrin hummed something quietly and turned over a card from her stack. Her clothes looked new, though not quite fashionable; her hippie ren faire style held strong, but something about it looked deliberate now, instead of being the product of shopping at thrift stores on a small budget. I brushed her hair back from her face and glanced up at Chloe. She shrugged and we both looked back at the little witch.

"Sweetie?" I ventured. Merrin turned to look at me but there was no recognition in her vacant eyes. I went to grab her hand but got shocked less than a finger's width away. I yelped and pulled back, rubbing my fingers on my skirt. I sometimes forget that Merrin's abilities are not only way more powerful than mine, but can also be legitimately, physically dangerous.

After waiting another minute, I looked down at her cards, trying to make sense of them. They didn't look like any tarot cards I recognized but they were quite pretty. Merrin started mumbling again before reaching out to take my wrist; when I didn't get shocked again, I let her close her fingers around me.

"You don't have to worry; Izzy likes you," she murmured. Her eyes were unfocused, her gaze sitting somewhere in the middle distance between her and my chin. I had no idea what she was talking about. I nodded, made a vague sound of interest, and switched my grip to hold her fingers. The action made her blink, her eyes clearing as she straightened her body minutely. "Gwen, hi. How are you?"

"I'm good." Letting go of her hand, I watched as she held it hovering, as if I was still supporting it. "What about you? Can we get out of this closet? This isn't the most comfortable position." I stood and took her hand again, but she remained still a second before standing.

"Oh. Okay." She stood up carefully, hopping out of the closet in a way that guaranteed she didn't disturb her cards. She shut the door silently and then tip-toed away like she'd left a baby sleeping. Chloe and I followed her into the living area, where she sat on the edge of the coffee table.

"Merrin? Can we ask you some questions?"

She nodded once, her eyes fixed on some point mid-ceiling, and said,

"About the fairies."

"Fairies?" I asked, worried we were having two entirely different conversations. Merrin remained robotic in her detachment.

"Spider fingers, tusks like an elephant." Merrin moved her hands to her face to mime a mixture of the two, pressing her knuckles to her lips as she wiggled her fingers.

I exchanged a glance with Chloe, who nodded encouragingly. "Yeah, I guess." The existence of fairies had never really been something I'd considered, but I had a werewolf hitting on me several times a week, so I couldn't really argue with the idea. Though under any other circumstances, I probably would have been happy to pick a fight. Who thinks of something like my monster employers when the word "fairy" is uttered? I was willing to bet no one. "Two… fairies… came to my office last night and asked for help. Do you know anything about that?"

"They don't want your help, they want *her* help. She refuses." Merrin's gaze slid from the ceiling to the door of her tiny pantry and her brows furrowed. "The future has drifted. Dark times. You will make the wrong choices."

I had no idea what she was talking about, but the latter half of the premonition came as no surprise. My choice was usually to eat copious amounts of junk food and watch reality TV; of course I was going to make the wrong one.

"Whose help do they want?" I asked, stepping into her view. This put her gaze at roughly my belly button, but I figured it was better than nothing. "Who do they think I am?"

"Another child will soon go missing. You can stop it. But you cannot stop her descent."

"Whose descent? The child's?"

"The child is a boy. You must reach his home." Her eyes rolled upward slowly, like balloons being filled with helium. "Tonight. Eight o'clock."

"Where does he live? What's his name?" Was she serious? Did I have the power to keep this kid safe? You could never quite tell with Merrin. Instead of answering me, she snapped her gaze to my face, her body going slightly stiff.

"Gwen, hello." Blinking, she turned to Chloe. "I didn't know you two were here. How are you?" Her expression went soft as she reached a hand toward Chloe. I could feel distress in Chloe, but she hid it perfectly, keeping her smile warm as she moved to take Merrin's hand.

"How are you feeling?"

"I'm well. Evadne keeps me." Still holding Chloe's hand, she turned to peer into the bedroom where the other woman lounged. Was she a fairy, too? I could tell by the pattern of her emotions that she certainly wasn't a werewolf, but past that I wasn't sure. I was going to just figure her a fairy unless she told me otherwise. Hell, I decided then and there that Madeline was a fairy, too. No one ever got hurt by generalizations, am I right?

"She's very kind," Merrin finished after a few moments.

I had nothing to say to that that wouldn't probably get the beautiful fairy mad at me, so I cleared my throat, stepping around to put myself between Merrin and Evadne to ensure she was looking at me again.

"Sweetie, you were telling me about a child being taken tonight. Do you remember?"

"Eight tonight." She looked distracted, like she was listening to something disturbing. "I see flowers. Oh." Her face fell and she turned to me. "I'm so sorry. I'll bring you something to help with that."

Despite the fact that I didn't know what she was talking about, I took a step back to let her get up and pass. She didn't move, just continued to watch me with pity and worry, as if I were detailing my injuries from a bad accident. After a second, Chloe dropped Merrin's hand to close in and elbow me. I caught up, realizing that Merrin had no intention of getting me anything at the moment. Swallowing, I nodded.

"I would appreciate that, thank you. Can you tell me more about where to find this child? How I can save him?"

"You haven't yet?" Merrin looked perplexed, her eyes widening as she tipped her head. "I'll find out for you."

This time she did stand, drifting toward the bedroom on bare feet. I frowned, lifting my hands to my hips. When she didn't reappear for over a minute, I turned to Chloe.

"What now?"

"Now you go," Evadne said, startling me. She sauntered toward us and held out a hand. "I understand you provide payment for services rendered?"

"Uh." I nodded, turning to Chloe. She'd been the one to get cash. Without hesitation, Chloe slid a small stack of twenties out of her bag, handing them to Evadne.

"I will contact you when she has what you're requesting." Still watching Chloe intently, she flicked her gaze to me almost faster than I could see before tipping her head ever so slightly toward Chloe.

"Pleasure."

Nervous energy slithered like an electric eel through Chloe and I jerked. I was definitely ready to get the hell out of there.

Six

We discussed the oddity of Merrin having a spectacularly gorgeous otherworldly roommate on the way back to the office, pausing occasionally to try to decipher all the things Merrin had said to us. We failed miserably but decided that if Evadne did in fact contact us with the location of the next kidnapping attempt, it hadn't been a wasted trip at all.

The rest of the day passed quickly; my last two Monday clients are nothing compared to the agony of spending an hour with Mrs. Q. Four-thirty rolled around and I was only too happy to shut down my computer and start getting ready to head home.

We chatted as I locked up, bantered as we rode the elevator down to street level, and said our goodbyes. The snow that had been tickling my office window glittered in my hair as I unlocked my car and tossed my bag into the back seat. My eyes flitted to my steering wheel as I slid into my seat and I sighed.

"Again?"

There was a pink sticky note in the center of the steering wheel. It said, *"Put up your shields!"*

I stared at it grumpily as I turned the car on and blasted the heater. Just as I was about to crumple the note and toss it in my little garbage bag, the passenger door opened and Mel slid his finely sculpted ass into my car. I was briefly stunned into silence as I did what the note had suggested and fortified my psychic wall. As at The Internets, it only helped so much. My muscles twinged, my skin protested, and insisted I was pressing a hot iron against each and every nerve. Luckily, I wasn't the only one in pain, at least for a few seconds.

Mel grunted in discomfort as he realized what a mistake it had been to

45

cram himself in without looking. Chloe must've adjusted the seat for herself earlier that day, so at least I got a chuckle watching Mel fold himself in where her small body had been so comfortable earlier. He was able to manage, but it required pressing his knees to his chest.

After some fumbling between his legs—and, of course, an obnoxious kissing sound directed at me as he did so—the seat shot back and he stretched out. I frowned at him and turned off the car to make it clear that I was not taking him anywhere.

"Hey, Jeeves, where we going?" Mel asked, his eyes roaming to watch my hand as I tucked the note into my jacket pocket.

"You're going to get out. I'm going home."

"I'll join you; we can warm the place up."

I sighed. "Mel."

He grinned at me and gave an amiable shrug. Turning my rearview mirror so he could poke at his Fillion-esque hair, he explained.

"I've got news. There are indeed children missing. While that's, unfortunately, not atypical, this batch has the cops scratching their heads. Three children, two girls and a boy, have been taken in the last few weeks. What makes these particular kidnappings interesting is that the police have no leads. Zilch. Nada."

"That's all you found out?"

"Let me finish before you run your mouth," Mel said. My eyelid gave a hearty spasm and I felt like smacking him. "All three children were removed from locked homes, where they should have been safe. First little girl was in bed and then she wasn't. Second was in the backyard; Mom swears she stepped inside just long enough to grab a pair of gloves off the counter. The little boy was home sick from school with his mother."

"No breaking and entering?"

"Nothing of the sort. If these aren't the kidnappings you're supposed to solve, I'll take a vow of celibacy."

"Oh, don't make this a choice between your abject misery and the safety of small children. I can't make that decision."

Mel snorted, rolling his eyes good-naturedly. "What about you? You're the one they hired; I'd better not be doing all the legwork here."

"Chloe and I went to see Merrin today. She spouted the usual foreboding nonsense, said she'd make me something, claimed we could stop a kidnapping—we're hoping to get a call about that sooner rather than later—and we gave her some cash."

Mel made a small, thoughtful sound before jerking his chin. "How's she doing?"

Despite Mel being, well, *Mel,* I wasn't surprised by his concern. Something about our little witch friend made her the only woman that Mel didn't shamelessly flirt with. I'd seen him hit on girls who had turned eighteen mere seconds before and also on women in their sixties. Merrin, however, had only gotten a pat on the shoulder and Mel's suggestion that she eat a nutritious dinner; he'd even offered to buy her the meal.

"She's... living with someone? Or someone's living with her. It was a not-person-someone, far as I can tell. Super hot, but off. I think she was a fairy."

"Ooh," Mel hissed, his face contorting like he'd been burned. "Super-hot fairies are generally bad news. Well, most are bad news, but the lookers you really don't wanna fuck with."

"Even *you* don't wanna fuck with them?" I asked, amused by the nervous frustration jangling through him like a can of pennies, even as I winced against the clamorous experience of being so close to it.

"Even I wouldn't risk it."

"Then it *must* be serious. I'll keep that in mind."

"Don't go getting your pretty little head ripped off," Mel suggested, reaching out to ruffle my hair.

"Okay," was all I could get out. His fingers tugged my hair lightly as he pulled away; lust flared up from his core and I jerked my head back to lessen the contact. "Anything else?"

"I'm going to see if I can get the parents to talk to me, offer my private eye services. Nothing seemed off to Julia—one of my hotter cop friends—but she doesn't exactly have our radar, does she?"

"How'd you pitch this, by the way?"

"What do you mean?"

"Well, I'm assuming you didn't just walk up to said hot cop and announce that you're a werewolf with an empath acquaintance who's been hired by two monsters to find kids. That wouldn't really fly, would it?"

"Some people pick up on what's going on around the spooky side of things, actually. Occasionally they're like you, with some mild power. Sometimes they're a few shades weaker than you, but still aware. Sensitives who get a tingle in the back of their mind when the phone's about to ring, or who just have a really well-developed lizard brain. Julia's the latter. She's been around enough conflicting eyewitness accounts of something hinky going down that she trusts me when I say something hinky's going down. Plus, it's tough not to believe me when I've made you see god." Mel winked, leaning forward with a predatory smile. "Interested?"

"Back off, Fido," I growled, pressing myself against my door. "It ain't happening." Mel watched me for a few moments before shrugging and sitting back. I took a deep breath, fought off the nausea he'd caused, and got back on track. "Look, if it's possible, I'd like to go with you when you meet the parents."

"In your capacity as Super Therapist?"

I ignored the dig. "Laurel and Hardy were scouts, right? They said their job is to check on kids with powers, to see if they're a threat. I'd like to go and see if the parents have any extra... oomph. If one or both of each pair have ..." I waggled my hands in front of me, unsure of how to describe it.

"A tendency toward dance?" Mel finished for me. I blinked and lowered my hands.

"Powers. See if any of them have any sort of abilities, even as mild as mine. We may have some sort of a zealot on our hands, someone who's learned that not everyone is a boring, useless human and that he—or she—has a problem with this. Someone with that overdeveloped lizard brain you mentioned, maybe. These kids could be in danger for being too powerful. Or maybe they're just sensitive, but this guy thinks they can bend reality or start fires with their hands, so he's killing them."

"You know, technically everyone can start fires with their hands," Mel observed. "You just need matches or a lighter, maybe some sticks to rub together."

My eye twitched again and I grunted at him. "Don't be pedantic."

"Alternately, we could rub our body parts together and see what heats up."

"Please shut up," I said, touching the jolt in my cheek.

Mel took a moment to enjoy my discomfort and annoyance before continuing. "You really gave this some thought."

"Should I not have?"

"I'm just not used to you *thinking* is all."

"I think all the time," I protested. "Usually about how I hope your testicles get mangled in some sort of industrial accident."

"You think about my testicles all the time?"

A fit of irritation and outrage ran through the entire right side of my face in a spasm and I reached up to press my hand to my cheek as if I could squelch my hatred of Mel if I squeezed hard enough. Mel laughed at me but got back to the real problem.

"What other theories did you generate while trying to fight your natural urge to picture me naked? You think he might go after someone like Merrin, who can actually do damage?"

The quake in my face died away and I waved him off. "I don't know. It's just a thought at this point. For all I know, this guy's just an asshole who likes hurting people and kids are the easiest targets. The fact that the fairies are after them means that they think these kids have powers, but I don't know how they determine that. Maybe they check the kids of parents with powers but not all kids get the powers. I really don't know."

I looked over and met Mel's eyes again. The car was still freezing and the windows were getting foggy. The light dusting of snow on the windows made the car oddly intimate. For once, though, Mel didn't invite me onto his lap or suggest he shove his hand up my shirt.

It was getting a little weird.

"I've got a date. I'll keep you posted," he said, breaking the silence.

"Not on the date."

He grinned. "You wish." After some more intense eye contact, he jumped out of the car and slammed the door. I did a roll of my shoulders, considered the note in my pocket, and wondered why the candy thief had decided to be helpful. I should have just been grateful the thing had taken a liking to me, especially considering everything that had fallen into my lap, but I couldn't bring myself to just run with it. I had a good thing going with my ignorance and if the candy thief was going to hang around, I might not be able to revel in it anymore.

I might have to start learning things about fairies and, god forbid, werewolves. I didn't want to know more about either, and this sticky note addict was putting a kink in my plans to avoid that side of things.

As I started the car again, I dipped a hand into the center console, aiming to soothe myself with a snack. When I found only an empty bag, my first reactions were a snarl and a hearty string of cuss words.

Then, when I remembered where the hard caramel candies had disappeared to, I thanked my past-self for having finished them a week before. They'd been gone well before the magical bastard could steal them, so there. Bolstered slightly by the fact that the thief hadn't gotten the best of me this time, I headed for home.

That evening I journeyed to a tiny vegan donut shop on the far side of Bellevue. Chloe had gotten me addicted months ago just by bringing me a single donut at work one morning, though I was sure that hadn't been her intention. While I usually didn't travel all this way for something as simple as a donut, I figured the last twenty-four hours called for it.

No one in the state—as far as I knew— other than Dulcet Donuts made a triple chocolate pastry stuffed with frosting and covered with a banana glaze. It could make your heart stop, but I figured the fact that the sugary coating was at least *flavored* with fruit meant it had to be good for me on some level.

The woman at the counter recognized me when I walked in, despite the fact that it had been over a month since I'd been there, and had my order ready.

"Long time!" Polly said, already ringing me up.

I shrugged. "Hard day, otherwise I probably wouldn't have made the drive."

"Well, that makes me feel special," she said, an edge of fake insult in her tone. I could tell, even without my psychic power, that she wasn't really bothered, but I made up for the accidental insult with a fat tip. I took a narrow two-top in the corner for myself and chowed down on my unhealthy delights, feeling all the better for it. After I finished, I realized that, if things got any crazier, I might not make it out this way again any time soon.

Just to be safe, I ordered five more of the heart-stoppers to go, cleaning them out.

I was strapping the box into my passenger seat—you can never be too cautious when protecting such valuable treasure as donuts—when my phone rang.

"Hello?" I answered without looking at the number on the screen.

"I have the address of your kidnapping." I blinked, my brain briefly too far gone in a glaze high to know what the silky voice was talking about, or who it belonged to. Evadne pressed on without waiting for me to acknowledge her, detailing an address that, to my surprise, was in the same city. I jumped, trying to find something write on. "Merrin will bring your trinket by later and we will be settled, is that understood?"

"Yeah. Wait, trinket?" I asked, still digging through my glovebox for something to write the quickly fading address on before my mind erased it. Evadne had already hung up, so I let the phone fall into the footwell of my car while I gave up on finding a clean piece of paper and scribbled directly onto the donut box.

"Crazy blue-haired hottie," I groused, flipping on the dome light to see what I'd scrawled. My writing was nearly illegible, but I was able to punch it into my phone to see where I'd be telling Chloe to meet me.

"Well, that's convenient." My phone claimed it would take me less than ten minutes to arrive at my destination. It was nearly seven-forty, but I figured Chloe could make it out my way if I got hold of her quickly enough. A revelation hit me as just before I hit the call button and I sat in the quiet car staring at her smiling face on the screen. Chloe could do wonders with an insurance company and make a damned fine cup of tea, but she wouldn't be any help in stopping a kidnapping. Chloe was, as she'd put it, just my assistant; what good was she at something like this?

I couldn't help anyone alone, though, regardless of how close I happened to be. Somehow I didn't think knocking on the door of someone's house and politely informing them that their child was about to be kidnapped was going to go well. I considered calling the police but instantly realized that was an even stupider idea than calling Chloe or trying to warn the parents.

So what the hell was I supposed to do?

When I realized what my only option was, I let out a resigned groan. I needed the big guns. Rather, I needed a werewolf *with* big guns. I rubbed my temples, then called Mel. To my surprise, he answered on the first ring.

"News?"

"Uh." I needed a second to adjust; I had expected him to answer with some crude come-on. "I just got the address of the supposed kidnapping. It's in Bellevue. I'm on my way there now. I was going to call Chloe but I figured you'd be more helpful. I'm assuming you can do more than howl at the moon."

"Please," he spat. "Send me the address and I'll be right there. Where are you?"

"Nearly there, actually. I was already in the area."

"Shit," Mel growled. There was an edge of an *actual* growl to it and my stomach did a flip-flop. Since it was currently stuffed to the brim with donuts, it was a heavy, unpleasant feeling. "Don't go near the place until I get there. I'll—I know someone in the Bellevue PD. I'll send her there. Don't be a hero."

"Not something you have to worry about with me. Just hurry. Merrin said eight and it's closing in fast."

"Already in the car," Mel said, hanging up. My headset went dead and I glanced at my phone on the seat as if it could answer my questions about when, exactly, Mel had become useful and heroic. This wasn't a side of him I had considered possible.

I paused at the first stop sign I came across, punching the address I'd been given into my phone and sending it on its way to Mel. I got a honk as I hit send, but I'd rather be honked at than accidentally crash myself into a tree because I'd been texting.

I planned on parking far down the street, but the closer I got, the more I realized that was unlikely. The street was packed with cars and, in an ironic twist of fate that never happened when I was, say, visiting a tiny vegan donut shop, I found parking right in front of the apartment building. It was run-down, though not as if it was neglected, just a little worse for wear. There were maybe twelve units in total. The paint was faded here and there and the sidewalks around it had seen better days, but the foliage was well kept and the windows actually looked new. It matched the address that Evadne had given me.

"Dammit," I said, darting across the other lane to take the spot, despite my misgivings. I was technically parked backwards, but I wasn't planning on being there long, so I decided not to worry about it.

I locked my doors, hunkered down in my seat, and tried not to be noticed by anything that looked like it wanted to kidnap small children. I sat in silence for ten minutes, too nervous to even contemplate digging into my box of donuts. The closest thing I saw to a kidnapper was a hipster with a giant mustache striding by. He looked harmless, but I decided not to trust him anyway, just to be thorough.

As was quickly becoming its habit, the universe decided to throw me a curveball. I was still hunched down in my seat, my gaze darting between my side mirrors, the front window, and out toward the apartment building, when I felt a peculiar emotional signature coming from far off to my left. It wasn't one I'd ever felt before, so I couldn't immediately recognize what the emotions meant. They felt liquid, thick and aggressive in a way that made me rub my hands over my arms as if I could wipe them away.

When I turned to see what exactly I was feeling, I found myself looking at a man. He was approaching the apartment building across the grass and the closer he got, the more I started to pull back, considering moving to sit in the passenger seat or getting out of the car and running away altogether.

Whatever he was feeling, my empathy was drowning in it, sucking under the thick, syrupy weight. I took a shaky breath and closed my eyes as I tried to build up my shields to block it out. Within a few seconds, I felt stronger, more aware of my own body and not just of how it felt to be near the creature outside. I opened my eyes, focused on him again, and tried to apply everything I'd ever learned from cop dramas on TV. Pay attention to details, notice the physical stuff, remember things I could pass on to Mel if necessary.

From my place slouched in my seat, he looked tall, reedy, like he was habitually underfed. His hair was pale, looking almost white even in the dark, and his features were shadowed, maybe a little gaunt. Despite the temperature outside, he was dressed in only jeans and a button-down long-sleeved shirt. Just the idea of standing out there in the cold without a heavy jacket made me uncomfortable. Shaking my head, I let out a small, unhappy sound of disgust.

As soon as I did, he tensed, perking up to look around as if he'd heard me. I pressed my hands over my mouth, terrified he'd detected me and was, at any moment, going to explode out of his skin into some horrid bat creature and fly across the distance between us to rip off my head. His gaze passed over my car but, to my surprise, he didn't seem to notice me. Seconds passed like eons, and when his shoulders relaxed and he shifted his footing, I let out my breath as quietly as I could, thanking the stars that I was still alive.

Where the hell was Mel?

Come to think of it, what the hell was this person-shaped creature even doing? I'd expected, should I run afoul of something, that it would spring into action, phasing through a wall or teleporting instantly into a home and reappearing seconds later with a stolen child in its arms. This thing, whatever it was, just stood there, almost like he was waiting for someone. Maybe I had it all wrong and this guy was harmless, unrelated to the kidnapping. Maybe it was the hipster with the 'stache I needed to be worried about, after all.

Taking a deep breath, I bit my lip and considered my options. Since none of them involved me getting out of the car, I figured I had only one way to satisfy my curiosity.

I extended my empathy toward the creature, reasoning with my fear about what I was trying. I'm not a cat, I figured; in fact, I don't even like the furry little bastards. But as sirens started to wail off in the distance and the creature with the liquid emotions turned to deliberately catch my eye, I considered that, while curiosity might not kill me, it could definitely rough me up.

Seven

I woke up in the car with a feeling like someone had driven a railroad spike through my sinuses and straight to the back of my brain. I was slumped over the steering wheel and something was tapping at my left ear with a sledgehammer. I groaned, shifting my gaze to the window.

Light blazed and, for an instant, I was sure someone had lit two road flares and jabbed them against my eyeballs. The sudden brightness was unbearable, swamping my entire nervous system. I shoved at the door, just barely able to aim my impending vomit outside the car. The violent heaving of my stomach did nothing positive to the chaotic destruction eating away at my brain and I was distantly aware that I was whimpering. When my body finally calmed, I didn't bother attempting to sit up straight and some small part of me realized that I would have fallen right out of the car if the seatbelt hadn't been there to stop me.

"Ms. Arthur?" a soft voice asked. I grunted in response but didn't have the fortitude yet to actually see what or who was questioning me. I couldn't feel anything except my own pain and I noticed after a moment that I was weeping. What the hell had happened?

"Gwen? Can you hear me?"

My eyes were closed but that didn't stop the swarm of angry bees going to town on my eyeballs. I felt a warm, gloved hand on my chin and my head lifted slowly. A light shined into my eyes, blinding me to details, but I took a deep breath of the scent of feminine soap. When she let my lids droop, I cracked an eye open on my own and saw a blurry, face-shaped blob. Whimpering, I let my eye close again and felt something soft come up to wipe across my mouth.

A radio squawked painfully next to my brain and the person tending me responded in cop-speak before dialing down the volume. I shifted, trying to turn myself over to lapse back into unconsciousness. Her now-bare hand rolled my face back toward her and she pushed one of my eyes open.

"No, you can't sleep. I don't know what's wrong with you." Gently cradling my head with one hand, she felt around my jaw and cheeks. On the surface, it wasn't a bad touch, but it seemed to aggravate something in my brain. Distantly, I realized it wasn't just me in my head anymore. Something else had surfaced in her presence, pounding at my skull from inside. I was still crying. She kept talking as she inspected me. I wasn't paying attention, though it was keeping me conscious; her voice was soothing but the thing in my brain was angry and fighting her, trying to drag me back down into darkness. Time passed as she felt around my body for injuries and checked the seat and car for blood, talking all the while.

"If we need to, I can call an ambulance and we'll get you checked out proper. I have a bit of first aid training and you don't seem to have a concussion, though. No injuries I can find. Honestly, if I could smell even a bit of alcohol on you, I'd guess you had the worst hangover I've ever come across." She leaned a hip on my seat next to my leg, facing me as her hands slid gently up my face, fingertips starting at my jaw and ending in my hair. "My name is Amy, and I wish we could have met under better circumstances. Now, breathe with me, Gwen."

As she took a breath, I took a breath. The thing inside me started to panic; she might have been human but that wasn't all and the parasite in my head knew it. It battered against the inside of my skull, trying to read her, trying to figure out what she was and what she was doing. As she breathed out, I did as well. The thing inside my psyche flailed spastically and then started to dissipate. My eyes snapped open and I found myself able to focus on a very pretty face.

Even with slightly frizzed hair and no makeup, she was lovely. Her blue eyes were vibrant over a straight, narrow nose and full lips. She had a trio of tiny beauty marks set back on her right cheek and I found myself concentrating on them as she continued what had to be some sort of psychic healing.

Amy's lips parted; she took a deep breath, seeming to call my attention from her cheek to her gaze. I couldn't look away and I couldn't resist whatever her power was. I took a breath with her and, when we breathed out, the thing in my head came out with it. Within a few more breaths, I was alone in my brain. I still felt like I'd been thrown off a cliff on fire, a la Lara Croft, but I could see my surroundings again and my empathy peeked out of whatever deep, dark crevice it had burrowed into. Concern and calm radiated from Amy; it was like being a small child sitting in my mother's lap again. I let out a small whimper of happiness and took a slow, long breath, on my own this time.

Still holding my face between her soft hands, she grinned at me from inches away. I swallowed thickly and gave her a small smile as I slurred at her.

"Thanks."

We stayed that way until something hot seared the edges of my consciousness.

"Why, hello, *ladies*," Mel said from nearby. Amy looked up at him without taking her hands away from my skin.

"Mel, dear, how are you?" She turned back to me without waiting for his answer and her face went sober. "I'm going to let go and you are going to feel it. Something was inside you and it left a nasty stain. Whatever it was, it's gone now, but you're going to need more than my modest little healing ability to feel back to normal. Are you ready?"

I swallowed hard and said a meek, "Yes."

She pulled her hands away and nausea rushed in. She jumped back just in time and I threw up just outside the car, where she'd been leaning. I wouldn't have figured I had anything left in me after the last time.

"I got here maybe ten minutes ago," Amy explained to Mel while I finished heaving. "I didn't see her at first, but I did a sweep of the area, checking around the building. Nothing out of the ordinary that I could see. Whatever you called about either ran off when it heard the sirens or had already done whatever it came for."

"Sirens, most likely," Mel murmured. I looked up at him from my seat, wondering why his emotions weren't affecting me as much as they usually did. I considered that maybe Amy was to thank, but I didn't have the energy to ask.

"That's the second time she's vomited and there's no clean street left for me to stand on." She looked away from the mess to Mel and her face warmed. "You'll need to take her home. Whatever's wrong with her, it's not something that a trip to the E.R. will fix."

"I did a lap around the area, too. I think the snow is screwing up my nose," Mel said, shaking his head. "I could've sworn I smelled vampire, but there's no way."

"Vampire?" Amy asked, her eyebrows shooting up. "I ... those really exist? I had no idea."

"There's a reason. Don't worry about it, they're not a threat to you or anyone else." Mel paused, cocking his head at her. "Will your bosses ask about your sudden detour?"

She shook her head, her expression going soft. "Don't worry about me. Just get her safe."

Mel nodded and took her hand off his arm, kissing it and giving her a wink. She smiled and I felt her flattery. Whatever was between them was warm, but she wasn't after sex. Mel leaned down to look into my eyes.

"You smell pretty awful. Slide over, I'm driving you home." When I didn't move, he frowned, then spread his legs on either side of the vomit and reached awkwardly into the car. "You're sure she's not hurt?" he asked Amy as he moved my box of donuts to the back seat.

She told him no and then I heard her radio squawk as the volume was turned up. She walked away without another word to us, addressing dispatch as she did.

"Up you go." He lifted me like a doll and sort of tossed me over the cup holders and e-brake. As I landed on the passenger's seat, one leg still draped across to the driver's side, Mel slid into the car. With a deft hand, he shoved the seat back and then reached over to gently cradle my leg, his grip more sexual than helpful as he put me completely on the passenger side. His hands flirted with impropriety as he reached across my body to buckle my seatbelt and he wasted no time turning the car on and blasting the heater.

"Mel," I muttered.

"Hmm?"

"You're an ass, but a nice one."

"I have a nice ass? Thank you, Gwen. I'm touched!" To demonstrate, he took my limp hand and dropped it in his lap.

I woke in the dark in an unfamiliar bed to the muffled sounds of a TV in the next room. The bed I lay in was decadent, the covers thick and plentiful. The room looked small, judging from what the sliver of light slipping through the doorway showed me. There was one narrow rectangular window set high in the wall to the right and I could see that the sun was sneaking a peek at the world. I couldn't tell if it was going down or coming up; I had no idea how long I'd been asleep.

Something shifted by my legs and I froze, panic taking over. A dark shape arched upward and I felt claws dig into my leg, even through the blankets. My heart pounding, I tried to force myself to think rationally. My brain was refusing the call to action and all I could do was picture horrible things about to happen to me.

The claws pulled back and little feet padded quickly over me before a furry head slammed into my face, shoving me further into the pillows I was propped against. A purr vibrated away my fear as a cat rubbed itself across my face, ending gracelessly with the side of its butt against my mouth. I blew out my breath—and likely a bit of spittle—and turned away, grumbling. The cat came back for more, stopping briefly to sniff my mouth before making another rear-ending pass. I couldn't feel any actual emotions coming from her, but that wasn't unusual for felines. They're often more of an enigma than the Riddler himself.

The door cracked open a bit more and Chloe peered inside. The light from the living room illuminated her, making me squint slightly.

"Poopy, leave her alone." She slipped in, closing the door just enough that it let light into the room but didn't blind me. She picked Poopy up—the cat let out a dissatisfied little rumble, but didn't fight her—and then perched on the bed next to me. "How are you feeling?"

"Naked." I answered. My throat was dry and I swallowed as much spit as I could generate. "Why am I naked?"

I was struggling to remember what had happened. I had vague memories of Mel in my car and I leaned my head back as I tried to piece things together. Suddenly I had a shocking thought, letting out a dry, strangled cry.

"We... am I naked because... did Mel do this? Did I have sex with Mel? Oh god. Oh, god!" I moaned, hugging the covers against my chest and wondering if I'd ever be able to chafe Mel's essence off my skin. My head was pounding; it felt like the worst hangover headache I'd ever gotten. I said nothing, waiting for Chloe to break the disgusting news that Mel had finally found the cheap pick-up line that I couldn't resist. After what felt like several days, she chuckled and sat up, setting the cat free on the floor.

"Relax. You threw up on yourself, so we had—"

"*We?*" I demanded squeakily. "What did Mel pay you to let him see me naked?"

"I wouldn't charge Mel to see you naked!"

"Wouldn't or didn't?" Chloe's snort dissolved into a fit of giggles and I relaxed. She took my hand and held it, giving a squeeze.

"You must be delirious. I undressed you to clean you up and you've been out for over a day. Whatever smacked you around really did a number. You feeling okay now?"

I took stock of my body, sucking in a breath, wiggling and moving my limbs from the toes up to see if everything worked. Other than the monstrous headache and fatigue, I actually felt reasonably normal.

What I didn't feel was Chloe. Panic surged right back in.

"I can't feel you!" I reversed her hold, taking her hand. I clutched it, seeking outward, trying to feel her emotions. There was an ebbing of something but it could have been the headache. I couldn't tell. "I—my empathy! It's gone!" I took a deep breath; I wanted to jump up, to run out and find whatever had done this to me and demand it give me back what was mine.

Chloe put a hand to my head.

"Calm down. It's not you." She pulled my hand to her chest, just below her collarbone, and I felt a lump of something smooth and hot, like glass left on a stove. She closed her hand around mine and tugged. The necklace left her skin and suddenly I could feel her. Concern washed over me and I gasped for air; it was like drowning in her worry. I felt myself flailing, trying to surface through the flood of mixed emotions, a torrent that I'd never felt from a person in one sitting before. After a few minutes, everything slowed and I adjusted, closing myself off to her emotions like I'd done a hundred times before.

"What was that?" I wheezed, putting a hand to my forehead.

"Merrin dropped it off. It protects the wearer from, um, probing. She said you'd need stillness to recover and told me to wear it until you woke up."

Evadne's words came back to me and I made a thoughtful sound. "The trinket, I guess."

"Merrin only stayed long enough to give you a once-over and tell me you'd be fine with rest and to come to her when you were ready."

"Ready for what?"

"She didn't say. You know Merrin."

I did know Merrin, so I left it there. Chloe dropped my hand, the stone still inside my grip. It was hot, but I didn't want to let it go.

"I rescheduled your appointments from yesterday and your only appointment for today cancelled so it's okay if you're not feeling up to going in."

"How'd Loraine sound?"

"Um." I could feel hesitation and worry in her and considered that she was about to lie—a waste of time around an empath. In the end, she answered truthfully. "As well as could be. She understood when I told her it was an emergency, that you feel really bad about having to put her off a few days."

Guilt chewed at my insides and it seemed to magnify the headache. When I didn't say anything else, Chloe pressed on.

"Can you eat?"

"Can I *eat*," I scoffed at her. "*Please*. It's one of the few things I can always do."

"Are you sure?" Chloe asked, leaning in. I opened my mouth to insist that I could, but reconsidered in an instant. Based on how I felt when I moved more than a tiny bit, I still wasn't doing very well. She continued: "What happened, anyway? Mel said you called to have him come out to meet you in Bellevue, that he sent a cop your way in case it was something bad. When he arrived, he claims he found you feeling each other up, that he had to tear you apart and bring you here."

"That *ass*," I growled.

Chloe laughed and I felt a spark of mischief in her. "Relax, Gwen, I'm just teasing. He told me she healed you, that something nasty had hopped inside your skull and messed you up. What was it?"

"I have no idea, but it wasn't human. It looked human, but it wasn't."

"Werewolf?"

"There wolf!" I quipped without thinking, pointing off to the right. Indulging me, Chloe twisted to look where I aimed and then back to me.

"There cat. That's just Poopy. Did you sense a werewolf?"

"No. This was something else. I've never felt it before, but that doesn't mean anything. I don't exactly have much of a track record with this... sort of stuff."

"Start from the beginning. What could make you drive all the way out to Bellevue?"

"What could make me drive all the way out to anywhere?" I asked sarcastically. "Donuts."

"Of course." She sighed and shook her head. "I made a mistake showing you that place. How many times a week do you sneak off and pick the cases clean?"

"I plead the Fifth," I said, unable to meet her eyes. "Speaking of, where are they? Did Mel eat them? I'll kill him."

"I brought the box in, but... don't worry about it. Just tell me what happened." Chloe was getting impatient, her concern for me shoving to the front of her psyche, which made me feel bad. Despite the niggling worry in the back of my brain that my sweets had been pilfered again, I pressed on.

"I was in Bellevue, making life worth living, when Evadne called with the address Merrin had sort of promised us. It was actually pretty close to where I was, so I headed straight there. I was going to call you, but I realized you wouldn't really be able to help." I jerked as a spike of irritation shot out of Chloe and stabbed me in the chest. "Mel said he'd rush right over, which you know, so I'll skip that part. I parked out in front of this little apartment building and waited, figuring I'd just hide out until Mel or the cops got there.

"And then this... dude-shaped thing rocked up, feeling all... wet and kind of slimy and proceeded to stand around suspiciously. I tried to sense him, to see what he was feeling, and then... nothing." I squinted, the memories floating together like lily pads. "I remember Amy waking me up and Mel being predictably inappropriate as he offered to drive me home. That's about it. Everything's still kind of a mess up here." I pointed to my head, as if she needed clarification.

"Like I said, you were pretty beaten up, at least psychically. You're doing better now though, I hope?" Chloe waited until I gave a nod and relief spilled out of her in a wave. It was a mild emotion, normally, but somehow it felt overwhelming now, crashing across me and making me feel for a moment like I was choking. I squeezed my eyes shut against it, willing the pounding in my head to ease up. When it did, it still wasn't nearly enough. I whimpered and tugged the covers up so I could press my face against them.

Chloe patted my knee. "Your clothes are clean if you want me to grab them."

"Yes, please," I mumbled into the blanket.

Chloe squeezed my knee and left Poopy and me alone in her room. The cat breathed out heavily through a purr, making it sound like she disapproved strongly of our conversation. I could feel a vague sense of irritation that might have been her emotion but could just as well have been my own. Cats are normally odd and often spastically unpredictable in their feelings, but Poopy was on another level entirely. I couldn't ever decide if that made me like her more or less than other cats.

The cat and I filled the next few minutes with a staring contest that she won several times over. When Chloe came back in, she had my clothes in one hand and my donut box in the other.

"I'm gonna turn the light on, are you ready?"

"Hit me," I said. The light came on and I squinted through the pain. Chloe set my clothes on the edge of the bed and rested a hand on top of the box. Her emotions spoke wildly of trepidation and pity. I narrowed my eyes at her. "What." It wasn't a question.

"I found it this way. You can't be mad at me." Without further ado, she set the box on my thighs. It weighed nothing.

"No," I hissed, yanking up the lid. Only crumbs and smears of glaze remained. "Mel!"

"I don't think it was Mel." Chloe tapped the inside of the lid and I lifted my gaze to a pink sticky note.

It said, *Get well soon!* in the familiar scrawl of the candy thief.

That *bastard!*

Eight

Chloe babied me for most of the day, bringing me thick socks to put over the thin ones I'd shown up wearing and feeding me like a queen. She explained that she'd spent most of the evening cooking for me and then dragged me to the fridge to show off an impressive stack of her colorful Tupperware.

We lazed around until early afternoon, when she suggested that I go home to check on Sonny; she'd apparently fed him while I was unconscious but she was no expert on birds and she was worried about him. As if I didn't trust her implicitly, she swore she would have called a bird expert friend of hers if I hadn't woken up when I did.

Loading up my car with the food she'd made for me, we headed out. I whined at her insistence that Mel come by so we could all talk through what had happened, but I didn't put too much effort into my protest. I was just happy not to risk driving alone in the post-snow city.

We got to my place and Sonny announced his displeasure at my absence the second he heard my voice. I went straight to him, pulling him out of his cage and resting him on my shoulder. He nipped at me and warbled. I cooed back at him while Chloe unpacked my haul in the kitchen and gathered some fresh vegetables for Sonny. I dropped onto the couch, still utterly exhausted.

Chloe came out, folding her empty tote bag; she looked confused.

"You have no candy," she said.

"I told you that," I said as I set Sonny on the perch where Chloe had left his snacks.

"But you have *none*! Not even a single caramel or one of those mini single-serve boxes of Diabetes-Os."

"Yes, "I repeated, "I told you that."

"Something ate *all* of your sugar! Gwen, you're practically a C&H factory. For something to eat everything you have with sugar in it, that's …" She trailed off, looking worried.

I nodded. "Yeah, tell me about it. I'm going to have to buy all of that again."

Frowning at me, she continued. "No, I mean … that night, you were only asleep, what, five hours tops?" I didn't bother answering. "What could eat *all* of your sugary snacks, fill your fridge with phrases, and not wake you up in that amount of time?"

"Didn't we have this conversation already? You're the one who convinced me it's a thing and not a person hiding in a crawlspace watching me sleep."

"I didn't realize you actually meant it ate *everything* everything. In this house, even half of everything is a lot. You have nothing. You actually meant *everything*." She shook her head, bewildered. "That's just way crazier than I was picturing before."

"Of course I meant everything. Why do you think I was so mad?"

Chloe's brows shot up. "And the office! Something ate all your honey packets and I'll have to restock your candy for the dish completely."

I squinted at her, suspicious of her sudden interest in restocking my sugar supply.

"You weren't worried before, so why are you nervous now?"

"This creature is clearly starving!" Chloe cried. "I'm just wondering if maybe we should leave something for it."

"Oh, don't do that. It's not a neighborhood squirrel. I'm not leaving Twinkies on the porch like peanuts. Not only because it would be a waste of Twinkies but because it may never leave me alone if we feed it." I felt Mel approach as I finished speaking, lust and hunger reaching scalding, sucking tentacles around me, wrapping me snugly in velvet nausea. I groaned and hugged my arms, squeezing my eyes shut and doing my best to protect myself as he came up the drive. Chloe realized immediately what was going on and Mel only got one knock out before she opened the door.

"I bring gifts," he said. I cracked open one eye, perking up when I recognized the box he was holding as being from The Internets. "I stopped by for coffee. Madeline asked where her best customer had been."

He stepped inside, elbowed the door shut, and set the pastry box down on the coffee table. He opened it, using his hand to waft the scent of treats my way. The smell of sweets was nearly enough to distract me from the pain of him being so close. I could feel my body tensing up, though, and it was all coming at me much faster than I was used to. Being around a werewolf was always bad, but the scalding slices of hunger tearing at my psyche felt as if he'd been pressed right up against me for at least an hour.

"Chloe?" I croaked, fighting a war between my desire for the marshmallow-covered chocolate donut and my body's desire to never stop vomiting. "Does that necklace still work?"

"Neck—oh! Oooh, good idea. I packed it. Let me get it." She fled down the hall toward my bedroom while I continued to focus all my energy on the donut, as if I could will it to my mouth. She was back quickly, the black-edged, square blue stone dangling from the skinny leather strap in her hand. Mel watched her approach, his lips quirking as she stood on tip-toe in front of him, wrapped arms and the necklace around his neck, and tied it off.

I caught sight of his arm sliding around her back, felt lust arc like a solar flare away from him ... and then it all stopped. The difference was so stark the world shut down and for a second, I felt like I had gone deaf, blind, and numb. I blinked as my living room seemed to melt back into being, looking down at my hands as I flexed my fingers. Sure that my other senses were working, I took a breath and let it out audibly to make sure my ears were okay. Still rediscovering the existence of the world, I leaned back with a sigh of relief.

Mel's emotions were barely there now, like sitting in a luxury hotel and listening to a heavy metal band play in the dingy bar next door. I could sense the chaos if I really tried, but it was better just to enjoy the calm. After maybe another minute, he was a blank slate, as though he wasn't there at all.

"Oh, thank god," I moaned, lifting my hands to press them against my eyes. I felt cool, comfortable, and better than I'd ever felt while so close to Mel. "Merrin is officially my new favorite person."

"Did Madeline send any vegan treats?" Chloe asked as she dropped onto the couch next to me.

"She said the little ones are from Mighty-O, just for you."

"Gwen?"

I removed my hands from my face and turned to look at her. She was holding the marshmallow donut out toward me; I must have looked pretty pathetic for her to be offering me pastry.

"Excellent," I said, smiling. "Thanks."

"First things first," Mel said, taking a seat in the chair to our left. "What is this blue thing and why am I wearing it?"

"Merrin made it for Gwen. It blocks her from reading the emotions of the wearer. She may actually be able to stand you now!"

"Fat chance," I groused, my mouth full of fluffy perfection. Disappointment bounced out of Chloe and off my shoulder like a pack of rubber balls, but I ignored it. "So, tell me from your point of view what happened."

"You'd mentioned you might be going to stop a kidnapping, so I kept myself available for when you inevitably realized you're completely incompetent and Chloe's skills mainly include alphabetizing and bullying insurance companies."

"I *am* excellent at both," she agreed, taking a tiny bite of a French toast donut. I wondered if she'd restrict me to my donuts or if she'd let me have one of hers.

"I was out the door as soon as you called, but I knew I wouldn't make it in time, so I called Amy. She's one of you, so—"

"One of me?"

"Someone with powers. Psychic healing." He waved off my question. "I told her we'd gotten otherworldly news that something was going to happen and passed on the address. She wasn't too far away, thankfully, and got to you just in time."

"Not just in time," I argued. "I still got knocked around. I mean, sort of."

"How much do you remember after you woke up that night?" Mel asked. I considered his question, trying to piece together the bits of images and sounds left by the jagged shards of pain in my head into an actual cohesive narrative.

"Um. I remember Amy waking me up and touching me a lot, which was nice. I threw up a few times—not so nice. You showed up, maybe flirted a bit."

"Sounds like me," Mel said with a smile. I ignored him.

"You told her you looked around, that you smelled vampires."

"Vampires?" Chloe demanded, shock and disbelief fracturing the peaceful interest that had settled over her. I grunted against the feeling, grabbed another donut—one of Chloe's, thank you very much—and chomped into it as aggressively as I could manage.

"I said I *thought* I smelled a vampire, but that's impossible." The sounds of Dave Matthews Band's *Crash into Me* rang through the room and Mel perked up, sliding his phone out of his pocket. "That's me."

"I wouldn't have guessed," I deadpanned, though I don't think anyone understood my mush-mouth retort. Mel was already answering, stepping outside as if he didn't want us eavesdropping. Chloe turned to me, eyebrows raised.

"He *did* say vampires, right? I didn't mishear him? He didn't claim he smelled, like ..." She trailed off, shaking her hand loosely in the air. "Shampires?"

"And what the hell would a shampire be?"

"If I had to guess, I'd say every goth kid at my high school."

I snorted, shook my head, and got back to the very serious business of eating my donut. Chloe stayed quiet as we waited for Mel. Sonny continued to snack, content to be near the action, even though I was sure he would have offered to help if he could. Mel came back inside a few minutes later, an excited grin on his face.

"That was Mrs. Morris, the mother of the second little girl who was taken. I called yesterday, asked if I could offer my services for free. She wasn't sure at first and I think she still doesn't entirely trust me, but she'd like to meet me to discuss the case. I told her I'd be bringing a consultant— it took some finagling, but I got her to agree. We're to be at the Bouncing Bunny café in an hour." Mel's gaze was fixed intently on me, but I didn't catch on until I took the last, massive bite of my donut.

"Wait, me?" I asked, dribbling crumbs down my front.

"You asked to go with me," he said. "I can bring Chloe instead, if you want."

"Can't you bring both of us?" she asked.

Mel shook his head. "Not likely. They weren't thrilled with me bringing along one person, let alone two."

"No, no." I sighed, swallowing the last of my mouthful. "It's okay. I'll get dressed and go with you. This is my problem, not Chloe's." She remained outwardly calm but I felt another jagged spike of irritation jab out of her. It held the razor edge of frustration, too.

"I'll hang here with Sonny," Chloe said, patting my leg. "Do you need me to pick an outfit for you?"

"I can dress myself," I protested, getting to my feet. Mel and Chloe exchanged a look that made me reconsider ever speaking to either one of them again. "Shut up. Both of you." I pointed aggressively at Mel. "Does this café have food?"

"That is generally what a café serves, yes."

His snark only made me loathe him more. "You're buying me the biggest, most delicious slice of cake they have." I headed toward my room. Mel gave it a beat, but spoke as I rounded the corner.

"Don't worry, baby. Anything I put in your mouth is guaranteed to be huge."

OLIVIA R. BURTON

Nine

I sat across from Mel in the Bouncing Bunny at a small rectangular table, my legs crossed in a way that might have been sexual. I'd conned Mel into springing for twice the amount of cake he'd promised me by vowing not to tell Chloe he'd done so. Turned out I hadn't really needed two pieces, though that wouldn't stop me from eating both. The massive slices of red velvet cake with cream cheese frosting could have fed a bevy of starving orphans, but they were mine, all mine. I took another giant bite, made a sound that was most definitely sexual, and closed my eyes.

Upon opening them, I found Mel leaning back toward a nearby shelf of condiments, utensils, and napkins, grabbing for a fork. This put him very close to an attractive brunette who wasn't a day under sixty and who looked at Mel like a cat might appraise a stupid dog trotting into its territory. Noticing her—but apparently not her attitude toward him—he gave an unsubtle wink. Even sitting so close to the action, I couldn't have told you exactly how she went from an angry feral to a purring pussycat.

I'd had the misfortune of knowing Mel for a whole year and, since he's not shy about his rakishness, I'd seen him work his magic before. Today, though, the experience was different. Rather than wanting to vomit from across the The Internets as he lured a patron up to his office, I found I was intrigued. With the necklace keeping his emotions from assaulting me, my empathy was finally able to pick up on the amount of raw arousal pumping off the woman as they spoke quietly and closely. I did my best not to let it affect me—even being turned on by Mel secondhand was unacceptable, and the cake was sexy enough—but it was still an interesting experience.

It took him less than three minutes to get her number and if either of them noticed the wedding ring on her finger, I didn't hear them mention it.

Though my head was mainly filled with the sounds of my contented chewing, so who knows what I missed?

Mission accomplished, Mel turned back to the table, fork in hand. Sensing what he wanted, I caught his eye and shook my head. To make things even clearer, I stuffed another forkful of cake into my mouth, even though I hadn't finished the previous bite. I was halfway through the fudgy delight and there was no way I was letting any of it go, not after losing so much sugar to the candy thief. Mel reached toward the plate with his fork and I grunted, very un-ladylike. Foolishly, he seemed to think my grunt was cute and non-threatening and went in for a bite.

So I jabbed him with the fork and pulled the plate closer, swallowing and grunting at him again. The attractive brunette turned to look at us; her eyes lingered on Mel, but she spared a rude glare for me. I pointed my fork at her threateningly.

"You can't have any of my cake, either."

Mel snorted, turning back to the woman with an apologetic look spread across his gorgeous face.

"Forgive my friend. She was raised by wolves."

I considered the irony of his words as the cougar got up to go. She dropped a hand on Mel's shoulder, whispered something lusty in his ear, and then sashayed out the door.

"Mel, she's twice your age," I managed around a mouthful of cake. He just watched me quietly, clearly waiting for me to explain the problem. I'd seen him go after all shapes, sizes, and ages of women but, despite watching him drum up her interest, I was having a hard time believing he had a shot. "She was wearing a wedding ring. She probably has kids your age and a husband."

"She's widowed," he clarified.

"Your spidey sense tell you that?"

"Spider-Man's an amateur compared to me. I'm like Sherlock Holmes when it comes to the fairer sex."

"You're a sloppy addict and you should quit cold turkey?"

Rather than addressing the comment, Mel snaked in and stole a chunk of my cake. I carped at him but he just smiled and rubbed his belly as if it was the best thing he'd ever tasted. I pulled the plate as close as I could, wrapping my arm around it like I was erecting a hulking stone wall to keep orcs out of Helm's Deep. After another bite, I waved away the discussion with a flap of my fork and changed the subject. "Tell me about vampires."

Instantly, Mel's demeanor changed. "I'd rather not. It isn't something you want to know anything about."

"Why not?"

"Gwen," he sighed, oddly exasperated. It made me smile. I gave him a few seconds to think while I ate more cake.

"Come on, give me something. Anything."

"I'll give you something …"

"I don't want that thing. Having nothing's better than having that thing."

"You're right, there is nothing better than—"

"Vampires, Mel," I ordered, reaching over to jab his hand with my fork again. He chuckled, rubbing his thumb over the indents I'd left in his skin. I found, as I watched him, that I was actually enjoying myself. It might have been because I was eating delicious pastry, but I think it was mostly the necklace.

"I know one. A vampire."

"What's he like?"

"Unpleasant."

I snorted, shaking my head. "Come on! I'll buy you some cake if you stop beating around the bush."

Rolling his eyes, Mel quipped, "I can buy my own cake. And beat around my own bush."

So help me, I actually laughed. Around another bite of cake, I asked, "What's your friend's name?"

"Dirk."

I nearly choked. "Dirk?" I coughed suddenly, my body warring between wanting to laugh and wanting to breathe. Hoping I wasn't going to die, I chewed and swallowed as fast as I could. "*Dirk*? Seriously?"

Mel sighed, leaning back in his chair and crossing his arms over his chest.

My mind exploded with vivid, darkly colored images of a mysterious figure in skin-tight leather and crimson silk. Smoldering eyes looked out of my imagination and into my very soul. What treasure trove of nocturnal delights had I stumbled on by asking such questions?

"What's he like? Does he live in a mausoleum?" My mouth ran on without my consent. "Sleep in a casket? Does he have pale skin and a flouncy little cravat? Is his hair *perfect*? Does he brood? Is he chock full of long-coated man-pain? *Does he dazzle you?*"

Mel was staring at me askance, his brows drawn together over wide eyes. He was silent for a full minute before he let out a long, irritated groan.

"Mr. Somerset?"

I twisted to face the voice and found a couple standing behind us. I was surprised that I hadn't felt their grief and worry the second they'd walked in. It was heavy, cloudy like a summer storm and a thick fog all at once. I wiped the smile off my face and set my fork down. Mel got to his feet immediately, offering his hand.

"Mr. and Mrs. Morris, hello. Please, have a seat. This is my associate, Gwen Arthur." I smiled, unsure if I should stand and shake or let them sit.

It was a tight squeeze at the small table, but we all managed it. Mel was the epitome of professionalism and I had to do my best not to gawk at his serious demeanor. All these new sides of Mel popping up were going to start giving me whiplash. He asked if he could get them anything to drink or eat, then got straight to the heart of things when they declined.

"Tell us about your daughter, about what's happened."

Mrs. Morris looked to me, her dark eyes slightly bloodshot, then nodded.

"Our daughter Ashley is four. I was home with her for the day. Duane was at work—we work opposite schedules so one of us is always home with her. Um. She wanted to play outside, and I know it's been cold, but the porch is covered and I brought a little space heater out so—anyway." She waved away whatever she was about to say. "I was reading and she was playing with her dolls. I wanted to get her some gloves because she kept getting up and going to put her hands in front of the heater. I knew she was cold. I couldn't—I *wasn't* away from her for more than a minute. It's imposs—I don't know *how* she's gone!"

Her eyes welled up, tears dropping down her cheeks. "I don't understand it. The kitchen is right inside the back door and I just leaned in, grabbed them, and came back and she was gone. I panicked. I checked the whole yard, the whole house. I checked *three times* and I couldn't find her. I asked the neighbors, I called the police. I just *kept checking*."

Her breath went wild, wracking her body like a paint shaker. Mr. Morris wrapped thick arms around her, pulling her to his chest, but he wasn't really calm, either. His eyes were puffy, his face unevenly shaved. As he held her, his tears fell into her hair. I was sitting as still as I could, fighting the torrent of their emotions as it swirled like a hurricane in my chest. My breathing had gone shaky, my jaw tight. It was small, selfish, and horrid, but I wanted to leave. I didn't want to sit there in that tempest of anguish. I was on the verge of breaking down. If I didn't leave soon, I was going to wail and melt into a heap on the floor.

Mel gave them a few seconds before speaking softly.

"The police are working as hard as they can to locate your daughter. I want to help. I can't imagine how awful it must be to lose a child, and I want to make sure Ashley gets home safe, sound, and happy. I'm offering my services completely free."

Mrs. Morris turned to us, composing herself as best she could.

"We appreciate that," she said. Her eyes drifted to me again and I felt a wiggle of suspicion root to the surface of her despair. "May we ask what it is your associate does, exactly?"

Before Mel could answer, I blurted out a question of my own. "What is it that you two do? Or what does your daughter do? You know, like, her power."

"*What?*" Duane demanded, worry and panic radiating from him in an acidic cloud masquerading as insult. I swallowed heavily, rubbing my hands over my arms.

"I'm an empath, I sense emotions in others. That's my power," I admitted. "Your daughter, she could do something special too, right? Did she get that from one of you? What's her power?"

"Her—" Mrs. Morris breathed. Panic had swelled inside the couple, their spines snapping straight at the same instant. I decided I didn't like that any better than the sadness.

"Look, just—I'm not here to tattle on you to the government or to some religious nutjob who might burn you at the stake. I want to help. I want to make sure your daughter is safe. I know you're both panicked. I can *feel* it. You don't have to be. I don't know how to prove to you that I'm—"

"Give me your hand," Mrs. Morris ordered abruptly. I flinched, knowing the emotions I was absorbing would only get more potent with physical contact. I had scared her, though, and I wanted her to know I wasn't there to hurt her or Ashley. If she had a power like my sister's that needed contact to work, I had to get over myself and let her touch me. Steeling myself, I put my hand in hers, wincing as her emotions seemed to suck up through my skin to flood my psyche. I had to take a deep breath and hold it for a moment. She watched me intently as I let it out in a wavering sob.

"Repeat what you said, about your power," she said, softer this time.

"I'm an empath," I said opening my eyes to meet hers. "I can feel what other people are feeling."

"Marion?" Mr. Morris asked. Mrs. Morris watched me for a second before giving a slow nod.

"She's telling the truth." Then, to me, "That's my power."

"Handy," I said. I can tell when people are lying too; it really is a useful ability. She let go of my hand, a bit of tension slipping from her.

"Ashley can start fires. They're small and she doesn't—I don't think she realizes she can do it. It's never anything big and they don't last. When she gets scared or unhappy, something … goes wrong. Usually your sleeve will start to smoke and if we don't distract her quickly enough, it'll light up."

"She's very happy, though!" Duane insisted. Marion had calmed some, but he was still unhappy, still didn't trust me. I was guessing he didn't have any abilities of his own and that the idea of superpowers and fire-starting pre-preschoolers still wasn't one he'd come to grips with. It made me wonder for a second how my parents had dealt with all of us. "It only started a few months ago. We didn't know what was happening at first, why we found some of her things melted, charred around the edges. She doesn't do it often."

"I'm not judging," I said, holding my hands up. "I just want to help."

73

"Does that have something to do with why she's gone?" Marion asked. She had gone still but her lip was quivering. The anguish was solidifying, the storm inside her slowing. "Did someone take her because of what she could do?"

"I don't know," I said. Wondering how much I should give away, I bit my lip. "I—when you were little, do you remember... I mean, I was four when I got a visit from—"

Marion jerked back and whispered, "The monsters."

Even though I'd been fishing for that exact response, I found myself briefly stunned that she'd dealt with them, too. I was quiet for a moment as we shared the remembered terror and I wondered if things in my life would have gone differently if I'd ever mentioned what I'd seen to anyone. Cowardice had kept me silent for years, but maybe bravery would have made me feel less alone.

"I guess we're on the same track," I said finally.

"You think they took her? You think the creatures that came to me—to us? You think they—"

"No! They don't have her," I assured her.

Duane was looking between us. "What? What monsters? What are you two talking about?"

"Kids like Marion and me, like Ashley, who have powers? We get a visit from, uh ..." How the hell do you explain something like this? Succinctly, I guessed. "Fairies. The monsters that came to me, that came to Marion when we were Ashley's age, they're fairies. Not the little, pretty, winged kind, but still fairies. They've come to me again, asking me to help find these kids. They're after whatever took—"

"These *kids*?" Duane demanded, loud enough that a couple a few tables over glanced at us. "Others are missing?"

"I thought you knew, I'm sorry," I admitted, trying not to feel stupid for assuming. "Yes. Three kids are missing and I've been... called on to help get them back. I'm going to do my best to do just that. Mel's going to help. He's good at what he does. We'll bring your daughter home."

Duane was a sticky, prickly mess of emotions. Outrage pestered me with thorny fingers, doubt clung to me like slime, and worry for his daughter rustled around us all like barbs. His proximity would have been bad enough on a normal day, but after the attack I'd suffered it was like being wrapped in a giant sheet of flypaper and thrown off a cliff.

Marion, though, just reached out, took my hand, and leaned in. She was serious, intent, desperate for my words to be the truth. I focused on her face, on the hope that had pushed through a crack in the stony heartache that surrounded her.

"You swear you'll bring her home safe?"

I nodded. "I swear."

Marion and Duane left before long. We went over what had happened when Ashley was taken once more, promised to keep them apprised, and then it was just Mel and me. My insides felt wrung dry when they left and I desperately wanted a nap.

"That went better than I thought it would once you started babbling about having magical powers," Mel admitted. I shrugged, digging into the remainder of my cake. It made me feel marginally better, at least. Behold, the healing power of sugar.

"I don't think it got us anywhere, though," I muttered.

"We know Ashley's a fire-starter, we know her mother's one of you. It's more than we had."

"So what's the plan now?" I took another bite. "What gumshoe tricks do you have up your sleeve?"

"Not gumshoe tricks," Mel said with a smile. "Werewolf tricks."

"Get out," I said, squinting at him. "What're you gonna do?"

"That's for me to know." He leaned back, looking smug and arrogant again. I didn't like it.

"Tell me more about vampires," I said. Mel's shoulders slumped. I couldn't feel it, but I could see the annoyance snap through him like a pair of cartoon wind-up teeth. It made me giggle.

"I told you already that you don't want to know anything about them. I don't know why you won't listen."

"I tell you things all the time and *you* never listen."

"That's because you tell me things like, 'No, I don't want to have sex with you' and 'No, you don't turn me on at all,' when I know neither of those things is true."

I jolted, suddenly self-conscious. I really don't want to have sex with Mel, I swear. I mean, my brain doesn't. Sometimes when I'm home alone, my hormones and my erogenous zones team up and get liquor involved and everyone plays a big trick on my body while my good sense is passed out in the corner. Okay, so sometimes I do wonder what he looks like naked, but only once these tricks have been played. That's absolutely the only time. I swear.

"That doesn't mean anything. Shut up."

He laughed but dropped the subject; he didn't even try to grope my knee under the table. It was like a whole new Mel. Figuring his good behavior deserved some from me in return, I finished my cake in silence, leaving him alone. We were quiet for awhile before, to my surprise, he broke.

"Vampires are *rare*. I've been all over the country, come across a number

75

of other inhuman creatures, but I've only ever met one vampire. I've known Dirk since we were kids, before he was turned. I've actually given him blood a few times. He'd gotten a scholarship to U-Dub, but got turned instead. He's been sick ever since. You haven't seen sick until you've seen Dirk. He was bone-skinny, wheezing like a leaky balloon the last time I saw him. He doesn't leave his house and doesn't usually let anyone in."

"And he's normal? He's—all vampires are sick?"

"I think so. That's what he told me, anyway. They have entire no-humans-allowed hospitals where they go to get treatment. Not just vampires, but anything—I could go if I had a problem. That's why Dirk's bald; he's currently got leukemia from a bad batch of blood and he's been going through chemo at the hospital. They've got support groups, even."

"Vampire... hospitals? Who *runs* something like that?"

"Fairies. It's pretty much all fairies, across the board. Upper fae with lots of property and the magic to keep humans the hell away."

I sat back, absorbing the soul-crushing news that vampires were nothing like I had hoped. I was never going to be able to read another paranormal romance without feeling a little bad and wondering if the heroine swapping spit with her undead lover was going to get him sick as a dog. I was going to have to tell my sister to stop buying me books.

"This is... wow. I still don't... So they don't heal fast and lift cars and seduce virgins?"

"Oh, they'll seduce virgins." He paused to elaborate. "On a good day." Another thoughtful pause. "Which probably means never, actually. Of all the people, virgins are their favorites, though. Less chance of—um. Contamination. That sounds bad. I don't mean like—"

I waved him off. "I know what you mean. Besides, you're the *last* person I would expect to hear complain about promiscuity."

Mel chuckled, apparently pleased that I understood, and continued. "As I was saying, there's probably nothing more annoying than a vampire with gonorrhea. They don't heal very well—I mean, not quickly—well, I mean ... it's hard to describe. They have all sorts of problems; I can't really go into it without keeping you here for awhile. Think of an untreated case of AIDs and you have your typical vampire. Only they don't die from disease, they just heal really slowly. Technically, their bodies can overcome anything, even beating the worst virus into submission. But it takes a long time, sometimes years, and in the meantime, they're overwhelmingly vulnerable to even the mildest disease. I've seen Dirk, at one time alone, with a cold, cancer, athlete's foot, and leprosy."

"Jeez." I shook my head. "How often do you give him blood? Does he ... uh ..."

"Oh, it's only been two or three times, and I donated at one of the hospitals he frequents. They're the only ones with the right tools." He tapped his inner elbow, but I didn't know what he was alluding to. "The only good side I can see is that vampires can't get the same strain of a disease twice. They can still get other strains, but I'm assuming if they live long enough, they could be immune to everything. Sadly, Dirk's not helping my theory in the state he's in now. You know, he had scurvy once."

I wanted to laugh, though it wasn't at the image of a sickly vampire yelling out for oranges and grapefruits; scurvy's just a funny word.

"If they're so frail, how did Dirk even get turned?"

"I never actually asked. He was in such bad shape it seemed uncouth to make him go into details. Maybe it was an accident."

This time I couldn't resist the laughter that bubbled up through my lips. "Like he got sent the wrong thing in the mail? This isn't the pair of pants I ordered!" I mimed opening a box and reacting to something shooting out and chewing on my face. Catching Mel's disapproving glare, I forced myself to sober up. A minute passed before I glanced up at Mel's expression and figured I still had a chance to get my questions answered if I played it cool.

"Does sunlight kill them?" I asked, thinking of Stoker.

"Oh, no, but they burn like an Irish baby. It's pathetic. No problems with garlic, mirrors, or running water, either." Mel paused before leaning close, evidently deciding he was done with the subject. "So, did you want more cake, or are you interested in beating around my bush?"

"Don't be gross,"

He laughed. "Well, then I guess there's nothing left to do except get you home to your wife."

"I'd make a terrible husband," I said as he helped me to my feet. Any other day I would have rather followed lemmings off a cliff than let Mel touch me, but we were getting along pretty well, all things considered. Plus, I'd felt lousy enough even before being pummeled by the emotions of grieving parents; I needed the assist. Mel didn't even make any comments about how getting to my feet made me groan like a dog being hugged too hard by an excitable child.

"Because you never want sex?" Mel asked once I could make my body cooperate with the orders to move. I almost would have preferred falling flat on my face.

"I never want sex with *you*," I corrected.

"But you want sex with Chloe? No wonder you're not interested in all of this," Mel said, and I didn't need to look over to know he was gesturing to his physique like it was an expensive car.

I rolled my eyes, but found myself laughing at his arrogance. "No matter what you say, I refuse to believe that the only women who turn you down do so because they're lesbians."

"Oh, I didn't mean to imply you're gay," Mel said, picking up the pace to open the car door for me. I paused next to him, eyeing him suspiciously for not only the nice gesture but also whatever was about to come out of his mouth. I knew it wasn't likely to be as nice.

"I'm almost afraid to ask what you *are* implying."

"Just that Chloe would kick my ass if I ever suggested I'm better in bed than she is."

"Is that so?" I asked, heaving myself into his ostentatious SUV with another groan of displeasure. "I like the mental image of Chloe knocking you around."

"Me too," he murmured with a grin. "I like it rough." I should have known better than to give his mind any chance to head for the gutter.

Ten

Mel offered to carry me into the house, but I couldn't tell if he was sincere or just looking for an excuse to cop a feel, so I declined.

"You look worse," Chloe said as we stepped inside. "Why do you look worse?"

"She ate half the cake at the café," Mel said. "Her insides are probably revolting."

"They're no less attractive than the rest of me," I countered, angry he'd ratted on me. Silence had been part of the deal, dammit. "And it wasn't that much cake."

"You didn't need *any* cake," Chloe chastised. "Now sit down before your legs give out."

"I look that bad?" I asked as I hit the couch. Chloe was already in the kitchen getting me some water.

"You look worse," Mel said and I turned to snarl his way.

"I didn't ask your opinion, so stuff it. No!" I held up a hand, anticipating his next comment. "No more gutter talk. If it doesn't have to do with the case, I don't want to hear it."

Mel watched me in silence, poised on the edge of innuendo and clearly trying to decide if he wanted to take orders and let me be. Chloe dropped down next to me and pressed the glass of water into my hand.

"We're not here to joke about your dick, Mel," she said, though her tone was much less aggressive than mine. "Keep it civil."

"No one jokes—"

"I will throw this water at you!" I threatened, my frustration at how quickly he could go from affable to insufferable making me forget how unpleasant I felt.

"You could, but then I'd have to take my shirt off, maybe my pants and—"

"Mel." Chloe's tone was still pleasant, no threat or irritation in her voice, but it shut him up instantly. I considered her and her impressive powers of persuasion and wondered if she would ever be willing to teach me how to get Mel to shut up with a single syllable.

"Right," he said after a few moments. "We met with the Morrises and learned that Ashley has recently developed fire powers. She's started melting toys, burning sleeves, that sort of thing."

"She's so young," Chloe said, distress waving out of her to splash against my shoulder like water at the edge of a lukewarm pool. "Is that what her parents do? Start fires?"

"Marion can tell when people are lying. It's the only reason they agreed to let us help, I think," I explained.

"Gwen nearly scared them off when she started rambling on about feelings."

"You told them you're an empath?" Chloe asked, the distress lapping against me harder. "You don't usually do that."

"I figured it would be fine to do with them. If Laurel and Hardy were headed over there, that meant there was a fifty-fifty shot the kid could do something and they'd seen it."

"And if they hadn't? If you just announced you're psychic and they didn't take it well, what then?" Disapproval slithered through Chloe's distress and I shrank back.

"Um. They'd think I was crazy?"

"Best case scenario, we would have lost out on a lead. Worst case, they might have reported you two to the police, worried you were in on the kidnapping somehow. You didn't think it through."

"What was I supposed to do? They were crying and I wanted to cry and I could tell they didn't really trust us so I just sort of blurted it out."

"It worked out in the end," Mel said, drawing Chloe's attention. She studied him for a moment, still unhappy that I'd revealed my power to the Morrises.

"It worked out fine. No one called the cops on us, as far as I know." I glanced at the picture window that sat behind Sonny's cage. "No feds parked on the street in a stakeout to catch the empath and smuggle her into a government lab."

"That you know of," Mel whispered.

"Shut up," I snapped. He laughed but didn't continue to tease. Chloe's emotions melted away from distress and she looked between us.

"I'm surprised you two convinced anyone to trust you. You're like children."

"Am not," I argued, stomping my foot as petulantly as I could manage.

"Hey, I'm all man," Mel said, lifting his arm to flex his bicep through his sweater. Chloe didn't look his way, her eyes on me as she gestured for me to keep going.

"Oh, ah …" I took a second to remember where I'd been before she'd gone all mom on me. "She—So, they agreed to let us help and we talked some about Laurel and Hardy and how we both saw them when we were kids. Then I promised to bring Ashley home safe and that was kind of it."

"I hope you can keep that promise," Chloe said.

"Me too. And not just because of what Laurel and Hardy might do to me if I don't."

Chloe rolled her eyes in disapproval but I trusted she knew I was joking. Mostly.

I spent the evening lounging, picking at the foods Chloe had left me—everything had vegetables in it; unbelievable! It was like living with my mother again—and communed with Sonny in front of the worst television programming mankind has to offer.

As the bird and I discussed the finer points of a TV movie about the ghost of a detective helping solve his own murder, I realized I needed to be more like the Inspectre. I couldn't just sit around mourning the loss of my candy-filled life of happiness; I needed to do something about it. I needed to get off my achy ass, head to the store, and restock my kitchen with all the junk food that had been stolen from me.

Sure, it wasn't as impressive or difficult as being incorporeal and leaving clues by ruffling papers or fogging up mirrors, but I felt it would be just as worthwhile.

I pulled into the parking lot of a gas station mini-mart several blocks from my house and wobbled inside, headed straight for the candy aisle. I held my reusable bag open and dumped in candy bars, crispy rice bars, and an entire bag of something that I recognized as chocolate but couldn't be bothered to consider any further. Then I made a beeline for the drinks and inspected my options. Straight cola didn't look intriguing, but I did spy a bottle of something claiming—with more exclamation marks than necessary, I thought—to be grape-flavored. My tongue turned purple just looking at it. I grabbed the largest size of it that I could find, heaved it into my bag, and turned toward the counter, foolishly thinking I was done shopping.

Then the siren song of the ice cream cooler called my name and I was powerless to resist.

I perused my options with the glee of a five-year-old given free rein and finally settled on something chocolate that was not only laden with a slightly different kind of chocolate but also swirled with utterly artificial "cherry" flavor and gummy bears, which were also covered in chocolate.

Just to be safe, I grabbed three containers.

I paid cash for my bounty and the boy behind the counter had a knowing look on his face. I realized he probably thought I was stoned, but I took his "solidarity, sister" expression and returned a small, proud smile. I don't need to be high to eat this way, buddy, but whatever floats your boat.

I ate an entire candy bar before I hit the door and, as the sugar permeated my system, I started to feel a bit better. I wouldn't have agreed to running a marathon, or even to watching someone else coordinate one, but I figured I could get through the evening without my head splitting in two and letting thousands of scorpions loose upon the city. I was maybe ten steps from my car, wondering about my sudden fascination with scorpions, when a familiar, liquid sensation oozed over the back of my neck, gripping my spine like an amorous slug. I froze, panic flaring up inside me as I spun around, convinced whatever had attacked me before had just shown up to finish the job.

I saw nothing.

The heavy, wet feeling was still there, terrifying me enough that I was having trouble concentrating. I didn't wait to see if I was imagining things. I took off at a run toward the mini-mart. It wasn't far; I was confident I could make it, even though running isn't exactly a specialty of mine. Turns out, that wasn't the problem. The problem was waiting for me in the shadows just before the front doors of the store.

I yelped and skidded to a halt, dropping my bag of goodies. My heart tripped over itself as my lungs forced a tiny secondary yelp out through my lips. The blond creature from Bellevue took his time, stopping on the sidewalk directly between me and the lights of the mini-mart. I took one step back and he shook his head.

"We didn't properly meet before, Gwen."

"Shit," I squeaked, frozen with one foot behind the other, my bag tipped on its side on the ground. It was late and, considering the fact that it was a bit frosty, with a dewy mist that couldn't quite bring itself to be rain blanketing the area, I wasn't going to bank on being noticed and saved. Who else but a sugar-mad empath would be out at this hour in this weather?

Blondie just watched me, a small smile warping his closed lips. I tried for another step back and he laughed, tipping his face so the shadows and light conspired to reveal gleaming fangs and pull my attention straight to them. It made my skin crawl both because of the threat of it all and because his emotions shifting felt like lines of custard dribbling down my scalp. I stopped moving, looked around for anything that might be of help. The contents of my bag shifted suddenly, drawing my gaze and Blondie's to it.

One of my pints of ice cream rolled crookedly out, spinning in the narrow circle its shape demanded. I stared at my out of season treat for a second before letting out a terrified, unintentional laugh.

"If any of my candy is broken, you're paying for it," I said, lifting my gaze. Blondie squinted at me, possibly confused by my bravado. I figured that, since he hadn't flown forward and ripped my throat out, I should take that as a sign from the universe that it wasn't yet my time to die. Plus, I had just come up with a plan. Sort of.

I moved to my bag, crouching down to tuck everything back inside and make sure my candy and ice cream were safe from the giant bottles of excitable soda.

"Everything looks fine," I said as I stood up. I just had to keep him off my throat for another few seconds. "Which is better than I can say for you. I mean, you might want to see a dentist about those canines."

My plan walked around the corner behind me, eight teenagers chatting about music, games, and someone named Mrs. Gulbranson who, according to them, needed to take her fat old ass and die in a fire. Kids these days, so delicate with words. Blondie's eyes flicked to the group as they approached, but he didn't move. I didn't move either, at least not until the kid at the front of the group was level with me.

Abruptly, I reached out, grabbing her coat.

"Hey!" I cried, dragging the word out, clinging close. "You know where there's a grocery store around here?"

The kids exploded into a chorus of irritated questions, demands that I back off, and slang that I didn't recognize but that I could figure out easily from the annoyance and shock clamoring around the crowd. Blondie stayed where he was, but I made as big an ass of myself as I could.

"I just need a grocery store, come on!"

At least three of the kids ordered, "Let go!"

"My friend here will juggle for you! Come on, let him show you." I pointed at Blondie. "Get a good look, too! He's quite the showman!"

"Lady, what the hell! We don't care about your friend!"

"Let go of her!"

"You're crazy, stop!"

"No, really!" I said, pressing as close to the group as I could. One of the kids, as teenagers in this day and age do, had pulled his phone out, aimed it my way. I pointed spastically toward Blondie. "Look! Look at him! Any second now he's—"

Blondie spun stiffly, crossed the street without another word, and hustled away. I stayed huddled next to the lead girl, who was still trying to shove me back. Despite the fact that she was slapping and pushing at me, I stayed close as I made sure Blondie was really leaving, letting my breath catch up to me. One of the bigger boys finally decided he'd had enough and grabbed my arm, yanking me hard.

"Jesus, lady! Take the hint!"

I let his friend go, grabbed my bag off the ground, and made a mad dash for my car before the kids and their phone cameras were out of range. I was cool with ending up all over the internet by morning. It was certainly better than ending up in Blondie's stomach.

I was sitting in my house, in the dark, all alone, a handful of gummy treats pressed close to my mouth as I inhaled them like a squirrel. I couldn't stop fidgeting, too scared to turn on anything that would draw attention to me. Sonny was happily snacking, occasionally ringing his bells or making tiny, curious noises. He was probably wondering why I was acting so strangely, but he at least had the tact not to ask about it.

How had Blondie *found* me? Would he be back? Would I be safe if he showed up at my home? Would Laurel and Hardy's promise of coming to me when I needed them—which hadn't been true the first time I'd seen Blondie—come through? Would the candy thief protect me?

Despite my mood, I snorted into the empty living room. At most, the little bastard would probably leave a sticky note with a sad face on my mangled corpse. Then it'd eat all the delicious food I'd just bought.

Cramming the last of the candy into my mouth, I got up, padding as silently as I could down the hall to my office. I dialed Mel's number, staying out of sight of the window as I did. I'd seen enough action movies to know the danger there.

"Gwen?" Mel answered after only two rings.

"Can vampires just come into your home, or do they have to be invited?"

"What?" he asked after a beat.

"Vampires! Could one walk into my home without an invitation?"

"If... if they're even healthy enough to walk, sure. What are you talking about? Did something happen?"

"Almost! I went to the store to get—" I faltered, fearing briefly that Chloe might get wind of what I'd bought and make me throw it all away and replace it with rutabagas and seaweed. "Supplies. The thing from Bellevue just *showed up!* I barely made it out of there alive!"

"I'll be there as soon as I can."

"Here? My house here? You don't—"

"Yep. Where else?" Mel hung up, not giving me the chance to argue. I blinked down at the phone, desperately torn between glee at the fact that someone would soon be around to protect me from any attacking creatures of the night and irritation over that someone being Mel. I consoled myself with chocolate.

I had no idea where Mel had been, but it took him around half an hour to arrive. I stayed huddled on my couch under a blanket with my candy, staring through the bars of Sonny's massive cage and out the front window. It was hard to miss Mel's SUV as it pulled up along the curb, taking up half my tiny street. I jumped and sprinted to the door, yanking it open before he even made it up my walkway. He stopped just inside the door, looking around. I could see the cord of Merrin's necklace poking out of his collar and I realized I hadn't even considered how miserable I would have been had he not still been wearing it.

"Why aren't there any lights on?"

"I was scared," I said, shutting the door.

"Of me seeing how bad you look in that outfit? Because darkness won't stop that, sweetheart."

I scoffed, scowled, and flipped on the light. It wasn't *that* bad, I thought. My clothes were a bit stained, the pants baggy around the crotch, but I hadn't dribbled any food on my shirt for once. I mean, not tonight, anyway.

"Shut up," I said after a few seconds, glaring at him.

"So, will we be sharing a bed?" he asked, waving a hand towards the hall.

"Who says you're sleeping over?"

"It's late. You need protection." He glanced back at me, waggling his brows. "And you really should take any chance you get to take off those clothes."

"You know, I'm going to just go stay at Chloe's instead. Get out."

Mel laughed. "What do you think she's going to do to keep you safe? She's not a werewolf."

"Which means she's not an insufferable ass. I'm better off—"

"Relax, I'll sleep in the guest room. Unless your extra rooms are just filled to the brim with cases and pallets of Hostess cupcakes?"

"I wish," I said, taking a second to genuinely fantasize about the idea. I didn't let the reality of the candy thief intrude, either; I just pictured myself rolling around in piles of spongy sugar and frosting like Scrooge McDuck in his money vault. Mel shook his head at me and strolled across the living room to take a seat in the center of the couch, draping his arms along the back. "Tell me more about what happened, what this thing looked like."

"It just looked human. It definitely wasn't, but you couldn't tell by looking at it. He just looked like... you know, a man. Except for the fangs."

"That doesn't narrow things down. Plenty of non-human creatures look human. Except those of us who," Mel gestured broadly to his body, lifting one brow, "look like gods."

"Get out," I said again. Mel laughed, settling his arm back across the couch.

"Tell me everything he did, everything he said. What happened?"

Sighing, I gave in, sitting down as far from him as I could before recounting my entire near-death experience. Mel listened patiently; he didn't make any smart remarks or ask to get me naked again. It wasn't as bad as I expected.

"So he didn't get close to you?" Mel asked as I finished.

"Nope. Only people who did were the kids. Why?"

"Because if he grabbed you or rubbed up against you, I might have been able to pick up a scent, tell you if I recognize what he is. As things are now, we still have no idea." Mel's face went tight with thought, the fingers of his left hand drumming twice along the couch. "Can you get ahold of your fairy contacts? What were you calling them? Harpo and Chico?"

"Laurel and Hardy. No, they didn't give me a way to contact them. They said they'd show up when I need them, but that hasn't worked out so far."

"For the fae, the definition of 'need' can vary wildly. Look, I'll hang with you for the next few days, until this gets sorted out. Make sure you don't get smacked around again."

"And what do I have to give you in return?"

Mel shrugged. "Don't worry about it. You can owe me something later."

"No." I held up both hands. "You either do this out of the goodness of your heart—assuming you have one—or I'll… I don't know. Buy a gun or something. I'm not *owing you* anything. Besides, we don't even know if this thing wants to hurt me. He didn't exactly leap on my skull and rip out my spine earlier. He kind of seemed like he wanted to talk."

"Maybe he wanted to talk about how he was going to leap onto your spine and rip your skull out."

"I'm not owing you anything," I repeated, refusing to give into the fear that he might have been right. We squared off for a bit before Mel broke, laughing as he put a hand up.

"Okay. Anything you say. This is your show. In fact, to that end, what's our next move?"

"What do you mean?"

"Do you want to go with me to meet the parents of the other missing children? Do you think you learned enough to go it on your own?"

"I don't know anything."

"Yes, but that's nothing new."

"I mean—dammit." I propped my elbow up on my knee, resting my chin in my hand as I considered what had happened so far. I'd been hired to find some missing children for an ugly pair of fairies. I'd stopped a kidnapping—or at least, I hoped I had. I realized I'd never actually asked if that had worked out.

"Hey." I sat up straight again. "We stopped Blondie from kidnapping that kid, right? He didn't leave me for dead to nab the little one and bolt?"

"Right. I had Amy make sure after I dropped you off at Chloe's."

"Oh, thank god. At least that went right. We should talk to Merrin again, see if she can give us another hint. If you're sticking to my side until this is done, then I won't be alone when she calls again. You and I can get to the place before Blondie does and you can wolf out and take him down."

Mel regarded me for a moment, then nodded once. "Not a bad plan, assuming Merrin can actually help."

"We'll go see her first thing tom—ah, shit. I have appointments in the morning." I bit my lip, thinking of Loraine. I'd give her a free session next week if necessary, but I figured keeping Seattle's children safe was going to have to take precedence. "This is more important, I think. I'll have Chloe reschedule my earlier clients for, what do you think? Monday?"

"Optimistic. I like it."

"All right. I'm gonna call her and then go to bed." At his look, I clarified. "*Alone*. I don't care what you do, but do it quietly. We'll go see Merrin first thing."

"Aye, aye, Boss."

I rolled my eyes, wishing there had been any other way at all to ensure my safety.

Eleven

I woke to Chloe sitting on the edge of my bed, brushing my hair off my face and saying my name. Cracking one eye open within the sea of my pillows, I grunted. Chloe laughed, pressed down the pillow that was puffed around my face, and leaned down to look into my eyes.

"How is it possible you're not suffocating?"

I grunted again, forcing my heavy body to roll over. Perking up when I noticed that Chloe held a reusable cup from The Internets in her hand, I got my elbows under me and sat up. "That hot chocolate? For me?"

"Only if you get up!" Chloe pushed to her feet, yanked the covers off my body, and headed for the hall. I whined, dropped back down onto the pillow, and figured sleep was the cure for the common morning. "I'll send Mel in to wake you up if I don't hear the shower in five minutes!" Chloe called.

Dammit.

After I was cleaned and dressed, I headed out to the kitchen and found that Chloe had made herself at home while I was busy. My kitchen looked... used. I was unaware such a thing was possible.

"I don't understand. What's that thing on the other thing? Why does the first thing have food in it?" I asked from the doorway.

"Tofu scramble," Chloe said, reaching into a bowl of sliced apple and bringing a piece up to her shoulder, where it disappeared. I peered around her and caught sight of Sonny chewing happily on his breakfast. Just for a second, I worried that she was trying to seduce him away from me.

"That sounds gooey," I said finally.

She laughed and pulled the pan off the stove, dumping the whole thing onto a plate to her right. Despite my opinion on the merits of a mix of vegetables and tofu, I was pleased to see that she'd at least thought to prepare a bunch of potatoes to go with it. I could probably pick those out of the rest if necessary.

"If you don't love it, I'll eat Sonny."

I frowned at that. "I don't think I like that ultimatum."

"Don't worry," she said, sliding the plate onto my dining table next to the cup she'd used to lure me out of bed. "You'll love it."

I discovered somewhere around the fourth forkful that I did love it. There was some blend of spices in there that I wasn't even sure I had in the house, and the addition of carbs made it impossible not to enjoy. I'll give vegans one thing: they love their carbs almost as much as I do. Once I was as conscious as possible, given the godawful hour, I jerked my chin at Chloe, remembering for once to swallow before speaking.

"Where's Mel?"

"Out running around."

"I didn't know werewolves had to exercise," I said.

Chloe shook her head, chuckling. "No, he's—"

The front door squeaked an announcement that someone had arrived and I had to assume from the lack of emotion it was Mel. I took the opportunity to stuff my face some more as Chloe leaned back in her chair, looked down the long kitchen, and gave him a little wave.

"She's up, almost ready. We'll head to Merrin's in five."

Mel approached, his gaze darting between the two of us. "You didn't make me anything?"

"Here." Chloe handed him her half-empty plate and got to her feet. "I'm going to try to call Jeremy one more time to reschedule. He didn't answer when I called earlier." Digging her phone out of her pocket, she headed out into the living room. Mel hunkered down and we ate quickly in silence together. It was a photo finish and Mel, still chewing, grabbed my plate and carried both to the sink.

I watched him as he gave them a quick rinse, loaded them into the dishwasher, and then turned to me. I couldn't quite get over the fact that the man I despised most in the world was standing in my kitchen, acting borderline domestic.

"Ready?"

"I guess," I said, wondering if I was going to have to reconsider my opinion of him. He continued to surprise me by being decent and, honestly, I was kind of starting to dig it.

We were on our way to Merrin's before long, Mel driving, Chloe in the front seat of his SUV. I sat in the middle of the second row, deciding to feel like I was being chauffeured instead of protected like the president's daughter or something.

"Did you find anything earlier?" Chloe asked Mel.

He shook his head. "Nope. Gwen's neighborhood smells like any other."

"You sniffed my neighborhood?" I asked. I suddenly wasn't sure which was weirder: having Mel in my kitchen or knowing that he'd been playing bloodhound.

Mel caught my eye in the rearview mirror and tapped his nose. "I mean I didn't sniff out any suspicious human-looking monsters roaming around, aiming to rip you limb from limb. You've got a family of werewolves living a few streets over, but I'm sure they're harmless."

"Werewolves? You sniffed my neighborhood and found werewolves?" I swiveled my head, inspecting the houses passing by as we drove. I didn't really expect to find a banner with, "Werewolves inside! Welcome!" but it seemed suddenly strange that all the houses looked so normal. Mel's emotions were impossible to miss; how had I not realized an entire family of his kind were so close?

Mel pressed on, turning to Chloe. "If Merrin has something, will you be joining us in our attempt to thwart another kidnapping?"

She hesitated for a moment, then gave a slow nod. "You're the muscle. If you think I'll be safe, I'll go with."

He was quiet, the silence between them saying something I couldn't quite decipher. "You'll be fine. I'm confident whatever this thing is, it won't be much of a threat."

"How do you know?" Chloe asked.

"It hasn't killed Gwen and it's seen her twice now. It looks human and didn't bother to approach her as something other than what it is, so we know it's not something that has glamour or the ability to shape-shift."

"I take it you don't mean the magazine," Chloe said.

Mel glanced her way and they shared another look that said they both knew something I didn't. Before I could ask, he caught my gaze in the rearview as if making sure I felt included.

"Not the magazine. It—certain fae can make you believe you're seeing something you're not, or not seeing something you are, as the case may be."

"What if he looks not-human, but did this magazine thing and showed up looking like a man, instead?" I asked. "Or is that now how that works?"

"Point," Mel said, going quiet for a second. "He could have six eyes and horns normally, but he flashed teeth, right?"

"I think that's what it was doing. It looked like a bad TV movie, actually, the way his lips pulled back and he flashed those—well, they weren't pearly white, but same idea."

"Then he probably looks just like what you saw last night. If he was trying to scare you and he could look scarier, he probably would have. If he was just trying to talk, why not hide the teeth?"

"But what if—"

91

"Gwen," Chloe interrupted, reaching back to pat my knee gently. "If we're gonna go over absolutely every possibility, we'll just run out of time. Mel's just picking the most likely scenario. If he's wrong, you can punish him later, okay?"

"You can spank me," Mel offered, winking. I wrinkled my nose and made a sound of disgust. Mel chuckled.

"Right. So we're sticking with assuming it can't change its appearance, so what does that leave?" Chloe asked. "What do you know of that looks human and would take children with magical abilities?"

"It's gotta be something that can crawl inside my head and wreck up the place, too. Amy said something was in my brain when she found me."

"Shit, yeah," Chloe pointed at me over her shoulder. "That, too."

"Not many things come to mind," Mel said thoughtfully. "Succubi look human, werewolves—but Gwen would have recognized that, I'm guessing?"

"Yep."

"Plus, we don't have any sort of mental powers." Catching my eye in the mirror , Mel winked. "We're all physical."

"Ugh," I groaned, again.

Mel pressed on as if I hadn't made a sound. "Demons look human, sirens too; it could be a—"

"Vampire?" I asked.

"Stop with that," Mel ordered, instantly agitated.

"I saw fangs!"

"That doesn't mean vampire," he said, his tone final.

"You're sure?" Chloe asked. Mel threw her a hard glare and she held her hands up. "Got it. So we're looking at a variety of things, but you're sure you can take down any one of them if we run afoul of it tonight?"

"I am." Mel was quiet for a few moments before he said petulantly, "It's not a vampire."

Chloe did her best to hold back a snort.

Merrin was standing just inside her open door when we approached. Her gaze went straight to me and I felt distress flap within her like a flag in heavy wind.

"Hey, Merrin," I said.

Before I could continue, Evadne called to us from inside. "She was expecting you, but we must take our leave soon."

"We'll be quick," Chloe said, stepping in as soon as Merrin moved to let us pass.

"You have five minutes," the fairy said briskly. She was dressed this time, sitting on the couch, legs crossed, fingers linked on her knee. I looked her over, probing to get a sense of what she was feeling about the situation, but she only smiled at me. Her eyes met mine and her expression said she could tell what I was trying. "I wouldn't."

"Sorry," I mumbled.

Mel shut the door and then turned, his entire stance shifting when he noticed Evadne. He took one step toward her and the fairy's body language changed. She was no longer concerned with me or my empathy and that was a very bad thing for Mel. Before he could even get a word out, she pointed at him.

"Halfling, you will not speak unless spoken to." Her tone was mild but the meaning behind it clearly wasn't. Mel froze, his eyes going wide as he looked down at himself. His skin seemed to pale and when he breathed out, the air from his lips was foggy.

Evadne had made her point; Mel said nothing for the rest of the meeting.

"Merrin, we're hoping you can tell us some more about—"

"Who's your friend?" Stepping close, she tipped her head, gaze on the front of my jacket.

"You mean Mel?" I asked, pointing. Merrin ignored my question, reaching out to unzip my coat. I looked to Chloe for guidance but she just shrugged. Without asking, Merrin tucked a hand into my inner breast pocket and pulled out a yellow square of paper that I hadn't known was there. I caught sight of the candy thief's familiar scrawl, but I couldn't make out any actual words.

"Not again," I moaned. Merrin stared at the paper, read it over without showing it to me, and then turned, walking dreamily over to Evadne. She stood still, her gaze aimless, and said nothing.

"What's this, pet?"

Merrin handed the paper over and Evadne looked at it, her lips curving. The temperature in the room dropped abruptly and I let out a little yelp. Before I could ask what had happened, Evadne threw back her head and laughed. Merrin stayed still, head tilted, staring out the window above the couch, unaffected. Mel inched away, but Chloe stayed where she was, watching with fascination as Evadne chuckled, crumpled up the piece of paper in her hand, and then squeezed her fist around it. Like magic—or maybe, not just *like* magic—her fingers uncurled to reveal that the paper had disappeared.

"It seems you are in a predicament," she said, pushing to her feet. "We will help, free of charge this time. You seek foresight, yes?" Evadne was focused directly on me, so I gave a minute nod. I had no idea what had changed the game, but her sudden cooperation made me nervous.

"Yeah, we're hoping to find out where else our bad guy is going to strike." An idea occurred to me and I decided to go for it. "Do you know what's been kidnapping children? Do you know how to stop it?"

"Not my place," Evadne sighed, disinterested in the question, as her gaze dropped to Merrin. "Pet, are you able to see the answer to their query? I'll give you a treat."

"I like treats," Merrin said, her eyes rolling upward until she was staring at the ceiling. Her hands lifted, her fingers wiggling gracefully in the air like a hula dancer miming waves. She turned her face to me, but her gaze remained upward. "The maiden will leave you at the tea party. Be careful of the bugs."

"Is... Are we going to—"

"Don't mind that," Evadne said, running her hand gently over Merrin's long red hair. "Pet, concentrate. What do you see in the here and soon?"

"I can." Merrin gave a small nod, turned her hands upward and put them together, cupping them like she'd scoop water to her lips. "You must save a little boy. Car. Red sedan. He's in the back seat when the woman grabs him. There's another. He is quite well. Don't look into the woman's eyes."

Merrin went quiet, reaching up to put her hand over her eyes. She stayed still for a few moments as we all watched her. When she finally dropped her hand, she looked directly at me, realization leaking in. I felt a tinge of confusion in her.

"Gwen, are you looking for the demon?"

"*Demon?*" I cried. "There's a demon?"

"She's ugly, though you will not see her real face. I can get you to her." Merrin's voice went lyrical as she crossed the room toward the tiny kitchen. "She comes soon."

"How soon?"

Merrin didn't answer me, just took a pen and a notepad from off the bar between the kitchen and the living area and started writing.

"We really appreciate this," Chloe said. I turned to find her looking directly at Evadne. "I can't say how much."

Evadne tipped her head at Chloe. "Of course."

"Here you go," Merrin said, handing me the slip of paper. "You'll find them there. I'd like my treat now."

"Of course, pet." Evadne didn't bother with politeness, just moved to wrap her arm around Merrin and lead her toward the bedroom. "Your five minutes are up. See yourselves out."

It felt wrong to spend the rest of my day as we would any other, but we didn't really have any other options. We didn't know enough about this creature to seek it out before it struck again—which wouldn't be until the next day—and we had no other leads. So Chloe and I went into the office as we normally would and I saw the clients I counseled every Friday afternoon. We figured Blondie wouldn't attack me with so many people around, so Mel headed up to his office to get some work of his own done.

The day passed slowly, ending after my last client at six. Chloe had gone downstairs and grabbed us lunch from The Internets earlier, but I still hadn't eaten for several hours. My stomach was definitely letting me know how it felt about that.

"What are we getting for dinner?" I asked as Chloe turned off the last of the lights and pulled her jacket off the hook.

"You and Mel? I have no idea. I have some things to take care of, though."

"Like what?"

"Unlike you, I have an actual life. Besides, we can't do much of anything right now, can we? We've got no leads except Merrin's note and that says we don't have to be in Everett to stop a kidnapping until tomorrow." She patted my shoulder and ushered me through the door. "You'll be fine. Make him buy you dinner."

"Then he'll think it's a date."

"So starve." She locked the door, hooked her arm around mine, and led us down the stairwell to the first floor. Mel was waiting there, leaning against the wall across from the windows to The Internets. With his leather jacket and perfectly coiffed hair, he looked like he'd strolled off the set of *Grease*. Chloe swung around in front of me, grabbing my hand and folding a square of paper into it.

"Don't do anything I wouldn't do!" Without giving me a chance for a snappy comeback, she headed out the side door. I watched her go and sighed after her, annoyed that she'd just leave me in such a situation. Forget the missing kids and mistaken identity; now I was expected to spend an entire evening—and night—alone with Mel? It was too early to avoid him by going to bed like I'd done the night before and I was too hungry to take that road anyway. As well as we'd been getting along, as decent as he'd been, I was no longer in the mood to ignore a whole year of experience telling me that Mel was *Mel* and that it wouldn't last.

"What's that?" Mel asked, stepping uncomfortably close. I lifted my hand, finding that Chloe had pressed a hundred-dollar bill into my palm.

"Cash."

"I think Chloe means for you to pay me for sex."

"What if she's paying me for sex?"

"Then I'll pay you to watch."

"Because you figure she's better than you are at pleasing a woman and you want tips?"

"Exactly. I can videotape the whole thing and watch it later for research."

"Research, my ass—no!" I hopped back, knowing in an instant I'd said exactly the wrong thing. "Don't even think about it!"

Mel laughed and gestured toward the front door. "Come on. You're probably hungry."

"What makes you say that?"

"You're *always* hungry."

"Ah," I said, falling into step with him. "That."

Twelve

"I am beginning to think you're kidnapping me for my kidneys."

"Nonsense. I can kill a deer if I'm craving organ meat."

I made a vomiting sound, which wasn't uncommon around Mel. Sometimes it just comes out at the sight of him. We'd been on the road for a while and the small talk had veered away from the supernatural problems we shared; you can only say so many ways that you have no new ideas or suggestions.

Mel was horrified by my lack of musical obsession and I was a little sad that he seemed mostly unaware of the internet. We learned we had practically no interests in common, except that we both loved pizza.

"Seriously, this is ridiculous. There hasn't been a house or driveway for—oh, speak of the devil."

Mel slowed and the headlights of his car lit up a loose collection of gravel that could have been considered a driveway if you were feeling generous. As the car turned off the paved road onto the death trap, I noticed a dilapidated sign that threatened trespassers with death.

I shifted in my seat, suddenly wondering if I should rip Merrin's necklace off Mel to see what his emotions were saying and if they would tell a different story than this horror movie cliché into which I was being driven.

"Mel?"

"One sec," he said, pulling over and fiddling with something on the driver's side door. As the car slowed, out of line of sight from the main road, I considered my options. The smart money was on trusting that I'd known Mel for over a year and he'd never shown signs of wanting to hurt anyone. Besides, despite irritatingly bragging about being a massive slut, he'd never lit up my lizard brain with feelings of, "Danger! Danger!"

After a moment, the car began to move again, turning onto the path. Within seconds, our ride changed dramatically. We'd transitioned onto another well-paved road far enough back from the main road that it wouldn't be seen.

"We're not going to a restaurant, are we?" I asked. Mel grinned at me and it was shark-like, all big teeth and taut lips. Sighing, I crossed my arms over my chest.

"Hey, if you were really bothered, you'd've asked more questions. You're just hungry and clearly you trust my superior pizza instincts."

"We'll see how superior your instincts are," I said, instantly annoyed that he had a point. I hadn't asked any questions because once it was clear food was imminent, I'd gone mostly on autopilot. But we were far enough away from my car and civilization that I was effectively trapped unless I wanted to spend a fortune on a taxi.

I considered the money Chloe had given me and it bolstered my mood slightly. If something really went wrong—for instance, if Mel tried to feed me something healthy—I had my escape. The road curved and then the forest opened up on a small home that looked much too modern for its location. Mel pulled in under a high awning and lights burst to life as we came to a stop. Turning off the car, he angled himself to give me an excited look. Whatever we were in for, he was pretty happy about it.

"Come on!" Without waiting for me, he climbed out of the car, strutting up a stone walkway along the side of the house. I sat in the quiet car, staring at his closed door and wondering if I wanted to go inside and see what he had planned.

With a shrug, I mumbled, "What the hell," and followed Mel. I saw light come through an open doorway and I followed it, noting that the recent snow was still clumped around the grounds.

I have no idea if I had any preconceived notions about what I'd find when entering Mel's home but if I did, they were probably similar to what I saw when I got there.

The interior was a lot of deep colors, red woods, granite countertops. A state-of-the-art entertainment and sound system made the living room look high-tech, while a closed laptop sat alone on a desk in an alcove to the right. The kitchen was huge and looked professional-grade. From the layout of the place, it seemed the door we'd come through was meant to be at the back of the house. Between me and an ornate glass and wood front door were the impressive kitchen and heavily furnished living room.

As I shut the door—and my dropped jaw—I noticed Mel had already gotten to work in the kitchen. He was laying opaque glass dishes on the gigantic black granite island, leaving the refrigerator door open as he bustled around. An incredible brick oven had been built into the left wall just past the stove and fridge; its metal doors were open, revealing a low flame. Wood was stacked in the storage alcove underneath and Mel pulled out three more logs and set to building the flame in the oven.

"Whoa," was all I could say.

"Best pizza you've ever had. Take a seat." Throwing a look back at me, he gestured with his elbow toward the living room. "Or put on music if you think you can figure out what that is."

"I don't know if I want to risk it. You've probably got Barry White queued up to lull a woman's underpants right off."

"Please," he spat, still arm-deep in the oven.

Before checking out the little office nook, I went to what I figured was the front of the house. I peered out the window but only saw a large porch and another walkway that disappeared into the dark of the forest. Nothing explained what we were doing in the middle of the woods, alone, about to share pizza.

I turned and frowned at Mel. I hadn't even taken my jacket off, but he had disrobed down to a white undershirt. His coat and button-up shirt were draped over one of the chairs set under the bar side of the kitchen island and he'd moved on to opening the containers he'd set out.

"This is weird," I announced.

"What is?"

"All of this. I don't like you," I said.

Mel grinned. "I hadn't noticed."

"That's part of what I don't like about you."

He chuckled this time and leaned back to grab a knife off the magnetic strip along the wall.

"I'm not kidding, Mel. This, among many other things, isn't something I ever saw happening between us. You don't offer to make me pizza or invite me into your home. Your bed, sure, but not your home."

"My bed is in my home," he said, pausing in the chopping of mushrooms to smirk at me. "In case you hadn't noticed."

"See, stuff like that," I said, deciding I might as well resign myself to the fact that Mel and I were acting friendly. He was okay with the situation, completely at ease even though I wouldn't have been surprised to find out it was all a hallucination. Mel and me getting along like grown-ups?

The very concept was nearly Greek to me.

Before pulling off my coat, I checked all the pockets for notes, wondering if the candy thief had left any explanation of what I'd let the evening come to. I found nothing and wondered why the thief had gone radio silent. It had warned me before about Mel, trying to get me to put up my shields so I wouldn't fry my brain. Maybe it foolishly believed that the necklace not only blocked Mel's emotions from me, but also made him completely tolerable.

Or maybe it hadn't warned me off of spending the evening with Mel because it was holed up in my house eating all the food I'd risked my life to buy from the mini-mart.

"Goddammit," I murmured.

"Pondering your own mental shortcomings?"

"What?" I asked, only half-sure he'd said something insulting. My mind was busy conjuring up images of a giant cartoon mouth—I can't even fathom what this candy thief looks like—chomping its way through piles of *my* sugar.

"The music, genius. You're just standing there when you should be picking out something to listen to."

"Shut up," I snapped. "I could be a genius. Maybe I'm solving complex math equations and calculating the exact square footage of your house. You don't know."

Mel wisely didn't address my comments, though I could see his lips fighting with a smile. I watched him chop vegetables for a few moments, worried that I was hungry enough to eat even those if it came to it, and then sighed, giving in. He had promised me pizza, after all, and I didn't want to ruin my chances at that.

"Where's your stereo?"

"It's the digital age, babe." With the knife, Mel pointed at another cabinet set into the side of the entertainment center. I opened it and found a slick monitor and a tray that slid a keyboard out toward me when the door opened completely. The screen flashed to life and I was greeted with an iTunes so packed with playlists I thought I'd never stop scrolling.

I picked one of the two dozen cooking playlists Mel had created and music floated out through the room from everywhere and nowhere; apparently he had hidden speakers. Then I decided I was going to snoop some more. Mel ignored me when I headed straight for the darkened hallway. I felt around for a switch and flicked it on to find that I was facing the bathroom door. The guest bath was long, narrow, and made up to look like a fancy hotel bathroom. It was very nice, but something about it clearly said, "Your visit here is temporary." Individually wrapped soaps and expertly folded fluffy towels were laid out on otherwise empty shelves. I wondered if Mel had a Zorg-esque army of tiny robots that did his bidding, since it all looked too well-maintained for me to believe he'd fancied the place up himself.

At the end of the hall was a closed door that I, of course, couldn't resist opening.

Mel's bedroom looked similarly inviting, without *actually* inviting anyone to stay. It had the same high ceilings as the rest of the house, as well as a lot of square edges and dark colors.

"What kind of meat do you like?" Mel asked, startling me into wheeling around. Normally you can't sneak up on me unless I'm eyeballs deep in pastry, because my empathy makes a sort of mental map of those around me. Merrin's necklace seemed to be affecting much more than I'd anticipated, though, and I realized I was going to have to learn to deal with the sort of blindness it imposed on me.

When I didn't answer immediately, Mel began thrusting his pelvis toward me to the beat of the music. "Because I have *all kinds*."

"I think you have one kind and I don't want it."

Mel laughed, taking my joke better than I took most of his, then stopped thrusting and gestured back down the hall.

"Come choose your toppings. Unless you'd rather we stay in here."

"No," I assured him, squeezing past when he continued to block most of the doorway rather than let me pass easily. I kept my gaze off his so he wouldn't see in my eyes that I was finding his behavior sliding down the spectrum away from objectionable and toward entertaining. I refused to consider that it was just because he was promising me pizza. I mean, I look at sex like I look at cupcakes and if great sex was as easy to get as great cupcakes, I would have it all the time. But this was still Mel and, necklace or not, I couldn't take that chance.

The kitchen looked like it was dressed for a TV crew to crowd in and shoot a culinary school commercial. I was pretty impressed, but rather than boost his ego by mentioning it, I sat at the counter and reached across to grab a handful of mushrooms. Any port in a storm. Ignoring my rudeness, Mel started opening paper-wrapped bundles of cubed meat. I jerked my chin toward them when he did a sliding dance toward the stove.

"What are those?"

"The different kinds of meat you claim you don't want. I've got venison and rabbit—very fresh—but if you prefer, I can pull some chicken, pork, or beef out."

It took me a moment to catch on to what he meant by fresh and I sat up straight when I did.

"Fresh? Like, you killed them?" I asked.

He nodded, still at the stove. The pizza oven made a crackling sound. "That's why I'm in the forest."

"There are chickens and cows in the forest?" I asked.

Mel took a second to throw me an annoyed glance. "I don't kill *those* myself, but I like variety. I have family all over; some of them have farms. Not all werewolves are as city-loving as I am."

"Yeah, you're a real Carrie Bradshaw out here in the dark of the forest, killing your own deer."

"You mock, but once you taste it …" He trailed off, grabbing a handful of the dark red meat and dumping the cubes into a pan that smelled like spices and wine.

I took a second to question my situation again, shaking my head. "I'm not kidding; this is weird. You haven't once tried to stick it in me in the last hour."

Mel shrugged. "How do you know that's not exactly what I'm doing now?"

I blinked, frowning. "This seems a bit elegant for you."

"Give me some credit, Arthur." Content with the way the meat in the pan was handling itself, he turned to me and leaned against the counter. "If it can somehow be used to seduce a woman, I am great at it."

"Really?" I asked, nabbing a few spinach leaves this time. I ate them quickly, leaning back in my chair. "Like what?"

"Oh, various instruments—though drums and bass are the top sellers. Cooking, singing—no, I will not demonstrate that for you. Yoga."

I was more taken aback by the yoga comment than the rest, but I vowed then and there to one day hear Mel belt out a cheesy love ballad. In my mind, he would don a long blond wig and possibly weep at the end of the song, before—of course—being pelted with panties.

"Yoga?"

"Oh, you have no idea. Especially out here." He whistled, looking at me like he'd just cracked the biggest secret in vagina history.

"You are …" I trailed off, unsure of what I could call him that I hadn't already called him a million times. "Actually, where is the wine? I need to talk to some wine about this." With Mel wearing the necklace, I could get as drunk as I wanted and I wouldn't have to worry about how my empathy might react. I hadn't gotten drunk around another person since I'd been dating my ex-husband and I liked the idea of company that couldn't fry my brain.

When he brought out a bottle of red and two glasses, I considered how the next hour might go and how different it was likely to be from the rest of our relationship.

"This isn't weird to you?" I asked.

Mel shrugged. "It's fun. Aren't you having fun?"

"I suppose. But this isn't how we do things. Your fun usually comes at my expense."

"True," he said, sipping his own wine and checking the meat in the pan. "But this is better. Why are you complaining?"

"I'm not complaining, I'm confused. I'm not used to being able to stand you. Generally just being in the same room with you makes me want to tear my—no, tear *your* hair out."

When he turned to unwrap one of the balls of dough he had on the counter, he was smiling.

"And that is exactly why I spend so much time in the same room as you. It's like a game where winning just requires me to stand there."

"You're an asshole."

He shrugged. "You just play hard to get really well."

"I'm not playing. And I'm not just hard to get, I'm impossible. At least for you."

"Never say never. With this necklace, who knows what might happen."

"I know what will happen and it's not sex. From the second we met, you've been insufferable and grating. And not just your emotions. You, as a person, tend to be a jerk. And besides, there's a world full of other women out there. Why is fucking me on your bucket list?"

"Wow," he said, his eyebrows shooting up as he worked the dough. "Language."

I went quiet, unsure if I'd offended him. After some contemplation, I realized that was unlikely. I watched him work, wondering why he wasn't addressing my comments about his jerkishness. He didn't look bothered but I couldn't be sure without being able to feel his emotions. For a brief moment, I kind of wished I could feel what was going on in his psyche. Deciding that way definitely lay not only madness but also rolling around on the floor clutching my skull and crying, I pressed on.

"So why me? From what I can tell, you don't have a type, so it's not that. You've, somehow, got no shortage of options and paying for sex would be way less work than you put into going after me." I took another drink of wine and a thought occurred to me. "Is it really just that I'm a woman?"

"Pretty much."

"Great," I said, shaking my head. "You're even simpler than I am."

"I wouldn't go that far," he said, lifting the dough and tossing it like a pro. "I don't think anyone's as simple as you. Maybe a dung beetle."

"Hey."

"That's not half as insulting as some of the things you've said to me," Mel pointed out, his tone gone harder than I'd been expecting.

"Well... you deserve it."

"And you deserve me driving you home without giving you any pizza."

I buttoned up, cowed by the idea that I wouldn't get to eat any of the spiced, boozy venison or the fresh mozzarella floating in cloudy water waiting to be made into delicious pizza. After another sip of wine and an internal admonishment at my growling stomach, I let my annoyance go.

"Well. I'm sorry," I offered. Mel nodded my way, ignoring the fact that my tone hadn't been entirely sincere.

"I appreciate that."

Trusting that he was back on the feeding-me train, I got back on topic. "If I looked like a rumpled bed sheet and weighed as much as a small horse, would you still try to have sex with me?"

"Yep." He nodded without hesitation.

"Well, that's something, at least."

"Meaning?"

"Meaning... you're actually less of a dick than I thought."

"My dick is less than no man's."

"Why does everything end up being about your dick?

"You'd understand if you'd just take a shot."

I wrinkled my nose. "It would take so much more than one shot to get me to have sex with you. I'd need the entire bottle." I glared at the wine as if it was conspiring against me. Mel caught my look and laughed.

As he moved on to adding sauce to the dough, I got up and went to the other side of the counter. Eyeing the options, I waited for him to finish with the sauce.

"Do I get to choose the toppings?"

"For one pizza, yes. I choose the second for you."

"I'll allow it," I said, risking my dignity and pouring another glass of wine.

By midnight, I was stretched out on the floor of Mel's living room, making undoubtedly sexual sounds. Both pizzas were divine, though I did cheerfully admit that the one Mel had crafted was better than the one I'd slapped together. At some point in the evening I'd lost my shoes and my socks and taken up residence on the floor next to the free-standing fireplace. The window at my back was impressively insulated; all I felt was the wine in my bloodstream and the heat from the fire.

Mel was on the floor across the coffee table from me, one long leg outstretched, one bent, his back to the part of his sectional that divided the living room from the kitchen. He was laughing at me. I couldn't recall the number of things we'd discussed, but none had been too personal. I wondered if skirting around subjects like siblings and life experiences was just his way of avoiding getting close to a woman.

Grabbing another slice of pizza, I chomped into it, moaning again.

"If I didn't have a year of experience warning me against it, I would *actually* be seduced by this. Come on, Somerset, let's hear you sing."

He laughed and shook his head, grabbing for a slice of the pizza I'd made—which I'd barely touched.

"Your experience is wrong. I could give you some better, though."

"No, no, despite your cooking prowess—which is impressive—I'm not interested. You're still an asshole."

"So are most of the men out there."

"I haven't slept with them, either," I mused, trying to decide if I wanted another glass of wine or another slice of pizza.

"Maybe you should give us all a chance."

"Each and every one of you?" I asked, feigning a childlike excitement. When he rolled his eyes, I let my tone fall flat. "That would probably just end in disappointment."

"Man," he said, finishing off his slice and shaking his head. "You have no faith in my gender."

"Eh," I shrugged, deciding against any more food. While I wasn't trying to impress Mel, I also wasn't really interested in barfing all over his house because I'd eaten and drank too much. "It's less a lack of faith and more a... discerning taste."

"Well, you should discern that I'm worth a taste."

I squinted his way. "Do you have a porn script writer in your ear, or something? You're like Cyrano de Blow Job."

Laughing, Mel got up, grabbing for the pizza pans. Winking at me, he padded into the kitchen. "I don't need anybody else; all this sexual cleverness is me and me alone. Unless you'd like to get a friend involved."

"I don't say it enough, but *ugh*." Grabbing the ceramic squares he'd set out for the formerly hot pizza pans, I followed him. "Besides, just because you've slept with a lot of women doesn't mean you're good at it."

"How does *that* logic work?"

"You're pretty, I'll give you that. Women are just as shallow as men and if I saw a picture of you, I'd probably want to bang you." Oops, that last bit had been the wine talking. Mel didn't seem to notice, which I thought spoke to how often he got told he was attractive.

"Yes, which means I practice sex a lot. Practice makes perfect. And then, once I became perfect, I kept having sex." Loading the pans and the few glass bowls he'd emptied into his dishwasher, he waved a hand as if everything had been explained and there were no more words.

"Practice on one woman, maybe. Practice on many is like ..." I had to pause to think of a good analogy. Mel let me, seemingly convinced I had no argument he couldn't deflect. "It's like building a lot of different things out of wood—" He paused in loading the dishwasher long enough to shoot me finger-guns. "But never focusing on one. You never get good at making birdhouses if you've made one birdhouse and thirty-five other objects."

"Bird hotel, bird ski chalet, bird liquor store."

I spoke over him, refusing to let him derail my point by making me laugh. "*My point* is that all women are different. We all like different things, especially in bed."

With the counter cleared of plates and bowls, Mel grabbed a rag, ran it under hot water, squirted some soap on it, and started cleaning.

Sitting in a silent haze of wine and pizza and surprisingly enjoyable conversation, I watched him work. I swear my eyes only drifted to the way his muscles moved once or twice. Or, like, four or five times, but it was all the wine, I swear. Good sense passed out in the corner, and all that.

When the island was clean of pizza debris, Mel turned to work on the stove and spoke with his back to me.

"I take it your argument has been made? No more animal-home-related analogies to throw my way?"

I shrugged, then realized he couldn't see it. "Yeah, I've made my point. You're good at stuff; I'll give you that. Cooking pizza is a stuff you're good at, but that doesn't make you a sex expert."

"It doesn't *make* me one, no," he admitted, starting in on the other counters closer to the sink. "But it helped get me what I needed to become one."

"Ladies," I stated, leaning a hip against the counter. After all the wine, I wasn't quite answering his questions with, "I love you, man!" but my motor skills had definitely taken a hit. Mel finished cleaning the kitchen, draped the rag over a bar mounted to the inside of the bucket sink so it could dry, and then turned to face me. Planting the heels of his hands on the counter, he leaned back.

"Lots of ladies," he said.

"And how many ladies have you slept with, uh ..." I paused, realizing my brain had gone even fuzzier and I had no idea what day of the week it was. Giving up, I waved a hand. "Last week."

"Let's see." His eyes squinted a bit and I watched the fingers of his left hand twitch, as if he were counting in his head and didn't realize his digits were helping. It was kind of adorable. Finally, he looked me in the eyes and said, matter-of-factly, "Twelve."

"Good god," I exclaimed. "That's—that can't be right."

"It was a good week!"

"So that's not normal?"

"No, that's about normal. It was just a *good week.*"

"Holy hell," I said. "My god!" I couldn't believe it. I knew he had no reason to lie but I still couldn't believe it. That meant he slept with scores of women a month, which meant... "Have you not gone through the entire eligible population of Seattle yet?"

"Well, I don't just date women in this city, you know." He seemed offended by the implication.

"But still! How the hell do you even have time for that?"

Tipping his head down to look at me through his lashes, he raised a brow and grinned devilishly. "How much time do you think each encounter takes, anyway?"

Immediately I felt my cheeks go red. I hadn't meant to imply what I'd practically made it my life's work to question.

"It's not even the sex *itself,*" I spat, my tone petty as I tried to regain my cynicism about his technique. "How many women can you even seduce in a day?"

"Like you said, women are shallow and I am ..." He paused, but went with my word, putting emphasis on it. "Pretty."

"Is it a werewolf pheromone? Do you put off something that makes a woman's undergarments run for the hills?"

"Do I?"

Frowning, I looked him up and down. All I ever felt around him was annoyance and aggravation. I couldn't imagine just seeing him and going, "All right, let's make with the humping." But other women were probably less uptight than me. And also couldn't feel how skin-crawlingly annoying it was to just be near him.

Mel let me inspect him. After a moment, I lifted a hand, quirking a finger to beckon him. Giving his shoulders a loose roll as if preparing for a fight, he pushed away from the counter. I only noticed then that he was barefoot, too. I ignored the fact that, for some reason, I found it really sexy to see his feet peek out from under his pants, and I twisted my hand. When he got close, I put the flat of my palm out; he stopped just before his shirt touched my skin and looked down at me.

"Don't try anything funny," I warned.

I lifted onto my toes, giving his neck a light sniff. Tipping his mouth near my ear, he whispered in a tone that not even the straightest man would fail to find sexy, "If I try something, it won't be laughter that has you out of breath."

I grinned, staying put long enough that he wouldn't see it. After a moment, I dropped flat to my feet again, circling him. He stayed perfectly still as I tried to see if I could detect some sort of sex-causing scent anywhere on his body. His neck, cheek, the backs of his shoulder blades— while all very nice to look at—didn't seem to smell like anything except... Mel.

"Hunh," I grunted in confusion. I stared at the back of his neck for a moment, fought my somewhat drunken urge to run my hands through his hair, and moved back around to face him. He watched me, seeming pleased that he was worth my inspection. I reminded myself that without Merrin's magic necklace, I wouldn't have set foot in the house, let alone be considering his well-shaped body and how he used it to get a woman into bed.

"You just smell like you. And kind of like pizza, but that might be the kitchen."

"You smell a little tipsy. And a little like lilac." Pausing, he wrinkled his nose slightly, then added, "And rose."

I stared up at him, very aware that at any moment things could get biblical. While Mel didn't move or physically indicate what he was feeling, I could see it in his eyes. If, in that moment, I chose to kiss him, or—as Chloe had suggested so many times—tried to climb him like a tree, he wouldn't have been opposed to it. I stayed flat on my feet, inches away.

"Well," I drawled. "Your sense of smell is better than mine. I can't smell *your* perfume."

Sensing that I'd broken the moment in two and tossed it out the window, Mel grinned. He stepped around me and headed toward the living room. I sighed out the tension that had built and caught a glimpse of the clock on the wall; it was telling me it was way later than I had realized.

"Wow."

"Looking at my ass again?" Mel asked, moving to the music cabinet, jiggling the mouse around on its tray.

"I didn't realize how late it is. We should probably go. I hadn't planned on being out this long."

"Stay here," he said, and the music stopped. My heart started thudding suddenly, apparently desperate to make up for the silence that had once again gone and gotten itself stuffed with tension. I swallowed audibly.

Mel and I made eye contact, watching each other across the empty room. After my eyeballs had been satisfactorily seared by the blue of his gaze, he continued, his tone dismissive. "It's not worth it to drive you home this late."

I opened my mouth, intent on arguing, but no words came to mind. I wasn't even sure why I wanted to pick a fight; was I angry that he wouldn't take me home or that his wanting me to stay was based purely on laziness?

Mel pressed on as if I wasn't watching him slack-jawed and confused. "There are plenty of blankets if you're cold, but the fire will burn for a few more hours. The heater—" he moved to a small panel on the wall near the hallway, "—is controlled here."

"That's... okay."

"What?" he asked, catching my eye with another net weaved of invitation and lust. "Were you looking to share my bed?"

"Not... usually." What had I just said?

"There you have it, then. I have to be up in a few hours and, since I'm guarding your body, so do you."

"Gotcha," I said slowly. Mel walked directly toward me, diverted at the last second, and brushed his bare arm by mine as he locked the back door. Once he'd turned the lights off and the only illumination came from a small lamp next to the couch, he paused next to me. His arm was pressed against mine, both of us staring into the living room. I dropped my gaze to the floor, waiting to see what was about to happen.

"You sure there's nothing else I can... *do* for you?" He was giving me an opening, but I wasn't convinced I should give him one back.

"No." I took a deep breath. "The wine will help me sleep and I'm sure I can find the blankets on my own."

"All righty." Without another word, Mel disappeared around the wall; I was left alone in the living room, pondering my life decisions.

Thirteen

I woke with a massive headache and a sore knee.

The combination of wine, a fireplace, a heated room, and too many blankets had shot my body temperature straight through the roof. Groaning, I lifted my face off the cushion, trying to figure out where I was and what I'd done the night before. I had vague, floating visions of pizza, and of getting very close to Mel.

The room was bathed in gray winter light and I stared at the wall between the living room and the hallway, wondering if I'd made the walk of shame from there to the couch at some point in the evening. Adjusting my leg, which was hanging off the wall-spanning couch from just above the knee, I did my best to sit up. My calf had gone mostly numb but my knee felt like Kathy Bates had been at it during the night.

Steeling myself, I got to my feet and hobbled toward the hall. I used the walls for support when I rounded the corner and made my way toward Mel's room. The door was ajar and I saw a light on inside. The end of the night crystallized in my brain.

"Oh," I grumbled, wondering if I was going to hate myself more for considering having sex with Mel, or for not going through with it.

"Mel?" I asked just before I pushed the door open. He was stark naked, his arms up and back, fingers on the tie of Merrin's necklace. Part of my brain started screaming a dramatic, slow-motion, "No!" while the rest was crowded around my eyeballs, taking in his physique and saying, "Oh *yes.*"

"You're up," he said, unbothered by what should have been a very awkward situation.

"So are *you*," I mumbled, unable to keep my gaze in respectable places. Then, as he pulled the necklace off, I collapsed.

Mel was naked, crouched like a marble statue of an Olympian over me. One knee was on the floor, the other pulled to his chest, blocking my view of most of his lower half. His face was smooth, dark bangs falling in a curtain to the end of his nose. The line of his shoulder was perfect, the muscles in his arms incredible as he moved to place his palm on my cheek.

"Overwhelmed by my hotness, I see."

I frowned, or tried to. My face didn't work and I couldn't feel the rest of my body. I had no memories, but my emotions were like bouncy house full of sugar-rushed children. Aggression, lust, frustration, affection, glee, lust (again and again) all slammed into the walls of my psyche as I stared up at Mel, trying to figure out what was happening.

I saw my hand come up, my fingers press against his shoulder. When Mel raised his eyebrows and asked again if I was all right, I clenched my fingers, scratching my nails across his skin. He glanced at my hand before looking back at my face with an eager smile.

The sugar rush wore off, the children tired, and the bouncy house deflated. My mind started to clear of the emotions that Mel had flooded out over me. I still didn't have any real idea of what was happening, but I could at least feel my own body and not just what had poured out of Mel like Gatorade when the necklace had come off.

"Did we have sex?" I asked. He blinked, pulled his hand in, and rested his elbow on his knee. He cocked his head and smirked at me.

"Do you feel satisfied in every *possible* way?"

"I feel sick," I said.

Mel shrugged and shifted, grabbing my shoulders with both hands. "I have a feeling that, for you, that doesn't rule anything out."

Then I was airborne in a drunken, spinning world. Mel placed me firmly on my feet but the spinning didn't stop. My head swiveled one way, my eyeballs the other, while the earth chose a completely different axis and took a nosedive.

"Ah," he murmured, before blurring away from me in one of the few displays of his werewolf speed that I'd seen. A metal bin was pressed against my chest as a hand slipped gently into my hair, tucking it out of the way and guiding my head down.

My body heaved and everything except the kitchen sink flew like a wrecking ball upward through my chest. When I finally stopped throwing up, I could barely stand. The bucket vanished and Mel wrapped an arm around my waist. Somehow, he managed to move me into the steamy bathroom and lean me over the sink. I coughed, spat, and pressed my hands to the warm counter.

Once he was sure I was stable enough to stand, Mel slipped out of the bathroom. I breathed in the steam, willing my mind to clear. The shower was running and I lifted my head to look at my reflection in the mirror. The steam made me a ghost and I glanced over at the shower stall. Without thinking about it, I pulled my shirt over my head, unhooked my bra, stripped down, and stepped in.

I lost track of how long I stood in the shower with my head bowed under the scalding water, but I jumped when I heard Mel's voice from outside the bathroom.

"I would join you, but you probably taste like vomit."

My mind had cleared enough for me to be mortified at being naked in Mel's home. I peered through the opening in the walls of the rounded stall and caught him leaning against the doorframe, still nude. Even in the steamy bathroom, I could feel my cheeks go hot with a mix of embarrassment and appreciation at the sight of him.

"Go away," I ordered.

He sighed, but I could tell it was for effect. "Oh sure, use all my hot water and don't even thank me."

"I'll thank you with a knee to the balls."

"How about something else to the balls?"

"Go!" I insisted, fighting off a smile and hoping it couldn't be heard in my voice.

By the time I got out to the kitchen, Mel had managed to start cooking what smelled to be the most delicious breakfast on the planet. His shirtless body was half-obscured by the island and I wondered if he was still naked. As I moved closer, I tried my best to peer over and check, while also doing my best to avoid seeing anything indecent should he be nude.

Relieved when I saw jogging pants resting halfway down his hips, I sighed and eased the rest of the way up to the island. Mel bobbed his head to the quiet music and then turned to face me, a seriously heavy-duty cast-iron skillet in his hand. He flipped an omelet impressively into the air, caught it on the other side, and then turned back to set the pan on the stove.

"You need filling up," he said, turning to catch my eye and let me know he meant it however I wanted to take it. When I just stood there, at a loss for a response, he continued. "So, I'm making breakfast."

"That doesn't look like much," I said, trying to play it cool. I was still reeling from the night, confused at how things had changed so much in such a short time. Twenty-four hours ago, I would have been horrified at the idea of having to see Mel naked. Now I was fighting off the desire to do it again. "Do I have to split it with you?"

He shook his head, wiggling his hips as a particularly energetic drum solo filled the air.

"I already ate; this is all for you."

111

"Thanks," I said when he set down an egg version of what Chloe had made me the day before. He'd filled the carb and protein mix with fewer vegetables and added cheese, which eased my discomfort slightly.

"My turn in the shower," he announced as he hit the hallway. I glanced back briefly but the siren song of food pulled my attention and kept me from admiring his ass as he walked away.

I mean, I'm not saying I would have done that or anything.

"I'm not wearing this necklace forever," Mel announced as we pulled into my neighborhood.

"Why?" I tensed, panicked at the idea that he might rip it off right then and knock me out again. To my relief, he kept his hands on the wheel, braking to let an orange tabby streak across the road.

"It doesn't really go with any of my most successful ensembles."

"You only mention this because you're never planning to stop by the office again, right?"

"I didn't say that," he said with a grin, pulling into my driveway.

"Jackass," I called after him as he climbed out of the car.

We found Chloe inside on my couch, Sonny perched on her shoulder as she fiddled with her phone and ignored the fluffy morning news show on the TV. Instantly, I felt guilt rush in when I realized I'd forgotten completely about Sonny the night before.

"I took care of your son," Chloe said without looking up.

"I'm home now, baby," I said, tucking my finger against Sonny's feet to entice him to come sit on my shoulder. He was happy to see me, even though I'd forgotten about him in a drunken haze the night before. Guilt over that sloshed around in my gut and I decided I wanted to run away. "I need to change."

"You two get dirty last night?" Chloe called after me as I hit the hallway. I walked faster so I wouldn't have to hear Mel's response. Whether he told the truth or made up a grand story about an eight-hour sexual marathon, I knew I'd be equally ashamed.

When I came back ten minutes later, changed and cleaned up, Mel had gone back outside.

"What's he doing?"

"He got a call, went out to take it. Dammit, Gwen, you didn't even get lucky?" Chloe demanded.

"How much did he tell you?"

"From the look you're giving me, I think not all of it. He said you just got really drunk and then busted in to catch him naked the next morning. Anything happen after that?"

"No. I didn't—I wouldn't sleep with Mel. He made some good pizza, we had some excellent wine, but I slept on the couch and woke up with a crick in my neck. Stop looking at me like that."

"You're hopeless," Chloe said with a shake of her head. Before I could retort, the door opened and we both looked over. Saved by the Mel.

"That was Mrs. Kraus, the mother of the first child taken. She's decided the police aren't doing enough and wants my help. I told her we'd meet her in an hour. That gives us a few hours before we have to get to Everett by three."

"Three-thirteen," Chloe corrected. "Merrin said three-thirteen."

"Well, then, we'll want to be there by two forty-five to make sure we have plenty of time to stake the place out."

"In Bellevue, Blondie didn't show up until five-till. We probably don't need to be there quite that early." Mel leveled a look my way and I nodded. "Yeah, okay, right. Earlier is probably better."

"Where are you two meeting the parents?"

"Their house. It's up kind of by Northgate."

"I'll go with you," Chloe said.

Mel shook his head. "Can't really—"

"I'll stay in the car. That way you don't have to swing by and pick me up after or anything. We can all just go straight up to Everett."

Mel was quiet for a moment, thinking it through, before he nodded. "Makes sense." And just like that, we were once again on our way.

We parked down the street so Chloe could hang in the car without being seen and Mel and I headed up the sidewalk toward the house. The neighborhood was a bit rundown, aged fences and long grass dominating most yards. It was still mid-morning, though, and people were milling about.

"This is it," Mel said, pausing in front of a small house with steps leading up to a covered porch. He pushed open the gate, let me go through first, and we headed for the door.

"You gonna blurt out that you have magical powers again this time?" Mel asked.

I shrugged. "Probably."

Heaving a sigh, he knocked. A woman answered immediately, which surprised me, since I hadn't felt anyone on the other side of the door. She was watching us with a blank sort of sadness on her face, but according to my empathy, no one was home.

Something was definitely wrong. Mel didn't seem to notice, holding out his hand and introducing himself.

"Mrs. Kraus, hello. I'm Mel and this is Gwen. We spoke on the phone?"

"Come in," Mrs. Kraus said absently, walking off into the house.

"Okay," Mel said, throwing me a confused look.

"Something's not right here," I whispered. Alarm bells were clanging through my head, making me want to turn and run back to the car. Mel ignored me, following Mrs. Kraus inside. I swore under my breath and went after him. Mel wasn't worried and, while I was sure this was a very bad idea, I figured I needed to trust the man. He was a werewolf and a private eye; he'd probably walked into stranger situations and come out unscathed.

"Would you like tea?" Mrs. Kraus asked in her hollow voice. I looked around, finding nothing suspicious in the tidy living room or the kitchen beyond. Mel followed her, completely at ease, but I hung back for a few seconds, pushing my empathy outward in an attempt to figure out what was going on.

My range isn't huge but I can shift it, pushing the radius outward with myself at the center or at the edge. I pushed it to the far end of the house and found that I could feel exactly one set of emotions within my range. They weren't human and, while they felt strangely familiar, I couldn't have put a label on them if my life depended on it.

My heart pounded as I started to wonder if maybe it would.

"Mel?" I called, backing towards the door. He twisted slightly to look my way just as a man stepped around the corner ahead of him, a baseball bat in his hand. "Mel!"

He flinched at my tone, turning back toward the kitchen just in time to get a face full of lumber.

I yelped, darting forward on instinct, even though there was no earthly thing I could do to help. The man moved with the swing, shifting his position as if he'd hit Mel again. To my surprise, Mel didn't go down. He stumbled a bit, brought a hand to his face as if he'd been hit with a spitball to the cheek, and swore, but he didn't fall. When the man went to swing again, Mel straightened, towering over him, and *growled*.

I stopped moving immediately, lurching as the sound seeped under my skin like smoke, settled in my belly like lead. Mel's attacker didn't seem to notice. His eyes were unfocused, staring into the distance as he kept swinging. This time, Mel caught the bat. As Mel yanked the weapon out of the smaller man's grip, a girl spoke from behind me.

"I had not anticipated a werewolf," she said. Her voice was light, a bit bored. I didn't get the chance to turn and see what she looked like; her arms came around me quickly, one wrapping around my waist, one pressing over my eyes. I shrieked, tried to struggle, but her grip was iron. Her fingers parted slightly over my left eye, letting me see Mel as he turned to me, shock naked on his face. He growled again but my captor wasn't intimidated.

"Hand the bat back or I break her neck."

I whimpered. Mel watched me, tension singing through him. He fought with the decision while I struggled, my normal irritation with him amplified tenfold by the situation.

"Just give it back!" I urged, at a loss as to why he would even consider keeping the damn thing. The attack had seemed to irritate him at best, but *I* was in mortal peril. Mel flicked his gaze to my face briefly before holding the bat out to the side. His attacker took it, lifting it across his shoulder, though he didn't swing.

The girl waved her hand forward, leaving my face uncovered for a moment.

"*Vis,*" she hissed, flicking her fingers like she was flinging water. The man shifted his grip on the bat and swung again in one smooth move. This time, Mel went down hard.

"No, no, no," I wailed, struggling in the girl's grip as if she might let me run to Mel and see if he was okay. Without him, I was toast.

"Better," she said. "Now we're all alone." We both winced at the sound of a window breaking and watched in stillness as the man with the bat crumpled in a heap on the floor. A colorful, feather-tipped dart stuck out of his cheek. "Or not."

The room was silent for a few seconds before a familiar voice called, "Gwen, you okay?"

I had to take a second to process before I called, "Chloe?"

"Stop speaking," my captor snapped. Her hand shifted from my belly upward and she gripped the sides of my face hard enough that I was afraid my skull would pop. I let out a whine and reached up in an attempt to pry her off, but her grip was no less sure than before. She mumbled one more word I didn't understand and it speared a shard of pain through my head. My vision short-circuited and everything went black.

Fourteen

This time, I woke up in my own bed. I was alone, it was dark, but I could hear the TV in the living room. My head was killing me and my stomach felt cavernous. I wanted ice cream, candy, sugar. As I rolled onto my side to clutch at my head and whimper, I felt Chloe close in from the hall.

"Gwen?"

In response, I let out a wordless groan.

"Good, you *are* awake," she said quietly. I felt the bed sag before her hand brushed over my cheek. "I'm not wearing the necklace this time. Mel's here, so I figured it's best he keep it."

"What happened?"

"You were attacked. Both of you. You're safe now."

"… did you shoot someone?"

"Tranquilized them. There's a difference."

I paused to process this information, opening my eyes to find that I was looking at her denim-clad hip. "I don't know what's going on."

"Not surprising. Come on, Mel should be back any minute with food and you'll need to eat."

That got me moving, though I didn't like it much. Chloe bundled me into slippers and my robe and helped me out into the living room, where I sank onto the couch. I was exhausted again—still? Who could even tell after the week I'd had.

"Mel called Amy and she came by, did what she could. Merrin wasn't answering, but we did our best. Whatever got you last time, it got you worse this time."

"I remember …" I trailed off, licked my lips, and swallowed; I could drool like a hungry baby while asleep, but without threat to my pillow, my mouth was dry as a bone. "I remember Mel getting hit with a bat. Then you shot—"

"Tranq'd."

"Whatever. You were there. And then I passed out. What happened?"

"That's most of it. The… girl … that had you was scared of guns. I threatened her and she scurried off."

"That's it?"

"Not really, but you're in no shape right now." The door opened and Mel came in carrying a large paper sack, his face lighting up when he saw me.

"Figured you for dead, Arthur."

"Shut up."

"I'm the one with the food," he said, passing us to head into the kitchen. "I'd be nicer to me if I were you."

"That doesn't look like a pizza," I pointed out.

"No," Chloe agreed. "So?"

"So unless that's something equally as delicious, I'm under no obligation to be nicer," I explained. Chloe rolled her eyes but didn't bother arguing with my logic. I turned to find Mel looking through my cabinets. "What's he doing?"

"Well, he's a mature, responsible adult, so he's probably assuming we're going to want to eat our food on plates with utensils." Catching my look, Chloe laughed. "Mel, just grab some forks."

Mel turned to her. "But—" Pausing as he noticed my expression, he nodded. "Right." Within seconds, he was seated on the floor across the coffee table from me, opening the paper bag and bringing out little cardboard boxes of food that I recognized from one of Chloe's favorite pan-Asian vegan places. I was too hungry to bother inspecting the containers; I just went with the one closest to me and flipped it open. Stabbing into the mystery meal, I began shoveling it vaguely toward my mouth, relieved when my aim was true and I didn't mash sauce and vegetables against my eye. After three mouthfuls, I was humming with pleasure when I figured out it was noodles and orangey meat-replacement. I'd managed to pick a container without vegetables; maybe my luck was turning.

I managed to finish off a box and a half of food along with three wontons before Chloe patted my thigh.

"Better?"

"Eh," I groaned, unwilling to say yes lest she make me trade in my sweet and sour for cabbage and carrots. We ate in silence for a few more minutes before the fog in my brain finally cleared enough that I felt human again. "Explain exactly what happened today. Yesterday? How long was I out this time?"

"Several hours."

Something occurred to me and I went stiff, looking at the clock. "Did we get the kid? The one Merrin—"

"They didn't show," Mel assured me. "I called in another favor and had a friend patrol the area and hang around the house in plainclothes. Francie said a woman did indeed bring her son out to her red sedan around three-fifteen, but that she buckled him in and left without incident."

"What if—"

"She followed them to the mall and made sure they were fine, and promised to check up on them for a few days. We didn't exactly do it the way we meant to, but we did manage to stop another kidnapping."

I settled back against the couch, trying to heave out the worry still twisting my guts into knots. After a few seconds I caught Mel's eye again. "Do you just sleep with so many women in hopes some of them will turn out to be cops who will do your detective work for you?"

"Not *just*, no." He winked. "But that is a side benefit."

I shook my head as if the situation was grave. "All those poor women suffering just so you don't have to work hard."

"You've got me all wrong, Gwen. Working long and hard is what I do best," Mel said, catching my eye. Chloe laughed at the tension that ran through me, my gaze glued to his. My brain seemed to shut down for a moment, sprinting away from the opportunity to make another cutting remark and toward the memory of standing next to Mel in the dark the night before.

"So," I said, stammering for a moment as I tried to regain my dignity. "What went down?" Realizing the double entendre in what I'd just said, I squeezed my eyes shut. "At the—earlier!"

Rather than look at either one of them, I slid my empty carton onto the table and grabbed another. Chloe let me stew for a few seconds, her emotions practically vibrating with delight at my embarrassment. I put all my attention into picking around the vegetables in the chow mein, refusing to admit anything pleasant about Mel had even crossed my mind.

"I was in the car," she said finally, a trace of laughter still threading through her voice. "And, of course, I didn't know how long you guys were going to take, so I told myself, 'Chloe, you're gonna go for a walk.'" She took a second to grab a quick bite of her food and I tried to analyze the barest hint of anomaly I was feeling within her. She had no reason to lie and it didn't exactly feel like deception, but it was odd nonetheless. I decided my brain had just been whacked around my skull too much and brushed it off as Chloe continued.

"I was in front of the house when you yelled at Mel. I went up, looked through the window to see what was going on, and saw him get hit. I went around the back to see if I could sneak in that way, but their door was locked. I broke the window, tranquilized the man and his wife, and then unlocked the door and came in."

"Hold up," I said, swallowing hastily. "Question. Why the hell do you have a tranq gun? Why the hell did you bring it with you?"

"You were attacked. Twice now. I figured having some sort of protection was smart."

"But a *gun*?" I demanded. "You're a vegan!"

"I don't shoot animals," Chloe said, taking a small bite of broccoli.

"What the hell do you shoot?"

"Targets?" I could tell from her tone she thought the question was a stupid one. "I've been shooting since I was little."

"Tranquilizers?"

"That was… I happened to be carrying both."

"Both?" I balked at her, my brain running in circles. In less than a week, I'd run into my childhood nightmares, been mistaken for someone with a mistress, nearly had my brain sucked out my eyeballs—twice!—and considered having sex with Mel. Now I was sitting across from the most liberal, compassionate person I'd ever met, talking with her about how she owns *and shoots* guns.

We see each other nearly every day, spend countless lunches and movie dates together, and she's never mentioned this hobby. It made me wonder if I should start randomly asking her if she did anything else supremely out of character.

Chloe, you don't happen to collect human heads, do you? Oh, no reason, I'm just asking.

Dropping my gaze down to look at my food, I let out a breath. Did it really matter that Chloe probably had a subscription to *Guns and Gams* magazine and spent her weekends away from me shooting things and ogling ladies? I'd known about the latter, but did I really need to focus so hard on the former? It had saved my life, after all.

"You okay?" Chloe asked, patting my knee. "You look a little green. Did you accidentally eat a chunk of broccoli?"

Mel chuckled around a bite of his own food and I met Chloe's gaze with a frown. "Just finish explaining what happened."

Chloe let it go a beat, still masking her mockery as concern before laughing and continuing her story.

"I came inside, hid around the corner in case I wasn't the only one with a gun, and told her to let you go or I'd shoot her. I guess she took me pretty seriously."

"She just dropped me and bolted?" I wondered if hitting the floor like a sack of potatoes accounted for feeling bruised and achy.

"Well, not at first. Even after she knocked you out, she didn't want to let you go. You were—ah—a bit too heavy for her to hold up, I guess, because when I looked again, you two were on the floor. She had you propped up like a human shield and I told her again that if she didn't back off, I'd shoot her."

"We should have called the police," I mumbled, irritated that Chloe had been forced to deal with my being held hostage. I twitched as twin bolts of electric displeasure arced out of Mel and Chloe to light up my insides.

"They wouldn't have reacted well to finding pod-people tranquilized into oblivion, an injured werewolf on the floor, and some crazy woman with the power to enchant a baseball bat trying to suck your brains out through your ears."

She had a point about the cops, but the rest still made no sense.

"I still don't understand why the parents called us over and asked for our help if they were just going—"

"Those people weren't the Krauses," Chloe explained. "The mail on the counter and the pictures on the walls say they're the Windhams—I made sure they were okay before we left, by the way—and I'm pretty sure they were just used to get to you."

"Well, that's just great." Sighing, I plopped my chow mein on the coffee table. "I don't think I can do this anymore."

"You can't eat?" Chloe asked, feigning horror. "You're worse off than we thought!"

For once I decided to be an adult and ignore her teasing. "It was just us before, trying to find out why some kids went missing so they wouldn't end up in the hands of Laurel and Hardy and whatever creepy, many-eyeballed slime monster they may work for. Now complete strangers are getting caught up in this just because we pissed off the wrong... whatever that chick was."

"Demon," Chloe clarified, her tone much too calm for the word.

"Merrin was serious?"

"You think she'd joke?"

"I—no, I mean ..." I trailed off, lacking an argument. Merrin wouldn't lie and I could count the number of times I'd heard her make a joke on Sonny's left foot, but still. A *demon*?

"I think that's why we need to keep going," Mel said when my silence stretched. "So we can figure out how to get the kids home safe in case this girl's planning on handing them off to some other slime monster."

"It's easy for you to be brave, you're nearly indestructible."

"Do you not remember the enchanted bat and the man who hit me in the face with it?"

I let out a low chuckle. "No, I remember that quite clearly. Almost makes the rest of this worth the trouble."

Mel rolled his eyes but didn't waste time on my attitude. "Look. I've got a meeting with the Carlyles tomorrow, the parents of the little boy who was taken."

"How you do know it's—"

"This time I checked. It's them. I'm not walking in blind again. We will solve this problem and get these kids back before anyone else is hurt." Mel watched me for a few moments as I considered his proclamation. I wasn't sure his confidence in us as a group was warranted. From where I stood, it felt like we'd just spent the last few days running repeatedly into walls.

Then again, we had already foiled two kidnappings, even if doing so had briefly come at the expensive of my sanity. Mel must have seen something in my face because he shifted gears from serious to silly.

"Besides, if you're that nervous, we can bring Chloe along. She can wear a trenchcoat and some sunglasses and stand behind us menacingly."

"I don't think that would go over too well with the parents," Chloe mused.

"Assuming they *are* the parents."

"I'll keep my eyes, ears, and nose open more carefully this time, I swear." Mel grabbed a fried wonton out of one of the boxes, shook it at me twice. "And if you yell my name in a terrified voice again, I'll actually listen."

My dreams were a jumbled mess. More so than usual, that is.

I was in the dark. I couldn't see anything, but I felt limbs and hands bumping me, shoving me, tugging me. I felt fear and glee and an immense hunger. My insides were empty, carved out until the edges of my flesh were ragged. The only thing that hadn't been taken was my heart. I ached with a despair that only comes from missing someone you love with all your soul but whom you know you'll never see again.

The floor of the kitchen was hard beneath my legs and my left hand was frozen. Sonny was squawking from the top of his cage to my right and I could feel tears on my skin. The front of my shirt was wet and the ice cream in my mouth tasted like snot.

I blinked twice before I realized I was awake, staring at the front of my fridge, blindly looking at the magnetic messages left for me by my mysterious visitor. A pint of ice cream was clutched tightly in my numb hand and I had eaten half of it. I was also covered in tears and my nose had been running for long enough that my shirt was already too soaked to clean it properly.

Sonny stopped talking; when I looked at him, he stared back, curiously silent. We watched each other for a minute before I realized that I really needed to get up and get moving. Despite how much I had enjoyed the idea of the gummy, chocolaty mess when I'd bought it, I didn't even want to look at the ice cream now. I knew I would never be able to eat it without also tasting my own runny nose.

"Gross," I mumbled, dumping the entire container in the garbage. Tearing off several handfuls of paper towels, I mopped at my face and neck, leaning against the counter for support. My knees hurt and the backs of my legs had gone numb from sitting splayed and hunched over for what must have been quite awhile.

"Gwen?" I spun around to find Mel standing just inside the kitchen. Chloe had gone home after we'd eaten, but Mel had stayed in the guest room again. I'd completely forgotten he was around. "Are you okay?"

"I don't think so. Jesus, I'm a mess."

"What happened? What are you doing?"

"I don't know. I don't remember. I was dreaming and then I woke up… It's fine. Go back to sleep."

"You look terrible," he said, straightening minutely. "But if you're having trouble sleeping, I can offer my services. I'm great at the art of wearing women out."

"You *are* exhausting," I said with a sigh. Mel just watched me quietly. I couldn't really decide what the expression on his face was without feeling his emotions to back it up, but I was leaning toward pity. "I'm going to take a shower and go back to bed. Did I wake you?"

"I heard the fridge opening and figured you were trying to sneak in some sugar this late because you figured I wouldn't notice and tattle on you to Chloe. I thought about letting you think you were getting away with it, but something didn't sound right, so I came out to check on you."

"I was sleepwalking. If you hear me again, wake me up. Or at least herd me back to my room and shut me in, Lassie."

"You sure you don't want me to join you? I'll make sure you stay put. I can tie you up if that's what you're into."

My eye twitched and, for once, it didn't have anything to do with his being a werewolf. "I will hit you with another bat."

Chloe called the next morning to say she'd meet us at the Carlyles' house after she picked some things up. I wondered if she was going to bring more guns, but then put it firmly out of my mind. Once everything else was solved, I could sit down and ask her a hundred questions. For now, I just had to trust my best friend.

We drove in silence but I was grateful for the quiet. There wasn't much I wanted to discuss and I still felt sore, sick, and tired, like my brain had hosted a series of bum fights in my skull.

Mel started whistling about fifteen minutes in. I tried to place what it was he had stuck in his head and decided it was a sad song. One from my youth, maybe. I thought about that car crash song, where the singer watches his lover die, and wondered if it was that tune.

No, that didn't seem gloomy enough. This song was about despair, tragedy, loss in the worst sense. The lyrics had to be about death or about being trapped. Why couldn't I place it? Why didn't I know what song this was? I wanted to be frustrated but I didn't have the energy. I didn't have anything. I couldn't even pay attention to the humming anymore. Were my eyes closed? Why was it so dark? Why was I so tired?

I forced my leaden eyes to open and rolled my head to the side. Mel was still humming and the tune was slow, tedious, depressing. My arms felt heavy. How long had we been driving?

"You asleep?" Mel reached over and grabbed my knee, giving it a squeeze. I tried to pull away but couldn't. When I didn't react, Mel turned, his brows knitted. As he switched his gaze between me and the road, I watched tension pull through him, his jaw going tight. I focused my eyes on the road outside and realized we were almost far enough north to be out of Seattle.

"Gwen, are you awake? You look like you're melting."

I blinked at him and that was all I could do. Where were we and what was I doing in this car?

Brow still furrowed, Mel checked the passenger's side blind spot and veered out of his lane. I watched the world move around me, feeling slow and tired and empty. I lost track of time, but when we stopped, I could see trees, houses, mailboxes. We were in a neighborhood and I felt something spark inside me.

Had I been here before?

"Come on, this isn't as fun as when you're berating me. I can take the abuse, but you look like you went ten rounds with Dalí. Gwen?"

Mel unbuckled his seatbelt and launched out of the car. I couldn't turn my head fast enough to watch him hustle around the hood but I felt his hand on my shoulder after he opened my door. His blue eyes met mine, his fingers moved to my chin, and warmth flooded through my skin.

We were on our way to a meeting regarding some missing children. I was an empath mistakenly hired by a pair of unpleasant fairies to locate said children. I'd been attacked twice by things that looked human but could sling around magic, and I definitely needed to get moving.

I grunted, shoving at Mel in the hopes he'd get the message that my mouth couldn't deliver. When he didn't move, I licked my lips, forcing a word out through them: "Move."

"Can *you*?" Mel asked, unbuckling my seatbelt. I shoved at him again and this time he let me move him. I tumbled out of the SUV onto the sidewalk, taking a huge gulp of air. My head was spinning, my stomach dropping into my feet. I took a few more deep breaths before I realized I was sucking in air faster than I should be. I felt Mel's hand on my belly and the other at the back of my neck, before he bent me double and crouched down to look into my eyes. "Slow down. If you pass out, Chloe's gonna blame me. Watch me, breathe like me."

Mel stayed close, sucking in air deliberately, slowly, leaning low to stay in my field of view. I watched him, tried to match him. As my panic subsided and the tightness in my chest eased, I wheezed out a laugh.

"Are you—" I took a deep breath, found I was calm enough to speak, and continued. "Are you doing Lamaze?"

"It worked, didn't it?" Mel looked seriously into my eyes. "Are you still dying?"

"I... I think I'm okay."

"Well, even if you're not, pretend. Chloe's pulling up and I don't want her yelling at me for letting you indulge in cheap dramatics."

I glowered up at him, but decided to save my breath for the meeting with the parents.

Fifteen

Both Mel and I managed to be appropriately composed and somber by the time we approached the front door of the house. Mel looked me over as we took the single step onto the porch, but whatever he might have said was interrupted when the door opened before he could even knock.

A giant pair of eyes took us in and I felt confusion edged with a tinge of hope. The eyes were a watery blue behind Coke-bottle glasses above a narrow rounded nose and thin-lipped mouth. We each got the once-over twice before the man in the sweater-vest and slacks reached out a hand. I wanted to grab it instantly, but didn't.

"You must be Mr. Somerset." The man shook Mel's hand. "And Ms. Arthur." Reaching for my hand, he cocked his head at me, confusion overtaking his birdlike features once again. As I touched his skin, I felt a rush of emotions. Joy, sadness, frustration, and anxiety all mixed inside me, turning my guts into a churning mess. Swallowing hard, I fought off the stinging sensation at the back of my throat. I realized that Mr. Carlyle and I weren't shaking hands, but holding them.

"Shannon?" I heard a voice from inside the house and my churning guts leapt into my throat. I wanted to run to that voice and... I wasn't sure, but it was a desperate feeling.

"Shall we go inside?" Mel asked. Mr. Carlyle and I turned in unison to blink at Mel as if we didn't understand him.

"Oh, of course. I'm ..." Mr. Carlyle glanced very briefly at me as he spoke. "I'm sorry."

Mel put a hand on the smaller man's shoulder and guided him inside, toward the garish living room. Tossing an annoyed glance my way, he made sure to enter the house before me, following on Mr. Carlyle's heels.

"It's okay, Christina, they're the ones here about Devon."

"Oh." A woman opposite her husband in every way stood just outside a hallway to our right. Her hair was jet black, falling in waves to her waist.

Deep brown eyes, steady and free of tears, watched us over a sharp nose and full lips. Her skin was dark, her clothes bright and bold. She smiled at us and it was a good mask, but I could feel the worry inside her.

I knew how strong she could be when it was necessary and it made me feel better.

I met Mel's concerned gaze again and started to wonder whose feelings I was actually channeling.

Taking a deep breath, I concentrated on my own thoughts, my own feelings, carefully separating my psyche from those around me. My first instinct was to sit in the chair closest to the TV, but when the Carlyles moved to the couch and Mel sat in one of the chairs directly across from them, I considered how rude I would appear by not sitting with everyone else. I sat next to Mel and clasped my hands in my lap, fidgety and unsure of myself.

"Let me begin by saying I'm sorry we had to meet under these circumstances," Mel began, his tone practiced and caring. "I know a few of the police officers working to bring your son home and I wanted to do my best to help them out. This whole situation is tragic and I just can't imagine what you must be going through."

"Thank you," Mr. Carlyle said, glancing over at me. I gave him what was undoubtedly a weak smile and swallowed thickly. I felt like I was in trouble, out of place in this big chair.

"Can you start by telling me how Devon went missing, maybe show me around so I can get a sense of the place?"

"Well," Mrs. Carlyle started, putting a hand over her husband's knee, as if steadying him. "He was home from school because he hadn't been feeling well. I stayed home with him and he was just there, watching TV." She gestured to the chair I'd considered taking.

"I'd gone upstairs to put away the laundry. I didn't think anything was wrong." She took a breath and I saw her fight back tears. Her jaw set for a moment and she glanced at the staircase to my left. "The TV was on but I didn't hear anything. Nothing suspicious, I mean. He was watching cartoons and I was thinking I should make him some soup, that it might make him feel better."

Mr. Carlyle turned his head to me sharply and I met his eyes as my mouth opened.

"Vegetable soup is the *best*," I announced, unaware until I'd spoken that I had any intention of doing so.

Silence fell over the room, as Mel, Shannon, and Christina all looked my way.

"I'm... I'm sorry," I apologized, feeling myself shrink back into the chair. "I just... like soup."

Suddenly embarrassed, I pushed out of the chair and stepped away from the parents. Mel urged Christina to continue.

"I came back down after the laundry was all put away and I couldn't find him. The door was locked—I checked as soon as I thought something might be wrong—but he wasn't in the house. I checked the garage and the bathroom, I even went upstairs and checked—" She swallowed. "Checked my closet. I didn't think he was—I mean, maybe he was playing."

"She called me as soon as she thought something was wrong and I came right home," Shannon said quietly.

The mantle held a picture of the Carlyle family in front of their Christmas tree. Devon was little, barely a toddler, and he was holding a toy truck up in the air like it had been the prize for fighting a dangerous and deadly battle. Something in me clenched but I couldn't tell if the sight of the truck made me happy or sad.

I reached for the picture and, as I pulled it forward, two odd things happened.

Shannon appeared next to me, annoyance slicing at my skin as he reached out toward the mid-point between the mantle and the fireplace. The corner of the picture I was grabbing hit the corner of another frame, knocking it forward.

"Please don't touch our things," Shannon said calmly as the fallen picture dropped right into his palm.

"Oh my god," I mumbled, meeting his eyes. "You *saw* that coming."

Shock and panic hit me at full force, like walking into a static forcefield. Just beyond it, barely hidden by the electric distress, lay a cold, hard wall of defensive anger. I took a step back, though I would have needed to leave the house entirely to avoid the sledgehammer of his emotions.

"I don't know what you're—" he began.

I interrupted, unable to stop myself. "Can Devon see the future, too? Did he inherit that?"

I felt Christina from across the room and before she could lash out, I turned to her.

"I'm not—I'm different, too!" Still holding the Christmas picture, I eased toward Devon's mother, stretching a hand out. "Right now, you're worried and angry, but you don't need to be. I'm not going to tell anyone about your husband or your son."

"I don't ..." Christina trailed off, staring at me. Her gaze moved past and I turned to watch her husband stare at me, slack-jawed.

"You can see the future?" he asked. I shook my head but he didn't seem to notice. "I thought it was just Devon and me."

"No, I can't—I do other things. I can sense emotions."

Mel had turned in his chair and was watching me intently, looking less concerned than he had with Marion and Duane.

Shannon stepped up next to me, reaching for the frame I still held.

When his skin touched mine, I felt that same storm light up my stomach. I wanted to hug him, to sit on his lap and have him read me a story. My adult self felt confused and vaguely uncomfortable at the almost fetishistic desire but my inner child was on the verge of desperate tears.

"I'm... I'm sorry, you can read emotions?" Christina asked, finally breaking the silence. Mel got to his feet, glancing between us.

"She's been rather ill lately, so her empathy is—well, out of whack. Like I said, *I* can't imagine what you're going through, but Gwen has no choice but to feel what you're feeling. I think it's knocked her off her game somewhat."

"Yeah," I said, watching Shannon carefully place the picture back on the mantle where it'd been. "I think I'm feeling echoes of what Devon felt, as well. It's like I know this place and I can't stop feeling ..." I trailed off. What was I feeling? Guilty?

I blinked and realized I'd lifted my head so I was staring at the staircase.

"You can feel my son?" Christina's voice broke as she mentioned Devon and I gave a small nod. I needed to go upstairs.

"I'll be right back," I murmured, heading toward the staircase. I felt my arm get tugged and I pulled against it, anxiety starting to brew in my belly. Upstairs, I needed to go upstairs!

"Please," Shannon insisted. "I can't let you just—"

"Shan, please." Christina stepped forward and I glanced over at her. The grip on my wrist disappeared and I tore up the stairs like a wild animal. If I could just get to my room, if I could just hide under the covers, I'd be safe. The man with the big eyes wouldn't be able to grab me. I just had—

I stopped just inside the door to a little boy's room, looking around as if I'd just woken from another nightmare. What was I doing? I wasn't going to climb into the bed of a missing child and hide under his blankets. Shannon grabbed my arm, yanked me back a step.

"You need to leave, you can't be in here!" he insisted. I could feel his panic and it nearly matched the lightning firing through my chest and zapping my heart. His eyes darted to Devon's bed and despair thundered through us both.

"I'm sorry," I cried, shocked at my own behavior. "I'm—I don't do this. I don't feel echoes. This isn't how I work. I'm—"

"Gwen, come down."

I snapped my head around and saw Mel through the slats of the staircase. Just seeing him, hearing his calm voice, helped me concentrate. I wasn't Devon and I wasn't missing. I hadn't been kidnapped. I was an adult, babbling at terrified parents about their lost son.

I was making an ass of myself.

"Oh my god, I am so sorry," I said again, pulling back into myself. "I am so, so sorry. I don't understand why I'm acting like this."

"Please!'" Shannon begged, slimy desperation hemorrhaging from him as his gaze pulled toward his son's room again. "You need to get out of here. This is *unacceptable*."

I stopped myself before I called him Dad. Barely. "I'm so sorry." Inside I was crying because they didn't believe me. They weren't going to find me. I was going to be stuck inside this blackness forever.

"Your son is alive and I'll—" My voice shook slightly as Mel grabbed my wrist and pulled me down the stairs. "I'll find him. I'll get him back. I'll come home!'"

Christina was talking over Mel's rapid stream of apologies, begging him not to leave even as Shannon was ordering him to do just that.

Everything blurred together as the werewolf shoved me through the front door; my resistance was no match for his strength. The further we got down the driveway, the less I fought. As we reached the car, I felt mortified, angry, embarrassed. I no longer felt young, desperate, and vulnerable; all I felt was the burn of my own regret.

Mel let go of me and I dropped to my feet, realizing for the first time that he'd been carrying me, an arm around my waist. He tugged my shoulder and turned me roughly, staring down into my eyes.

When I simply stared back, unsure of what needed to come tumbling out of my mouth, he lifted a hand and flicked my forehead.

"Ow!" I cried.

"Gwen?"

"Yes! Dammit, that hurt."

"You are one big bucket of crazy."

I rolled my gaze to the house behind Mel, saw Mrs. Carlyle staring at me through the front window. I swallowed my embarrassment and shifted to place Mel between us as a shield against her despair.

"Oh my god, did I really just lose it in front of them?"

"Yep," Mel said, straightening up. He crossed his arms over his chest but didn't move; he let me use him as a wall.

"Oh my god, oh my god," I wailed, dropping my head into my hands. "I should be locked up, or put to sleep. I am a nutcase. I am—I should be carted off in a stretchcoat."

"In a what?"

"In a—um." I couldn't think of the word, so I shook my head, lifted it, and then wrapped my arms around myself to demonstrate. "You know! One of those things!"

"What happened? Are you okay?" I twisted to find Chloe rushing down the sidewalk toward us.

"She's had another breakdown."

"*Another*?" Chloe demanded.

"Look, we should do this somewhere the parents can't watch," Mel pointed out.

"Right," Chloe glanced toward the house, nodding.

"I'm driving with Chloe," I said. "I don't want another—I can't be alone with you right now."

"You sure?" Mel asked.

I nodded rapidly. "Unless something's going to flip the car, I think I'll be safe without you. Let's just go." I stepped around Chloe, heading toward her car as fast as I could manage.

We ended up pulling into a nearby hotel parking lot, driving around the back to park next to each other. Chloe grilled me the entire time we were driving but I didn't have much to say. I couldn't explain my behavior, or the tiny, screaming part of me that wanted to curl up in a ball and cry myself to sleep.

Mel yanked open the back door and climbed in behind me.

Chloe turned to him. "She's not saying much."

"I'm not surprised. I think she's cracked."

"I'm not ..." I trailed off, lacking an argument.

"What happened?" Chloe asked. I remained quiet, but Mel assumed she was talking to him and detailed everything from finding me crying in the kitchen to my breakdown in the car to my show at the Carlyles'. Chloe's worry dissipated as he spoke, hardening into resolve and making me lift my head to watch her curiously. When Mel finished, she nodded.

"We're going to Merrin's."

"I tried calling and she's not answering," Mel offered.

"I'll take care of it," Chloe said, sliding her phone out of her pocket.

"And how will you do that?" Mel asked.

Chloe ignored his question. "You riding with us, or taking your own car?"

Mel was quiet for a few seconds before muttering, "I'll meet you guys there."

"Then get out." Chloe started the car.

Mel stayed stubbornly motionless for a few seconds, but when Chloe put the car into gear, he did as she ordered. I turned to watch her as she hit a few buttons and put her phone to her ear. When she spoke again, she was all business.

"It's me." She was quiet for a moment but, when she started speaking again, it was in a language I didn't recognize. Seconds later, she hung up and I felt her try to mold the rigid concern inside her into something softer. I didn't know what had her so serious, but she could tell I'd caught on and didn't want me to worry. "You'll be fine."

Sixteen

Merrin opened the door before we even knocked, looked right at me, and said, "There are lots of you. You have company."

"Okay." I wasn't sure what that meant. "Hi."

Chloe shuffled me inside, left the door cracked for when Mel arrived, and jerked her chin at Evadne. They shared a look I didn't understand before I turned back to Merrin. She was still watching me, her focus much more intense than I was used to from her. A slim line of curiosity dripped between her forehead and mine and I swatted at it without realizing it was a feeling and not a spiderweb.

"All of them are asleep. Am I asleep?" she asked.

"All of who?"

"Let her touch you. Give her permission." Evadne gestured at Merrin's hand with her long blue nails.

I nodded. "Merrin, you can touch me if you need to."

She blinked, her dreamy eyes clearing. "Oh, Gwen." Her tone was conversational, as if she'd just stated something utterly relevant to a discussion that we'd been having for hours. Lifting her left hand, she pressed it to my cheek like a mother looking upon her child. After a moment she shifted, moving her fingers into a specific pattern along my jaw, cheekbones, and temple. I saw Chloe bolt toward me but before I could register what was happening, my eyes rolled back and I felt myself plummet into unconsciousness.

My body was on its back on the floor, head cradled in Chloe's lap. I knew it was my body and yet I wasn't in it. In fact, the more conscious I became of my surroundings, the more I started to wonder how my body was no longer that of an adult woman.

I was staring at a tiny blond boy with giant brown eyes that were focused on Chloe's face. I could hear a vague, muffled sound that I recognized as speech but couldn't understand. From my position, I couldn't see Chloe's expression and it made me wonder if she noticed that I was no longer myself.

Shifting my focus was instant, like changing camera angles in a movie. I was no longer looking at Chloe, but at Mel across the room. I wanted to laugh at the expression on his face; he was cold and irritated, shivering ever so slightly. His exposed skin had goosebumps, despite the heavy leather jacket he wore.

His arms were pulled tight against his chest and he was perched awkwardly on a barstool, like a pro wrestler asked to sit at a plastic kids' table. My focus changed again and I found Merrin sitting across from the me on the floor, her legs tucked under her butt, her ankles crossed. Behind her Evadne watched me—the floating me—a small smile on her stunning face.

She spoke but her mouth didn't move. I could understand her, even though her words had no sound and felt like snowflakes on my eyelids.

"Yours is a funny-looking soul."

I glanced down at myself and I saw nothing but the floor and the young boy's body. The laugh that came from the fairy was sharp and I shivered, pulling my hands up to clutch my ears. If I didn't get back in my body soon, I was going to freeze to death.

This time, her mouth moved and her words were room temperature. "Pet, she needs to come back. Any longer and that little boy is going to grow up very confused about his place in the world."

I turned to look down at my body again and found I no longer looked like a small blond boy. I was an adult woman now: dark chin-length hair, shapely legs, and just a little too much pudge around the hips and thighs for my personal taste. Frowning down at my body, I resolved to let the candy thief's lesson be to eat less crap.

I felt a disorienting sucking sensation, like pressing a vacuum hose over each of my eyes. It started at my temples and moved along my body until I was staring up into Chloe's heart-shaped face, her blue eyes comforting.

My hearing popped in and I heard Merrin mumbling near my feet, followed by Mel's voice asking if we were almost done. Evadne hissed a command for silence and I cringed, expecting to feel my ears freeze again.

Chloe's hand moved from my cheek to my forehead. "She's gone a little cold, is that natural?"

"That's my fault," Evadne said. She didn't sound sorry.

"Oh, gotcha," Chloe nodded, looking up at Merrin. "Is she good to go?"

I could feel my body again, but it felt loose, like I was wearing a jumpsuit that was three sizes too big. When I tried to touch my face, I overshot and smashed my knuckle against Chloe's breast. When I tried to say "oops," it came out a shapeless moan.

Chloe laughed but I could tell she was trying not to. Instead of frowning like I wanted to, I felt my nose wrinkle, my teeth clench.

"Never mind," Chloe said as I struggled to make my face work. "I don't think she's okay. Gwen?"

I moaned up at her again and Chloe rubbed my shoulder. Her expression bloomed into one of shock before I felt the front of my jacket yanked upward. My body followed it and I found myself staring at Merrin's freckled face. Her expression was stern, but it was her hand I was suddenly concerned about.

Mel cried, "What the hell?" as I felt her palm crack against my cheek, knocking me to the side. My chin barely missed the coffee table, but when my forehead collided with the hardwood floor, I felt normal again. My skin fit, my body was my own, and the stinging in my cheek was exactly where it needed to be.

"Thanks," I mumbled, just to make sure I could actually speak. As I got my arms under me, I glanced over and found Mel on his feet, his expression tight.

"Down, boy. She wasn't settled." As Evadne spoke, I felt a breeze blow past me. Mel took an uncomfortable step back, as if bracing against the sudden onslaught of a blizzard, and bumped the counter bar.

"I think I'm okay. Am I making sense?" As I got to my feet, Chloe draped a hand on my shoulder and I leaned against her. She nodded, touching my face before dropping her hand down to my chest. Her fingers tucked into my jacket and under my shirt, warm against my skin. I glanced down and wondered briefly if she was getting fresh.

"Her heart rate is pretty slow."

"It'll speed up once you leave. Pet, please let them know where it is they'll be going. The—Chloe and I need to speak privately for a moment."

"Mel?" Chloe asked, and before I knew it he was stepping up next to me, wrapping an arm around my waist and taking the burden of keeping me upright off Chloe's hands. Chloe followed Evadne into the bedroom once she was sure I wouldn't topple, but I was still too foggy to think much of their conference. Surprisingly, standing in Mel's arms was an altogether pleasant experience. I tipped my head up to look at him and thought about how handsome he was and how nice his body felt against mine.

Noticing I was admiring him, Mel winked and grinned. I felt a little spark of my usual annoyance but most of me was just happy to be touched.

When I looked back at Merrin, she was staring at me in a way I recognized but hadn't seen from her before. It was a look Chloe had given me many times when I'd eaten too much candy and made myself sick, but Merrin wasn't usually aware enough of my presence to give it. I frowned at her and forced myself to straighten up, to stop relying on Mel to fight my battle with gravity.

"What's that face?" I asked.

She shook her head. "It won't last."

At her words, Mel snorted and announced, "Bite your tongue; Mel Somerset has no trouble lasting."

Merrin said nothing but wrinkled her nose as she tucked a folded piece of paper into my jacket pocket. She headed toward the bedroom just as Chloe emerged.

"Come on, G," Chloe said, her voice a song. "We should hurry up; we're headed out to Tacoma."

Mel and I groaned in disgust at the same time.

Ten minutes later, my mind had cleared enough to consider my experience in Merrin's living room. Chloe was driving, Mel had taken the back seat, and I stared at each of them in turn. I wanted to ask what had just happened, where we were going, and what the hell was going on, but another question elbowed its way to the front of my psyche.

"I can feel you, but not all of you," I said to Chloe.

"You can feel all of me whenever you want, sweetheart," Mel announced. To demonstrate, he thrust his hips toward me as far as the seat belt would allow.

"Not you, moron. Chloe. I feel like I've got all my mental shields up, but… I don't think I do. Not on purpose, anyway."

"That was Merrin. She had to do some minor repairs before she could get to communicating with the kids," Chloe explained.

"The kids?" I demanded. "What ki—the kidnapped—okay." I waved my hand in the air, brought it to my forehead. Rubbing the bridge of my nose, I took a deep breath. I didn't feel the baseline of awful that had been running through me since the first attack but something still wasn't right. I was still missing time and unable to work through the fog in my mind. "You have to explain what's going on. I'm lost."

"There's a demon kidnapping children, specifically children with powers. They've taken three, tried for one more."

"I know that much, though I'd like to just forget all of this and go bury myself in some sand until it's all over."

"Shh," Chloe said. "Let me finish before you jump out the window and start digging. Demons aren't terribly common and this isn't the sort of thing they usually do. Generally their antics just involve conning people out of their souls, adult people specifically. This one, though, is taking children. We're not completely sure why, yet, but the why doesn't matter nearly as much as the 'how do we stop it?'"

"Did Merrin tell you all this?"

"I told you to let me finish. It's odd that the demon wants children, since anyone under eighteen doesn't really, um, *own* their own soul. It's the magic number, literally. Before you're an adult, your parents have claim, which means demons can't get a child to give up its soul for a piece of candy."

"Strange coincidence," Mel piped up.

"Not one at all," Chloe said, though she didn't explain further. "Now for the important part: the kids are alive. Whatever this demon wants with them, it doesn't involve killing them."

"Good! Excellent! Let's find out where they are and send Laurel and Hardy their way!"

"I'm getting there. When Mel told me about your breakdown at the Carlyles' place, I started to think that maybe it wasn't you. You're prone to hysterics and you love a good tantrum, but this wasn't normal. Even that time Poopy shoved an entire cake off the counter and rolled around in it, you didn't go this nuts."

I felt rumblings of my previous rage over Chloe's cat ruining my day— she'd wantonly destroyed an entire, perfectly good cake! That *I had paid for!*—burble in my stomach but I didn't say anything as Chloe continued.

"Maybe whatever took the kids and scrambled your brain left some sort of accidental connection. I called Merrin's place—"

I interrupted her. "In what, Russian?"

"Nope," Choe said, pushing on. Her tone was calm but I felt the barest hint of worry run through her, like she was scared I might ask more. "And told her we'd be coming over. She noticed right away something was wrong and once you were out, she got to work. My guess was right. You're connected through the demon to the kids. So Merrin was able to draw on that connection and get a location. We're headed there now."

"By ourselves?" I demanded, suddenly horrified. "We have to call someone else. We have to bring someone who won't pass out at the first enchanted bat that hits him in the face."

"Hey," Mel protested.

"Laurel and Hardy said they'd be there when you need them, didn't they?" Chloe asked, ignoring Mel's outrage.

"I wouldn't bet on it."

"Let's just get to where the kids are and see what happens."

"I don't like that plan. What if what happens is more enchanted bats?"

"Will you *please* let that go?" Mel griped. I waved my hand dismissively. He let out a growl and I ignored the tiny flutter that it kicked up in my belly.

"Look. I talked a lot with Evadne about this stuff while you were out. You need to trust me here."

Chloe was confident, which was nothing new, and no matter how hard I tried, I couldn't overcome my knee-jerk reaction of bitterness over it. There was no good reason for me to argue; there never was. When Chloe's put her mind to something, she's never wrong and no amount of jealousy over her competence and intelligence is going to make a difference.

As I fought off the desire to bicker with her, to demand we turn around and go back to Evadne for clarification, I asked myself what it would accomplish. The only answer I could come up with was, nothing. Getting a solid promise from Evadne that everything would be fine wouldn't do anything except prolong the inevitable. Either we'd show up and Laurel and Hardy would be there with bells on or Mel would get hit in the face with another bat.

Smiling to myself at that thought, I gave in. "Okay, let's do it."

We pulled up outside a run-down motel in Tacoma, parking at the edge of the lot.

Chloe turned to Mel. "I'm going to take a walk around the perimeter and make sure no one's hanging around. Keep an eye out, and for god's sake, don't hand anyone any bats this time."

"What about me?" I asked.

"You get to tell Mel what door to break down."

"How am I supposed to do that?"

Pity nudged against me and Chloe tapped my temple. "You have but three skills and eating cake and napping aren't going to help here."

With a wink, Chloe hopped out of the car and headed toward the hotel. I watched her go, the entire plan she'd laid out suddenly becoming clear.

"What the hell does she think she's doing? What if something's out there, waiting for her? What if she gets hurt?"

"She brought her guns."

"This isn't target practice!" A dozen awful scenarios ran through my mind, not all of them involving Chloe being the only one to get hurt. "What if she accidentally shoots a maid?"

"Come on, let's go figure out where these kids are." Mel climbed out, not waiting for me to answer or argue.

I had a spastic little fit in the passenger's seat, swearing and flailing before forcing myself to remember what was at stake. It wasn't only the kids in danger anymore. The kidnappers knew what we looked like and if Chloe was going to throw herself into danger with us, I needed to get out and do my damnedest to make sure she didn't get knocked around like I had. I couldn't just hide in the car; I had to protect my best friend. And Mel, though I didn't feel he needed it as much as Chloe.

No matter how much I wanted to find a bed and hide under it until this all blew over, I had to be brave and do everything I could to make sure everyone made it out of this alive.

Being mature sucks.

Mel caught the back of my jacket as I stormed past him, determined steam coming out of my ears.

"Be cool," he murmured.

"I hate you," I said. He laughed under his breath and jerked his thumb at the first door we came to.

"Do your thing."

My determination petered out, leaving me staring at the scuffed and dirty door. Yes, I wanted to find these kids and keep Chloe safe, but courage was harder to call up in the moment. Back in the car I hadn't been seconds away from possible doom. Now there was nothing stopping me from focusing my empathy on an unseen hotel room that might contain a demon that had climbed into my head twice before and scrambled my brain.

"If I faint, get me the hell out of here."

Mel just shrugged noncommittally and I snarled, whacking him in the belly with the back of my hand. He grinned and I got the feeling he was amping up the attitude for my benefit. I actually appreciated it for once.

It was easier to be mad at Mel than scared of the unknown.

After a calming breath, I lowered my gaze to the ground, concentrated on reaching outward with my sixth sense. To my relief, there was no one inside. We moved on to the next room, and the next, all the way down the line of the first floor. Most rooms were empty, a few were occupied, none were suspicious.

Four rooms into the second floor, though, I found what we were looking for: three sleeping people, likely children, definitely enchanted and under extreme stress from the feel of it. The kids were alone, their emotions clumped together like they were all sleeping practically on top of one another. I used my keen powers of deduction to decide this was the room we wanted. And Mel had said I was dumber than a dung beetle.

"This is it!" I cried, not quite managing the whisper I was trying for. Mel tipped his head, listened to the door for a second, and nodded.

"Gotcha." Without hesitation, he took a step back, lifted his leg, and kicked in the motel door. I yelled wordlessly as it bounced off the wall, rebounding back toward him. He caught it easily and I hopped back, shocked.

"Mel!"

Ignoring my outburst, he leaned in, looking cautiously around the room before leaning back to check the rooms on either side. The one to the left was empty and a quick psychic poke into the one on the right revealed that whomever was in there was no threat. I could tell from the soupy mess of pleasant intoxication that unless I sent Mel inside to get shirtless and sing "Hotel California," we weren't in any danger of being noticed.

For the first time since we'd gotten wrapped up in this mess, we'd gotten lucky.

"Stay out here for a second," Mel said quietly. "I'm going to check it out real quick."

"Careful," I whispered back, watching him. He was thorough, checking under the beds and in the narrow closet. He even opened the cabinets under the sink at the back of the room and then went in to check the bathroom. I took a look around the lot for Chloe, but couldn't see her. I hoped she was okay.

When Mel stepped back out and nodded the all clear, I went inside, feeling along the wall for the light switch. I found it right as I felt a familiar sort of gooiness seep over my limbs, latching on and making me let out a small whine. I flipped the light on just before jerking to the side, twisting to see Blondie step around the corner and into the room.

"We meet again," he said, his eyes on me.

"Crap!" I squeaked, trying my best to back up as far as I could. Panic was yelling at me to run and hide in the empty cabinet under the sink but my legs were ignoring the orders. Blondie grinned, revealing fangs that weren't hidden by shadow this time. They were real and they were *deadly*.

Panic made way for terror and its voice was louder, convincing my legs it was time to *move*. I scrambled back maybe three steps before my calves hit the bed and my ankle smashed against the metal frame. Pain squeaked through my lips and Blondie laughed before rolling his gaze past me to the back of the room.

"Mel, it's been awhile," he said, smugness scalding along my skin like I'd spilled a pan of hot oil down my front. I whimpered and twitched as if I'd find escape if I just tried once more.

"Dirk?" The shock in Mel's voice pulled my gaze toward him and hope started to murmur beneath the terror still gibbering in my mind. Mel didn't look sure, but if this was in fact the vampire he'd spoken fondly about at The Bouncing Bunny, maybe we weren't in trouble after all.

"In the flesh," Blondie said, the smugness I'd felt before boiling along my skin as it congealed into what I could only guess was envy. "You've been quite a pain in my ass this week."

"Imagine how *we* feel."

I whipped around and found Chloe crouched low at the edge of the doorway, a small gun aimed at Dirk's head, hiding as much of her body behind the doorjamb as she could. I looked back to the vampire and flinched at the sizzle of annoyance that splashed out of him.

"What the hell, Dirk?" Mel asked.

"What the hell what?" Dirk wasn't watching Mel; he was staring at Chloe's gun but the envy still seared my limbs, refusing to give way to worry or fear. My eyes darted twice to the weapon and I wondered how he was unbothered. Chloe's my best friend and I trust her more than nearly anyone, but if she'd aimed a gun my way and made that face, I would have at least been concerned.

"What the hell, 'why am I not a walking germ bag?'" Dirk continued, turning back to Mel to give a small smile. The envy warped again, disdain spewing forth like a burst water main. "I made a new friend. And here she is."

Dirk didn't gesture but I felt a spike of shock from Chloe and looked over just in time to see a girl close in on her like a snake. Gun still in hand, Chloe reacted impressively fast, her shock burning away in a flash of anger as she was forced to block and deflect the girl's attacks.

My hope that we weren't in trouble was gone, squashed to bits by the gibbering terror. Confusion wedged itself at the edge of my mind, too, mumbling small questions about Chloe and her impressive fighting moves. I knew she could wrestle me to the ground before I raided her fridge for a chocolate-filled vegan croissant but I'm not exactly Chun-Li.

This was a whole other level of skill that I'd never seen outside of an action movie.

A growl drew my attention back to the other end of the room and I caught sight of Mel before he charged forward, teeth bared. Dirk tensed, readying himself for the attack, but he needn't have bothered.

"*Debilus!*" the demon yelled, her voice strained. Mel's attack slowed to a crawl but he didn't seem to notice. His movements, while extremely lagged, remained determined, his expression dangerous. Dirk's tension melted away and his emotions cooled to a pleasant, bubbling warmth as he laughed at Mel's predicament. We both watched Mel move like cooled molasses and after a few seconds I felt frustration burble through Dirk. Sick of waiting, he stepped forward, balled up his fist, and punched the bigger man square in the jaw.

Mel dropped to the floor at the same time Chloe's gun went off and I gasped, whipping around expecting to see Chloe standing triumphantly over the girl-shaped demon. I saw only her feet instead, the rest of her out of sight on the ground outside. The demon stood over her, Chloe's gun in her hand.

"Chloe!" I yelped, the threat of losing my best friend breaking my paralysis. Dirk got to me before I could make it even a step, grabbing my hand and yanking me close like a dance. I bumped against his chest and, while my instinct was to struggle, he wouldn't let me. His arm locked around my back, forcing the air out of my lungs, and when I tried again to fight, he just smiled his sharp smile and bent close.

"This worked out well for us."

I managed to squeak out my last bit of breath before he nudged my face to the side. His dizzy pleasure swamped my psyche, doing its best to drown my manic anxiety as I felt the heat of his breath against my skin. Little seeds of panic sprouted in my stomach and, as I felt the pressure of Dirk's fangs, a beanstalk of terror grew out of them. With incredible speed, it speared its way into my internal organs, wrapped its razor-sharp leaves through my screaming lungs, and stabbed its thorny branches into my heart. I felt cold.

When his fangs pierced my skin, the pressure on my chest let up and I felt air suck into my bruised ribcage. I took two great breaths before I let out a sound that might have been a call for help. I was losing my voice, my vision, my hearing. Sluggishness swept over my body and I was becoming less and less aware of anything outside of the two of us. All I felt was the icy stab of the terror inside and the wound at my neck.

Dirk loosened his grip on me so the last thing I saw was his face and my blood on his lips.

Seventeen

My body was in paralyzing pain, though my mind still frolicked through a bloody, sharp dreamscape. My limbs felt bent at all the wrong angles and tiny wounds dotted my skin. Distantly, I could feel patches of dried blood and scabs on my stomach, along my arms and legs. The sound of a voice ordering me to wake pulled me closer to consciousness, out of one nightmare and into another.

When I finally fluttered opened my eyelids, I could see darkness and the corona of a bare bulb. Before I had consciously decided to do so, I was pulling and kicking against the bands of pressure holding me in place.

If my mind was a factory and my thoughts were its workers, every one of them was slacking off, getting high by the water cooler instead of pulling levers and answering phones. I couldn't entirely tell why, but I knew my struggling was accomplishing nothing.

"She's awake!"

The voice was high, young, and excited like a teen set free with a credit card in a trendy clothing store.

Shock and terror pulled through my lips in a quick shriek. After another attempt at pulling out of my bonds, I discovered I could only move my head. Wildly, I looked left, right, letting out another cry when I noticed a needle of terrifying size sticking out of the inside of my elbow. A dark red cord was trailing off the side of the cross-shaped table, channeling my blood out of my body and out of sight.

"Up you go!" The voice sang from behind me just before I heard metal scream. The world flew by and then I was upright, my head spinning as my slacker thoughts stumbled against each other and tumbled around in my head like drunken astronauts.

Dirk stood across from me. He had no expression on his face but the young woman who stepped into my field of view held enough excitement on her own for the both of them. I recognized her expression, the smile and the wide eyes, but it was meaner than any excitement I'd seen before.

This wasn't just glee, this was a bully advancing on the scrawniest kid on the schoolyard because he knows who's got the most lunch money.

"Welcome!" she announced. I struggled against the straps again, sure despite my weakness that I could make headway this time. The girl shook her head, her eyes darting to my right arm as I tried to fight. "Nice try, dummy. He's got you well and truly tucked."

Dirk caught my attention by baring his fangs, tilting his head as if he knew the exact angle to make them appear their most menacing. Her slang was odd, not entirely descriptive on its own, but Dirk made the point for her. Even with a head full of lazy thoughts, I could put together that the weakness holding me back and Dirk's fangs were related.

The girl—the *demon*—looked about my height, with brown hair and solid, inhumanly black eyes like Laurel's. She was wearing jeans, ripped at the knee, and a plain black t-shirt. She seemed young, early twenties at most, and her nails were painted a chipped baby pink. Her features were average, her nose a little too bulbous to be beautiful, though her full lips tried to make up for it.

She jabbed me in the kidney with a hard left and I grunted, swore, and tried again to fight. When I lowered my gaze to measure my progress, I realized I was worse off than I'd previously assumed. When I tried to pull my left arm out of the straps, nothing happened—nothing at all. Despite screaming orders for my muscles to move, I couldn't even manage to flex my bicep or pop a vein. My pinky finger twitched a bit but my arm lay otherwise dead.

"I think she's gotten it, D," the girl said.

"She isn't too bright."

"Hey," I said, more out of habit than actual offense. Having my intelligence insulted was the least of my problems, but it was something I heard so often I argued without thinking.

"You'll be fun to keep around, I think. Not to mention useful!" She bounced forward and lifted her hands to my face. I felt her fingertips on my skin and she met my eyes. Wooziness flooded through me before a brick cracked my skull right between my eyes.

My lashes fluttered open after what could have been minutes or days and I found myself staring down at the top of her head. She'd tucked her hands up into my hair, pressing her palms to my temples as she rested her head on my chest. I wasn't bleeding and I didn't feel any more battered than I had before she'd touched me, but it was clear that whatever she'd done hadn't been as passive as it appeared.

"You have potential, but it's wasted," she said, her tone distracted. I felt the pressure of her fingers change slightly as if she'd give me a scalp massage and it sent a wave of fear through me. I didn't want to lose consciousness again, to be left completely at their mercy. I couldn't fight, thanks to Dirk's paralyzing bites and the aged leather pinning me to the table, but that didn't beat back the fear of oblivion.

"Get off me!" I tried to struggle again, not because I hoped it would help but because terror had found my rational mind and socked it right in the face. "Get away, get away!"

The girl laughed, rolling her head up so she could meet my eyes with her chin on my chest. She watched me for a few moments, as if trying to decide if she wanted to take my order, before she shook her head.

"I can feel your real abilities, thick like sludge below the surface of your sanity," she said, her voice much too young, much too casual for the content. "You're more than you will ever be, but such is the problem with so many humans. You waste what you've got, ignoring it rather than calling it forth and using your true power."

"Speaking of below the surface, may I?" Dirk asked, though he didn't gesture or advance. The demon stayed pressed close, her eyes still on mine. Seconds passed before her expression twitched toward irritation.

"It's half the reason we brought her here, isn't it?" Backing away from me, she flicked her wrist in a "go ahead" gesture. "Make it fast."

Dirk stepped wide around us both to crouch down by the side of the table out of view. The girl watched him for a moment before a tremor of impatience ran through her and she began to tap her foot. I struggled to see what Dirk was doing but my neck wouldn't bend that far. Despite the fact that he wasn't hurting me, that he seemed to be concentrating on something on the floor rather than planning to slit my throat, I let out a whimper. When Dirk stood abruptly and spoke, the sight of a bag of my blood in his hand turned my whimpering into a long whine.

"Do you need me to—"

"Get out," the girl snapped, stomping her foot. I saw the rumblings of a tantrum in her—even though I'm usually the one throwing them, I can recognize the signs in others—though I couldn't feel anything to back it up. I wasn't sure if my empathy was being repressed in some way or if I just couldn't read her.

I racked my brain at the realization, trying to remember what I'd felt at the hotel. Had I sensed her then? I couldn't remember. My other senses were still having trouble fighting off disorientation and I couldn't be sure what I was or wasn't feeling. It was rather like wondering if you've gone colorblind in a black and white room. I wasn't sure if my brain was to be trusted, considering my situation.

Dirk didn't need to be told twice and had fled the second the first syllable was free of her lips. I heard a door open and shut and I tried to see where he'd gone, but I couldn't strain my neck enough. Dirk was gone, I didn't know where, and I was alone with the demon.

I didn't want to look at her. I wanted to shut my eyes and click my heels together and murmur, "There's no place like home, there's no place like home," and find myself in Chloe's bed again. I'd even take being assaulted by her cake-destroying cat over sitting here and discussing my empathy with a demon.

Something familiar slithered through my brain, bumping a slippery shoulder against my thoughts before weaving back into the darkness. I turned to the girl, my eyes wide as the moon as I realized why I recognized the feeling.

"Did you miss me?" she asked. "I wasn't completely gone, but the witch was only as thorough as can be expected."

"You—it was you? In my head?"

"Of course." She narrowed her eyes. "Are you always this stupid?"

Fear, frustration, and pain collided in my chest, splashing out through my mouth in an insulted rush.

"You've had your pet vampire chew holes in me, you've sucked out half my brain, I'm tied to a fucking table, and you're draining my blood out through a straw!" I shrieked. "I think I have an excuse to be stupid!"

Rather than punish me for yelling, the girl laughed, hopping around and clapping her hands together like an excited audience member at a taping of *The Price is Right*. She gave a happy wiggle of her shoulders as she watched me thrash my head, struggling against futility.

When I exhausted myself and met her gaze again, she lifted a knee, dropped it, and then did a complicated dance move that reminded me of Fred Astaire. Soft-shoeing her way over to me, she stopped with a flourish, one hand held up as if asking me to join her. I just stared down, wishing I could at least punch her in the face or something.

Being paralyzed really blows.

I didn't know why she looked like she expected something from me. We both knew I couldn't move and, while I was now aware enough to really consider my situation, I couldn't think of anything else to say.

I could have sworn about it, yowled and complained until I was blue in the face, but I didn't think it would get her to let me down. In fact, I would have bet my—er, something definitely less significant than my life that my complaining would just make her laugh at me some more.

Shifting out of her stance, she half turned to make a show of surveying the darkness of the room. The part of her wriggling in my brain seemed to nudge me toward something and I got the feeling I was supposed to follow her lead.

Craning my neck, I searched what little I could see, curious despite myself about what it was she wanted to show me. I couldn't see much past the bright light of the bare bulb, but the place smelled like dust and old cardboard. Dilapidated wooden shelves along the right wall held dented banker boxes and the curve of a rusting water heater peeked out of the darkness at the edge of my view.

Recognition dawned and for a moment I wasn't sure how to feel about my predicament. Was this nightmare taking place in a plain old dirty garage?

"There you go," she said, pleased with me even though I hadn't said anything. "You're coming around. There may be hope for you yet, though it took you awhile to really figure out the obvious."

I rolled my gaze to her, wondering what she was talking about. What was obvious? That I was in a garage? That the water heater was leaking and probably needed to be replaced?

"Maybe your soul isn't worth taking after all," she said, narrowing her eyes at me.

"You want my soul?"

"Just the important part," she clarified. "I don't need as much as your buddy once did. I've been at this a long time and I know how to take what I need without leaving a corpse." I'd barely begun to relax at the idea of not being murdered before she met my eyes. "That doesn't mean I won't kill you eventually."

"Kill—but you shouldn't—you can't—"

"I *can*, but I'm not going to *yet*." She interrupted my panicked blubbering, raising her voice above mine until I'd quieted. "I wouldn't have bothered waking you up just to cut you in half."

"Really?" I squeaked, relief washing through me. She didn't assure me again, simply watching me with a knowing smile on her face. I took a few moments to calm my breathing, to back away from the fear and force myself to take stock of the situation. I wasn't about to die, so that was something.

Although, as somethings go, it wasn't much. I was still trapped in a garage with a psycho who looked like she should be fighting with teenagers on Tumblr over Benedict Cumberbatch being hotter than Chris Evans. I was still bound and paralyzed, slightly light-headed from blood loss.

I was still going to die, just not right at that moment.

The realization made me sad and angry all at the same time. What had my life come to that I was patting myself on the back for not being dead *yet?*

Something must have shown in my face because the girl started laughing.

"That's better! Now we can chat. You've got spirit, at least when you're not whining or freaking out." She rolled her eyes and it reminded me of the looks I'd gotten from my big sister when she'd been at that "too cool" age. "The vampire's been holed up alone in a house for fifteen years and he's so *boring*. He doesn't know how to listen and he gets distracted, like, really easily. But, since you're here for awhile, you might as well entertain me."

Her immaturity was bordering on offensive and it was driving away my panic, filling me with me a bitchy bravado. My rational mind knew it was a bad idea to mouth off, that she could probably kill me in an instant, but it was still smarting from the hit it had taken before and that made it easy for me to ignore its advice to stay quiet.

"I'm not really in a position to juggle for you, but you could untie me and give me some flaming knives and we'll see what happens."

"See! Spirit." Something seemed to occur to her then and she snorted out a laugh as she clapped her hands once. "*Spirit.*"

I just watched her, lost and frustrated that I wasn't in on the joke. I didn't feel like giggling along with her like two friends splitting a bottle of wine, but she seemed to be laughing at me rather than with me and that's never a good feeling.

"Spirit!" she repeated, really hitting the word as if that would make me get it. "Like soul? You're—I give up. Let's talk about me instead, what *I've* been up to. I've already told the vampire and he *so* wasn't impressed once he started to feel better. Now all he wants to do is run around the city sucking on virgins and terrorizing his old high school teachers. He never wants to talk about me."

"How sad for you," I deadpanned. She took it as if I was serious.

"I know! So how much do you know about me? It doesn't seem like much from what I can tell." The thing in my mind shifted again, getting comfortable in the folds of my brain. I cringed, shaking my head as if I could knock it out through my ears. The sensation wasn't much different from the fizzy feeling of getting soda backed up in my sinuses.

"You're a demon," I offered, hoping she'd back off whatever mojo was bubbling through my skull.

"Excellent!" She clapped again. "Do you know what demons *do*?"

"Are you going to make me guess?" I asked, irritated by how excited she seemed. I'd never faced a maniacal villain before; I wasn't sure if I wanted to hear her blather out a monologue about how great she was. I don't have James Bond's skills. Time would not reveal an escape for me.

"You're right. I'm giving you too much credit. Your powers are weak enough that no one's ever bothered to school you. You were, what, four when the scouts showed up?" I didn't answer, but the question was probably rhetorical, anyway. "When you're judged useless, they let you be. It's only when you're of interest to them, when you could be used against them in some way, that they would bother to pluck you out of obscurity. I wasn't useless."

Despite myself, I found I was curious. Hardy had mentioned something similar when we'd met, but I'd been so distracted by their sudden appearance and by the raucous feeling of standing too close to Laurel that I hadn't taken much of it in. Sensing I was now interested in participating in her one-demon show, she paused to watch me expectantly. I considered that she'd known before I had what I was about to ask, but I went ahead anyway.

"Are demons and fairies … like, buddies?"

Once again pleased with me, she pointed her finger like a weapon, jabbing it forward as if she'd spear my chest. I flinched.

"Not a bad question for a nitwit. We are not friends, no. They would have wanted me bad for what I could do, but they never got the chance. Someone else got to me first, much like I got to little …" She waved her hand. "What's the kid's name, Andy? With the fire starting?"

"Ashley?" I asked. Rage boiled inside me at her attitude, at the fact that she couldn't even be bothered to learn the names of the children she'd kidnapped and held hostage.

"Sure, like that one. Like how I got to them before the scouts could. It's like that, but I'm not wasting their time with deals and lies. I'm just gonna take what I want."

"You stupid—" I didn't get far with my tirade before she held up a hand, her expression hard.

"This isn't about you," she said, squeezing her hand into a fist as if she was crushing my heart. I struggled for a millisecond, but whatever power she held over me coursed through my body, slowing my pulse to the point where I started to drift off. Consciousness ebbed away for a moment before the pressure in my chest let up slightly and I opened my heavy eyes to find her considering me. "You're gonna listen this time. No more *insults*, you got it?"

"Sure," I slurred, blinking against the desire to pass out.

"Excellent! Where was I? Well, so, demons, of course, have existed for ages. We were all like you, once upon a time. We were all human, all special." Her eyes did a quick pass, taking all of me in. "Some more so than others. We were all approached by the same man, though some of us undoubtedly realized quickly he wasn't a man at all."

"He was an elephant!" I interjected, the slowness of my brain making me feel silly. I giggled but the demon was too wrapped up in her performance to notice my stupid joke. When she spoke again, her voice boomed through the garage like she was on stage, speaking to thousands.

"He was a liar, one of the most well-known, in fact. To those of us whom *he* found useful, he offered help, love, riches, whatever we desired. All we needed to do was promise to come to him after a period of time and agree to give him one thing. He would tell us what that one thing was to be, but not before we promised to give it."

She sighed, shook her head, a bitter smile on her lips. "My deal was different. My deal was special. Not many get *my* deal. I didn't have to give him anything of my own. I got all the riches, all the goodies, and I didn't have to promise him my soul. The souls of others, sure, but I got to keep my own. Until he got stingy." She caught my eye, her jaw tight like she'd suddenly decided her miserly boss was my fault. "I didn't like the deal anymore, so I told him I was out, I was done with him and his contracts."

"Did you at least give your two weeks' notice?"

Her eyes narrowed to slits and, despite my fuzzy mind, I winced.

"It probably goes without saying, but he didn't want to let me go. I mean, would you?"

"I think you should definitely go," I agreed, still trying to rouse my sluggish thoughts. I'd been high a few times in college, but this was nothing like sucking at a bong and eating so much candy I couldn't move. I hadn't done this to myself; it had been impressed upon me by something alien inside my own mind.

My head lolled back as I felt my eyes roll around in my head, out of control in their sockets, and I squeezed them shut. I wanted to fight against her control, but my thoughts were as paralyzed as my limbs. I needed help.

"You're not funny," she said. After a moment, she sighed and reached out to grab my chin. "But I liked you better when you were asking better questions." Life rushed into me, making me yelp as the nerves in my neck, face, and scalp sparked to action. I swore, shook her hand off, and looked back at her, my brain buzzed from her touch.

"I'm not sure if you're better or worse than an energy drink."

"Are you ready to listen now, or are you too busy thinking stupid thoughts about your glory days getting stoned in your boyfriend's dirty apartment?"

I jolted, trying to sort through the rapid stream of thoughts zipping through my head. Most of them concentrated on my predicament, trying to figure out if escape was possible, demanding I test my bonds again to see if my arms or legs would work. The most logical thoughts, though, concentrated on the fact that she was in my head, that she knew what I was thinking at any moment, and that, if she really wanted to ruin my day, she might bring up everything about those supposed glory days.

They had been anything but glorious. I had a lot of bad memories from that period in my life and I didn't want her pulling them out of my head one by one and rubbing them in my face like steel wool.

"I'm ready to listen!" I insisted. "Go on, keep talking. You're great and your boss was a dick. Start from there."

She eyed me for a moment, a smile tugging at her lips before she stood straight and slipped back into her performance.

"He *was* a dick! He thought he had it all figured out, that he could control us if he just plied us with riches and pretty clothes. But it wasn't enough for me. I caught on to what was really going on behind the scenes, why he really wanted all those contracts. I figured out that souls are more than just wiggling little lines of energy. They're *power*. If you get souls, you have power. I just need souls and I can boot him out and take over! It took me some time to figure out how to do it, but I'm on it now. I've got it all planned out. With the right assistant—say, a desperate vampire who's *sick* of being confined to a sterile room—I can gather more than enough souls to rock right up to the boss himself and punch him in his dick face."

She lifted her arms to box the air in front of me, breathing out delicate puffs of onomatopoeia to match each jab of her fists. I watched her shuffle her feet like Mohammed Ali as she mimed punching me and it just made me frustrated at her freedom.

"So where did we land on you going?" I asked when one of her hits barely missed my already bruised kidney. Her eyes darted to my face before lowering back to her imaginary opponent. She danced minutely forward, close enough that I worried for my stomach with every move of her fists. "You know, far away from here?"

Rolling her upper body like a snake, she weaved, hooking her left fist toward my face in an arc. When I yelped and tried to flinch away, she shifted tactics and slapped me hard with her other hand. I tasted blood inside my cheek and my ear hurt from being smashed between my skull and the wood.

"Dammit," I hissed.

"Damn what? Damn you? All done! You're with us until we're done with you. I wasn't going to go after an empath, especially not a level *three* who doesn't even know what the hell she's doing, but I can make an exception. With a little finesse, your empathy could be so much more than a sponge."

I wiggled my jaw, wanting to make sure the pain radiating down from my ear didn't mean she'd broken my pretty face. My silence seemed to annoy her and she shook her head.

"There's a ritual involved with this, one I didn't used to need to tug out souls, but Bossman knows his stuff, unfortunately. So, I'm stuck doing things the hard way. It's going to take some time and a whole lot more sad little kids but—what's that they say? New year, new you? Come January first, my new me will be part you!"

That broke the camel's back. A bevy of emotions exploded inside me: fear, anger, despair, and a tiny thread of hope that suggested I try to escape just one more time. I shot into another round of struggling, fighting against the paralysis.

The demon just watched me, her shoulders sagging as if her interest in me was waning. She let me thrash my head a few times before she leaned close to catch my eye.

"I think you need some time to yourself. You're clearly having issues right now." Straightening, she lifted her hand to give me a cutesy little wave from next to her cheek, then stepped past me and out of view. A door opened and almost immediately slammed. It made me jump, which amounted to my head jerking to the side in shock.

And there I was. Strapped to a table, bitten everywhere, with a gigantic needle sticking out of my arm. I did my best to concentrate, to try to figure out my chances for survival. Chloe had been shot, probably killed. I had no idea if Mel had made it out of the hotel room at all.

If he was alive, what had he awoken to find? What had the demon done to him that allowed Dirk to knock him out with one punch? If he'd survived, had he woken in time to get Chloe to a hospital? And where were the children? Had the demon gathered them up and brought them to remain captive alongside me? My empathy was still no help and I still had no idea why.

The demon had said that my powers weren't enough to make me important and so no one had taken much notice of me. Maybe there were tons of special humans out there, meeting to change the world for the greater good. Maybe I was just a few shades away from being in some real-world version of the X-Men. Was there a chance they'd find out I'd been smacked around and abducted and come rescue me?

"Shut up," I told myself, trying to think through the blood loss and psychic abuse. Mulling over what-ifs wasn't getting me anywhere. I made the conscious effort not to struggle anymore, not to waste my energy, but I did let myself swear like it was my job. Anger generally makes my vocabulary more limited, though, and my cuss concoctions came out nonsensical, physically impossible and, at one point, heavily reliant on dessert foods.

Judging by the pit in my stomach, I figured that I'd been out for probably five or six hours. That gave me a starting point for doing something useful.

"Okay. So you've been kidnapped by a demon," I said to myself, trying not to dwell on the fact that I sounded like the worst educational video ever. "You're strapped to a table, unable to even struggle properly. This bitch is aiming to snatch your soul and a vampire is bleeding you dry. Chloe and Mel might be dead and there's a chance no one even knows you're missing. Your pet bird is home alone, for god's sake, with no one around to feed him. He may starve—no. Stop that. Let's look at the upsides, Gwen. Come on." I blinked into the darkness, my mind a blank. "Any upsides. Come on. You can do it."

I couldn't.

Eighteen

"I brought you a present."

The pain in my neck was excruciating.

"Don't you want to see what it is?"

"What?" I asked, groggy. I had no idea how much blood I'd lost, but it was getting pretty bad. I wondered how much more I could lose without dropping into a coma from which not even the snarkiest voice could wake me.

"Over here."

"What?" I asked again. For a second, I was fuzzy on the details of what was happening, but when I finally got my eyes to focus on Dirk's face, I remembered. I let out an exhausted whimper, squeezing my eyes shut against the urge to start crying. I was so tired, hungry, and sick. I wasn't sure how long I could last before my body just gave up and I passed out again.

"Hey," Dirk said, snapping his fingers a few times to call my attention. I considered sinking back into sleep instead of giving him the satisfaction of answering. "You might want to take one last look at your boyfriend before the demon carves up his eyeballs."

Boyfriend?

Curious despite myself, I opened my eyes, doing my best to focus my bleary gaze on Dirk and the bundle at his feet. It looked kind of human-shaped the longer I stared at it. Even in the shadows, I could make out the curve of a shoulder and dark hair peeking up from beyond.

Recognition snapped it into focus and I gasped, going tense.

"Mel!" I yelped, leaning forward to fight as hard as my paralysis would let me. "Mel! Wake up!"

"He can't hear you. He was harder to bite than you were, what with the werewolf skin and all—I nearly cracked a tooth." Dirk lifted a finger, curled up his lip like Elvis, and pointed to his exposed fang. "Nys threw out a little magic, though, and now he's sleeping like a baby."

I darted my gaze to Dirk, anger simmering in my belly, bubbling upward through my throat like heartburn. It wasn't just that he was talking so casually about chewing on Mel—a few days ago, I probably would have encouraged it, maybe taken pictures and posted them online—but that it represented a larger problem.

Mel was *right there*, absolutely lousy with car-crushing strength and blurry speed, and yet we were both looking pretty screwed.

"Come on, Mel," I mumbled, eyeballing him harder than I'd ever done before. Had this been any other situation, he'd have woken up and assumed I was propositioning him with just the strength of my will. Unfortunately for me, he didn't budge, remaining an unconscious lump of stylish clothes and sculpted muscle.

I called his name a few more times, getting louder when Dirk started laughing. Chloe had said Mel had woken up quickly the last time he'd been knocked out. That had to mean something now, didn't it? Fate wouldn't send him to me, drop him nearly at my feet, and leave him to snooze through my execution.

Dirk was still laughing at me, his amusement rumbling through his lips in fitful, snorting jerks like he'd never seen anything funnier.

I paused long enough in my rescue attempts to throw him a glare and in the bad light, I could see what I hadn't really noticed before.

His features held an echo of the bony, cancer-ridden vampire Mel had described. He was healthy, whole and strong, but with the extra shadows along his eyes and below his cheekbones, I could see the history of illness in him. Without thinking, I jerked my body—well, my head and neck—toward him, as if posturing.

"I'm going to wake him up and he's going to kick your sorry, sickly ass. Whatever you got from the demon or whatever virgin you sucked dry, it isn't going to help you when he beats you to a cancerous pulp." Dirk's laughter trailed off and his grin retreated. I sneered. "That's right, Bubble Boy. I'm going to laugh so hard when you're back to the bald, germ-phobic *weakling* Mel and I laughed over just the other day."

Mel still wasn't stirring, but something in me was. Nerves were firing like lightning through my arms and my left foot. When I lashed out once more, I felt the rope press against my bicep ever so slightly. My victory was short-lived, however, as Dirk took a step over Mel's head and stalked toward me. I tried my best to stay tough but I couldn't stop the butterflies in my belly. Dirk stopped a breath away, baring his teeth.

I stared at him, feeling my emotions run from anger to panic. When he snapped his jaws, I felt the scrape of one of his fangs against the top of my lip. I cried out, jerked my head back, and felt it crack against the table. Immediately I regretted the pain of the impact, even while the area around the scratch went numb.

I tried to swear at him but my lips were no longer under my control, numbness spreading through the bottom half of my face. Dirk stood there, still close enough that I could smell my blood on his breath, and laughed.

"Nys likes you talking, but I think this is a better look on you." I did my best to glower but the paralytic had probably kept my expression several shades away from "die in a fire!" and left it somewhere around, "did you hear something?"

The door opened behind me again and as the demon approached, I felt something tickle the back of my throat. It was subtle, like taking too deep a sniff of freshly lit incense, but it felt familiar. She spoke and stepped into view, distracting me from investigating the new sensation.

"Why is he out?"

"I thought you'd—"

"Just because you're walking around like a big man again doesn't mean you get to *think*. I give the orders and you follow them. I didn't give this order."

"Nys—" He was cut off as she shoved into his space, jamming a finger into his chest. The tickle in my throat grew into an itch, a smoky feeling of… of… what was it? Why couldn't I put two and two together?

The demon started in on a lecture that I had the feeling she'd given time and time again and I did my best to tune her out. My face seemed to be waking up, judging by all the pins and needles being repeatedly stabbed through it. I could move my jaw again, and bite my tongue in an attempt to quell the itching. I sucked my lips into my mouth, trying to get rid of the slimy feeling that reminded me of putting on too much of my mom's lipstick as a child. The irritation was growing, spreading through my throat and along my tongue, but my lips and cheeks felt overly gooey.

I watched my captors turn on each other, Nys giving Dirk a piece of her mind and him looking like he'd had enough pieces and he'd like to give this one back. Hoping they didn't see my wincing attempt at bringing life back into my mouth, I opened and shut my jaw a few times. If it was anything like coming home from the dentist, I hoped I could solve my vampire Novocain problem with a little extra blood flow.

I failed to remember, in that moment, that I had no extra blood to flow.

"If you'd just let me explain!" Dirk argued.

"Oh, sure, let's hear what you think you've accomplished by letting the werewolf out of his cage!"

"It's fine," Dirk insisted. The gooey feeling on my mouth had spread to the rest of my face and it warmed. I stopped dead, my jaw hanging open, when I realized what was happening. "I got him good and—uh, tucked."

"You think you slobbering on his neck one time is enough to keep him out of my hair for the whole day?" Nys demanded. The irritation in my throat intensified, expanding through my mouth like smoke until even my teeth itched. My empathy was waking up much quicker than the rest of me, but I was really wishing it would conk out again.

I gagged hard against the itching of the demon's emotions, recognizing them as frustration just as she shot a hand out and gripped Dirk's throat. He choked out a strangled cry and their distraction urged me to be bold. I concentrated on my right hand, doing my best to wiggle my fingers. My wrist twitched, my bicep tensed, and then, with a flood of pride, I bent my index finger a few degrees. The paralysis was finally wearing off! Happy visions of a demonic murder-suicide danced through my mind, followed by images of me freeing myself, waking Mel, and dancing into the sunset.

"Get him out of here before he wakes up," the demon ordered.

"Relax," Dirk wheezed, his hands fighting against her little fingers. "He's still out."

The sharp sound of glass cracking made me jolt as Dirk's head snapped to the side. It was dark, hard to see, but I thought I caught sight of blood blossoming out the other side of his face.

Nys's arm was forced to follow and she dropped her captive. I blinked at them and then she and I sat in silence, watching Dirk crumple to the ground. After a second, she turned to me, one eyebrow up. I felt a single puff of what I decided was her confusion and I did my best not to turn it to something worse. When I appeared to be no threat—strapped in and numbed as I was—Nys swiveled to look around the room and consider the source of the bloody hole in Dirk's temple.

Almost casually, she twisted, her hands up in front of her like a magician coaxing a rabbit out of a hat. When Dirk groaned and struggled, another low *thud* sounded and his head jerked again. He went still and his emotions flatlined, all the wet slimy feelings retreating from my face like I'd wiped away a smear of honey.

Nys shifted like lightning, grabbing the side of my table and yanking it back. My body screamed in pain as it hit its mark and I found myself staring up at the ceiling. The demon crouched next to me, completely silent. The murky cloud of her emotions grew out through my mouth, spreading along my neck and shoulders. Whatever was holding my power at bay seemed to be waning, and I was entirely sure if that was a good thing. At that moment, she was all I could sense and it wasn't a pleasant experience. Even Mel was a void, though he was still breathing, so optimism demanded I assume he was still wearing the necklace.

Nys peered up and moved her gaze past me to the opposite wall. Swallowing the lump in my throat, I turned to follow her line of sight. A tiny hole had appeared in what I had previously thought was a solid wall.

The demon hissed out something guttural and a smoky wave of anger threatened to choke me. I coughed and fought to flex my hands some more. With Dirk catching some Zs and the demon distracted, I figured there would be no better time to free myself. Sunset, here I come!

I could feel something above me, to my right. It was coming from behind Nys but she seemed oblivious to it. The ebb of it was familiar, a pattern I'd spent plenty of time with. It was faint, though, and I wasn't entirely convinced it was even there until I heard Nys gasp.

"Trash!" she yelled as I saw her pop back, dropping slightly into a loose stance, knees bent, hands held out as if gripping an invisible basketball. She swirled her hands around each other but nearly the instant a purple glow appeared between her palms, there was a whistle and the handle of a small blade appeared, sticking out of her neck. She stumbled away from me and I lifted my head to follow her trajectory.

Her arms pinwheeled, sending power crashing off clumsily into the walls. I yelped as a bolt came toward me and I did my best to avoid it. My best, of course, went as far as twisting my head to the right and closing my eyes. Adrenaline was making my sluggish body feel light and cold. I had honestly never been this scared before in my life.

"Nysgrogh, Queen Orlagh is none too happy with thee."

My eyes snapped open when a deep voice rumbled through my chest. A very large, furry hand had stopped one of Nys's wayward bolts of energy from slicing into me. The hand moved, taking the power with it, and I jerked my head around to find Hardy to my left, a stern look on his tusked face. The demon girl screeched and threw herself at him, hands crackling with purple electricity.

"I do not answer to the *fae*," she hissed. Hardy lifted one arm to block her swing, sweeping his other under her guard to press the stolen purple power against her ribcage. She yowled but kept coming at him. Her arms waved, her nails looking especially sharp, as he used one hand to hold her off while the other blocked her swings toward his face. Her body was jerking as he continued to shove his own dark red power against her chest, right above her heart. Meanwhile, she was scratching his arms, drawing blood even through the fur. His blood was red, which surprised me, and his wide face betrayed the pain he was in.

I was too busy watching their struggle to notice that someone was undoing my bonds. At about the third power-backed punch that Hardy blocked, I heard a whisper from my right.

"Psst!"

Yelping, I turned to see the top of Chloe's head poking up from next to the table. Dizziness rode through my body as my ribcage tried to compensate for the rave my heart was throwing in my chest. I whispered frantically, catching Chloe's determined expression as she unbuckled the last strap near my wrist.

"You're alive! You're—I thought you were—"

"Don't call attention over here," Chloe warned, reaching up to press a finger against my lips. "They don't usually deal with demons but Syham should be able to handle her. I'll get you out of here, get this shit out of your arm."

I wanted to ask who Syham was, but I was too light-headed, too concerned with the fact that Chloe was *alive* and *here* to *rescue* me! I was saved! Within moments the straps along my left arm were gone, leaving only the needle and cord. When she shifted to crouch-walk toward my feet, I noticed movement behind her.

"Behind—" I started. Chloe's expression changed in an instant and I felt a brief stab of anger arc out of her. She darted right, twisting and pushing to her feet. Dirk's grab missed by a hair's breadth and she shoved her own hand up, slamming the heel of her hand toward his face. Dirk avoided her attempt to break his nose, dropping downward and reaching out. I missed exactly how he managed it but, to Chloe's credit, she didn't scream as Dirk lifted her and flung her backward. She twisted in midair like a cat and went down protecting her skull.

Unfortunately for Mel, she used his body as a landing pad. He grunted but Dirk didn't seem to notice. He and his badly injured head were making their way past me to assist Nysgrogh in her fight with Hardy. The wicked holes in his skull had decimated his right ear and part of his left eye socket. I was betting the only reason he had missed Chloe was that he was half-blind.

Mel's voice, raspy with confusion, called out by my feet.

"Chloe?"

"Mel?"

"Help!" I demanded, my body sprouting fresh panic through my skin. I was sweating and the fact that I kept glimpsing the needle in my arm was only making things worse. If I'd been a rabbit, I definitely would have already died of, like, six heart attacks.

"Gwen?" Mel asked. Chloe got to her feet and attempted to heave Mel to his. He made it to his knees before gravity seemed to yank him to the side. "Whoa."

"Help!" I repeated, willing my free arm to wave in case he couldn't locate me. It remained draped across the table.

"Help her," Chloe barked, dropping Mel's heavy arm and darting past me. I looked up, tried to follow her, but it was too dark and she was too fast.

"So bossy," Mel complained and I turned away from where Chloe had gone. Mel pushed to his feet, but stumbled.

I shrieked out a terrified, "No!" as I saw him bring his hand up, trying to grab for the foot of the table. His brows shot into his hair as the heel of his hand hit the edge but continued downward. He didn't know the table was meant to be both vertical and horizontal, and Nysgrogh hadn't locked it into the down position.

I screamed as his weight carried the foot of the table down, lifting me to a standing position yet again. I felt the table hit something by my head and it made a clacking sound, like when Dirk had snapped his teeth at me.

I jerked my head over, caught sight of Hardy dodging a two-by-four swung by the demon. Shortly after, Dirk shambled into view, hands pressed to his face, which had spouted a cascade of blood. He managed a mumbled string of what might have been cuss words before one of Nys's swings hit him in the shoulder. She spared him a glance, spat something his way that sounded to me like gibberish, and then turned back to Hardy.

The furry fairy and the diminutive demon eyed each other in silence for a moment and I had the briefest of hopes that she was about to give in. Hardy, however, had no such illusions; he was ready for her as she launched herself once again toward his face, fresh, smoky power oozing from her hands and arms. She gripped the front of his chest fur and jammed her feet into his gut, holding herself close to him as her free hand went for one of his giant eyeballs.

Past them, I caught a glimpse of Chloe as she popped up behind Dirk. She was patient, her face stern as she mimicked his movements to stay behind him without touching. Finally, as he leaned back, possibly to stop the blood gushing from his broken nose, she carpe'd her diem. A knife glinted in the light as she reached around his upturned neck. I cried out in shock as she pressed, dragged, and slit his throat.

Nys screamed as a white blur appeared behind her, wrapping long limbs around her torso and pulling her away from her target. She kicked out, hitting Hardy in his barrel chest, but he barely grunted. Too busy calling more of his own red, soupy power to his hands, he shrugged off the blow and attempted to close in. Nys kept kicking out, her hands a flurry above her head. Her attempt at attacking Laurel with raw power was pointless; it hit his skin, but dissipated immediately. Even the scratching of her nails didn't seem to faze him, sliding fast like water down a freshly waxed car. His grip was tight around her chest, his other arm attempting to grab at least one of her wild legs.

Past Laurel and his struggling captive, Dirk was pressing his hands against his bloody neck, backing up as if he could simply step away from the gushing wound. After slitting his throat and planting the knife right into Dirk's heart, Chloe had disappeared again.

Mel groaned from near my feet. Blinking down toward him, I felt the vibration of the table as he gripped the edge next to my knee and tried to pull himself up. My free arm had flopped to my side but I still did my best to reach out and grab him. Nothing happened.

"Hurry, hurry!" I demanded, my voice a high whine. Mel had gotten one foot under him, trying to push off his knee, when Nysgrogh shrieked an unholy sound. I whipped my head over, catching sight of Laurel being knocked slightly off balance. Nys's foot shot out and Mel's luck continued to go from bad to worse.

Without so much as a grunt of pain, he dropped out of sight, keeling over backward: he'd taken an energetic steel-toe right to the face. I blinked down at where he'd been, noting the faint blood spray across my legs.

"No!" I shrieked, turning to concentrate on my own arm. Chloe was still missing, Mel seemed to be down for the count, and Laurel and Hardy had their arms full with the screaming demon. I *had* to be able to get myself free, but no matter how much I tried, I couldn't move my limbs.

I considered, after far more struggling than was comfortable, that I was trying very hard to make a very stupid mistake. Chloe had gotten my left arm free but the only reasons I was still upright were the straps on my right arm and my legs. I was still mostly paralyzed and if I managed to get unbound, I would likely just collapse straight into the concrete floor, face first. Then I'd be no better off than Mel or Dirk.

A gun barked again, three quick times, and I heard a grunt from Nysgrogh. Laurel growled out something that, if I had to guess, was the alphabet sneezing, and Hardy sighed. Just as quickly as it had exploded to life, the fighting died. The only sounds in the room were heavy breathing and a pathetic gurgling coming from Dirk.

"You got it?" Chloe asked. Laurel made an insulted sniffing sound and I turned to watch him adjust the body of the girl in his arms. Her limbs were twitching, dark, smoky power puffing out of her fingers at random intervals. Even as I watched, the three wounds across her skull were healing.

"Of course I have, human. You need not have interfered."

"Stick a cork in it, scout," Chloe ordered, as if she did this sort of thing every day. "Just get her out of here."

"Give her to me," Hardy said. Irritation and insult fizzed out of Laurel and along my skin but rather than argue, he dumped the girl into Hardy's arms. Hardy cradled her surprisingly gently and pressed a hand over her face.

"Cease," he said, his tone calm, almost sweet. Instantly, the spasms wracking her body stopped. She went limp and the lack of movement seemed to startle Laurel. He hissed and jerked back. Once he was sure she wasn't about to attack him, I watched his body loosen; he straightened up and I was reminded of a cat that had stumbled but tried to make it look deliberate.

The power rippling around the demon died down and I felt a peculiar sensation in my head. I managed a small, uncomfortable grunt before the feeling of a bubble expanding in my brain became too much to bear, and I went under.

Nineteen

There was a furnace next to me and it seemed to be breathing. I shoved at it but my attack was weak, ineffective. I whimpered and tried to roll away. Slowly, and with great effort, I pushed back the layers of thick blankets determined to cook me alive.

As I had before, I felt the tiny claws of Poopy the cat press into my leg before she made her way up my body and hit me in the face like a truck. A puff of affection and relief might have come out of her, but the cat couldn't seem to sustain such unselfish emotions; they were gone in an instant and for a second I wondered if my empathy hadn't come back to me after all.

"Ugh," I mumbled, but the cat wasn't deterred. She reminded me of Mel in that moment, especially when she shifted positions, jabbed two paws into my cleavage, and started methodically massaging just above my left nipple.

"Ow, ow! Claws!" I yelped, pulling away. My back pressed against a solid line of heat as I fought the cat. She was determined; when I moved her paws, she switched tactics and shoved them into my throat. I let out a strangled gurgle and then felt a single paw press against my lips. Both the cat and I froze, though she had the advantage of being able to see me in the dark. We stayed that way for a few moments, one paw still digging claws into my neck, the other forcing my silence. Finally, as disappointment clouded through her, she huffed out a contemptuous rumble and took off. Relief at not being cowed by the cat meshed with happiness at my empathy working again and I grinned.

The furnace at my back shifted and I felt an arm wrap around my waist, cutting my contentment off at the knees. I rolled over to fight the grip as the arm pulled me against a broad chest and I found myself brushing noses with Mel. When I pushed at him again, he gave in with a sleepy mumble of assent, pulled his arm away, and rolled over. He didn't say anything else, but he did tug hard at the covers until I was nearly free of their weight.

"What the hell?" I demanded, doing my best to sit up. My balance refused to cooperate, though, and I got halfway before collapsing back into the pillow. My skin started waking up in sections and I could feel a dozen small, sticky lines of plastic along my arms, legs, and stomach.

"Gwen?" Chloe asked as the door opened.

Mel mumbled an order for silence and pulled the covers even more tightly over his shoulders.

"What the *hell*?" I demanded again, still trying to fight my inner ear for dominance. Chloe laughed when she saw me and moved quickly to my side, crouching down. She put a hand on my head, pressed gently.

"You need to stay calm, lay down for a little longer. The paralytic isn't out of your system yet and you're still healing. Dirk took a lot out of you. Likewise the demon."

"Shh," Mel grumbled again. It made me want to shove him off the side of the bed. Or the side of a building.

"What—"

"The hell, yes, I heard you," Chloe interrupted. "Do you remember anything?"

"I remember—" I paused. What did I remember? What was going on? Why was I *starving*? "I don't remember."

"You don't remember anything? Not major world events? Who's our president? What's the eighth letter of the alphabet? How did you get all these scratches?" Chloe poked me hard on one of my bandages. The pain sliced up through me, making me whine and writhe. By the time it finished arcing up my body into my brain, things started to come back to me.

"Oh god!" I yowled as the last few hours snapped into focus. "Dirk? The girl? Are they—"

"Dirk's handled."

"Dead?"

"Don't worry about him."

"The demon?"

"Also handled, for the moment. How do you feel?"

I considered that, investigating how I felt, tucked against the warm covers next to Mel. I felt bad, but no worse than I'd felt over the last few days. Bad luck had taken a liking to me and I sincerely hoped that, with the demon and Dirk "handled," it would move on to someone else. I didn't have it in me to live in this much pain for the rest of my life.

"I guess I'm okay," I said after a few moments, still trying to discern my chances of ever feeling better.

"Wonderful. Then, since we have some important things to discuss, I'm going to bring you a cookie."

I blinked at her, my train of thought switching tracks at the mention of sweets.

"I love you," I said.

She smiled, rubbed a hand over my forehead and cheek, and then headed for the other room. I heard the cat meow and Chloe cooed back.

I took the silence as a chance to take stock of myself. I was fully clothed, but not in the clothes that had been ruined by Dirk and Nysgrogh. I had several bandages along my limbs and a wad of cotton taped to my inner elbow. Swallowing my discomfort, I slipped a hand under the blanket and walked it hesitantly toward Mel's back. When I brushed my fingertips along the fabric of his jeans and sighed in relief, he shifted.

"Gwen?" he asked, his voice groggy.

"No?" I answered, hoping he'd believe me. He remained still for a moment but I could tell he was awake. After a second, he rolled onto his back, lifting his arms and resting his head in his interlocked hands. I glared at him in the darkness, wondered how well he could see my expression.

"I recognize that scent," he said with a grin in his voice. "Can't fool me."

He didn't make any other moves toward me and didn't elaborate on how I smelled. I was sure after all I'd been through that it was no longer roses and lilac, but I couldn't tell how Mel was feeling about it either way. Without asking permission, I reached over, felt along his chest and neck until I found the smooth stone of Merrin's necklace.

"Now go lower," he purred.

"Down boy," Chloe murmured from the door, a plate of cookies in one hand and a pair of juice boxes in the other. Despite the fact that most of my mind was concerned with only drooling over the incoming sugar I could feel a flutter of concern within her. When she was close enough I reached out and grabbed for the cookies without asking. I was able to stuff two of them in my mouth before Chloe pulled the plate away and set it at the foot of the bed. I pouted but let her tuck pillows behind me so I was sitting up.

Mel sat up on his own, swinging his legs off the side of the bed. He took a second to stand, waited a moment, and then padded toward the door.

"Nature calls," he explained, making me scowl again. It wasn't really what he said, just that he was there at all.

"Cookie," I demanded. Chloe shook her head and shoved a juice box toward me. I slurped at it and then sighed. My throat felt dry but the juice was helping.

"How do you feel?" She touched my forehead again, reminding me of my big sister. I wondered, for a second, if I would ever be able to tell Robin about what had become the weirdest week of my life.

"I'm still dizzy. And hungry. Cookie." I pointed toward the plate and watched Chloe's shoulders slump. She leaned forward, pulling me into a tight hug. She squeezed me and, after a moment, I heard her breath catch. Sadness and relief welled like an overflowing jug.

"Hey," I said, shocked. "Are you crying?"

"No," she insisted, her voice betraying the lie. Empty juice box in hand,

I wrapped my arms around her, hugging her back.

"I'm okay," she said, but still wouldn't let go. I settled against her, resting my head on her shoulder with my nose in the crook of her neck. I felt her body shudder as worried relief and tears rolled out of her. I didn't have the energy to shield against the sadness as it tried to leech into my skin like radiation, and I felt a few falling tears of my own. Chloe's sadness wasn't entirely to blame, though; I had a lot to cry about.

After a few sobbing hiccups, she seemed to calm.

"I'm sorry," she said, her voice shaky. "I can't believe I let you get taken and sucked nearly dry. I should have been paying more attention, realized the demon was sneaking up on me."

"You couldn't have known. Me, on the other hand... *I* should have known Dirk was around. I don't know why I didn't feel him until he was right there—I couldn't feel him when I woke up, either. Him or the demon. Not until you guys showed up."

I mulled it over as Chloe sniffled and steadied herself. It had to have been the demon's doing. She'd been in my head reorganizing, after all. I couldn't figure out what she would have gotten out of blocking me from knowing how happy she was to torture me, but it was the only thing I could think of.

"Well, then, it's *all* your fault," Chloe said, and I could feel the smile even if I couldn't see it. "The kidnapping, the blood loss, the fact that Mel got his butt beaten six ways from Sunday." I snorted, taking a second to enjoy the mental image of him getting kicked in the face by a girl. Truce or not, Mel had spent over a year abusing me whenever he got the chance and had flat out told me he wasn't planning to stop. I needed that mental image to keep me strong in the future.

Chloe squeezed me again and we stayed like that, breathing against each other's necks for another few minutes.

Mel stepped back into the room and I saw him blink his eyes in the light from the living room. When he got a good look at the two of us wrapped in each other's arms, he waggled his brows at me.

"Mind if I join you?" he asked, his hands going to the button on his jeans. Chloe shifted out of the hug and grabbed the juice box from my hand, heaving it at his head. Mel weaved as if it was a bowling ball and not a juice box, but caught it. "Fine, then. Be that way." He sniffed and strolled out of the room, head held high. Chloe snorted and turned back to me.

"I was so worried about you."

"What the hell *happened?* I thought you got shot!"

"I did. Bulletproof vest. Hurts like a bitch, though. I hit my head when I went down, which was unacceptable. By the time I came around enough to realize what was going on, I was the only one left. I wasn't even out long, but the demon has tricks I don't."

"How the hell did you find me?"

She went silent and I wished I could see her expression in the darkened room. After a tense moment, she shook her head. Taking another second for herself, she spoke.

"Merrin," she lied.

I didn't call her on it. She'd saved my life, after all.

Mel and I sat around Chloe's retro kitchen table, slow music playing quietly through the room. I wasn't sure why Mel was still hanging out, but with the necklace, I actually wasn't too bothered by him staying. He looked worse than I'd ever seen him, his face filled with splotches of black and blue, his chin scraped up. He managed to avoid complaining, which was better than I would have done in his situation. If my face had looked like his, I would have been wailing, demanding all manner of treats to distract me from the pain.

Chloe brought me hot chocolate in a giant mug stamped with *Luke's Diner*. Mel looked up at her with a frown.

"Where's mine?"

"You can get it yourself, you're an adult," she said as she settled in next to me. Mel let out a small snort and the look they shared was friendly, despite her rudeness. Getting to his feet like it was an incredible effort, he moved to the kitchen, picked through Chloe's rack of individual portion coffee cups, and popped one into her machine. He leaned against the counter, arms crossed as he waited for his drink to brew.

"That was some nice shooting today, Tex," he said after a bit. Chloe shrugged like it was no big deal.

"I'm just glad Laurel and Hardy did most of the heavy lifting. Without them, I can't say rescuing our girl would have gone as well." Chloe caught my eye. "I mean, I don't consider myself a demon expert and Mel wasn't exactly any help either, lying there on the floor, getting kicked in the face."

"I helped," he grumbled.

After a giant gulp of chocolaty goodness, I nodded his way. "The way you fell right on your nose and hit him with the table? That was aces."

Mel pouted in the kitchen and I felt Chloe's amusement mix with pity.

"Normally a vampire his age wouldn't be an issue to any of us, but Nysgrogh fixed that. I do feel bad about the girl the demon's possessed, but she was lost well before I got there. Besides, my whole goal was just to get in, not die, and make off with Gwen. Once Laurel and Hardy had the demon distracted, she wasn't my problem."

"Make out with Gwen, you say?" Mel asked, coming back to the table. I rolled my eyes as Chloe took another sip of her coffee, ignoring him. He plopped down in the chair across from me and took a giant gulp of his coffee. On a sound of disgust, he pursed and swished his lips, trying to overcome the taste before popping back to his feet.

"We have to talk," Chloe said quietly, elbowing me gently. I cringed, mostly at the twinge of pain in my side, but also at her tone. There was no threat of Chloe dumping me for another cake addict, but nothing good ever came from that phrase.

"About how much you love and missed me?" I tried for a grin, failed miserably. Chloe looked down into her cup and let out a slow breath. Mel had started picking through her kitchen, yanking open cabinets at random.

"The kids are still missing."

"So I'm still on the hook with Laurel and Hardy?"

"I'm not actually worried about them. They took care of Dirk and they have the demon, but they don't exactly have much power over her. They can't cancel out any enchantments she's laid down, including anything she's done to you and the children. I brought you here to sleep it off, but you need to go back to Merrin. We need to use you to track the kids again before we can truly stop Nysgrogh for good."

"Doesn't sound so bad." Mel had found a liquor bottle that had been de-labeled and filled with cane sugar; he upended it over the cup. I watched him dump a mountain of sugar into his coffee and found myself grinning his way.

I scolded my brain as I realized it was once again thinking pleasant thoughts about a man I had decided long ago I despised. Thankfully, Chloe distracted me from the slimy feeling of not disliking Mel.

"It might not be as simple as it was before," she said. "We searched the house where they were keeping you and the kids weren't around. Considering the fact that we were able to track them through you, there's a good chance that they used harsher enchantments when they moved you all in order to guard them better. It may not be as easy as kicking in a door this time. Though I guess it wasn't that easy last time, either."

I went quiet, considering her words. It wasn't that I had qualms about being used to locate the kids. I could suffer through floating about as a ghost and getting slapped around a bit if it was for the greater good. But I wasn't sure how much use I'd be if things were as dire as Chloe suspected. Mel had come back to the table, watching me carefully as he stirred his coffee. When I didn't say anything after a few minutes, he piped up.

"Plus I'm still weak as a kitten. It'd be nice if we could take care of that."

I didn't bother fighting off a smile. "Maybe my payment for finding these kids can be to make sure you stay that way."

Mel scoffed but Chloe jumped in before he could pick a fight. "So you're game? We can't do this without you agreeing."

"We could," Mel insisted. "I may not be myself, but I could still stuff her in a sack, drag her there, and hold her down while Merrin does her thing."

"Mel," Chloe said, her expression a warning. He couldn't quite manage to hide a smile as he held his hands up in surrender.

I thought about little Devon and his parents, Ashley and hers. We hadn't actually met the parents of the third girl, Felicity, but that didn't mean she meant any less to me. I nodded.

"Whatever you need, Annie Oakley."

Chloe grinned and yanked me into a hug hard enough that I was briefly reminded of being in Dirk's arms. Chloe smelled much better, though, and had never once tried to bite me.

"What did they do to Dirk?" Mel asked as Chloe started the car.

She shrugged.

"I didn't really ask the details, but they assured me he won't be kidnapping any more children or hanging around any more demons."

"Goddamn dick," Mel growled.

Chloe caught his reflection in the rearview mirror, eyebrow up. "You mean Dirk?"

"I didn't stutter."

She snorted, but silence fell over the car again. We were quiet for a few more minutes before curiosity got the better of me.

"You said earlier that a vampire *Dirk's age* wouldn't be trouble. If he were older, we'd have to watch our backs? Do vampires go through a particularly bad mid-life crisis?"

Chloe was quiet for a second, discomfort billowing out of her. After a moment, she nodded.

"Um. Yeah. Mel didn't tell you that?" Her tone suggested this was common knowledge, something you learn in grade school around the time you hear all about how Batman smells.

"No," Mel said, leaning forward. "My only vampire knowledge is through Dirk, though."

"Well, when they get to be old—I mean, really old—they're pretty impressive specimens. Evadne and I talked about a vampire who was several thousand years old. I'm talking B.C. here."

"Jesus," Mel mumbled and I wondered if it was intentional. Instead of letting the silence fall, I spoke up.

"Will this be like last time? With the fainting and the slapping? I don't know if I'm in any shape for more physical comedy."

"It *was* pretty funny when you fell into a heap and then started stuttering in the voice of a little boy," Chloe teased. When I frowned her way, she let out a small chuckle. "I don't know what Merrin will do. I just know that once she gets us a location, we're gonna go in full bore."

"Tusks and all?"

"If that's your thing, sure."

"I just mean, what are we expecting? And how the hell are we supposed to be prepared for this? Is Evadne coming with us? Laurel and Hardy?"

"I think it's just the three of us. I'm sure we can get hold of some gadgets that will help."

"Gadgets? Like a remote-control pillow and an electric back massager? I don't think those will do us much good against magic."

"*Back* massager?" Mel asked, his voice low and throaty. Without hesitating, I reached between the seats, whacked him in the chest. He grunted out a laugh and leaned out of my personal space.

"Just trust me, okay? I'm confident we can handle this," Chloe insisted.

I tapped my foot impatiently. She had saved my life multiple times already and besides, Chloe was nothing if not competence personified. I considered the last few days and realized that the only times I'd been really hurt or in danger had been with Mel or while waiting for Mel. I nodded.

"I trust you."

Twenty

I *did* pass out, but there was no slapping involved and we left Merrin's armed with an address that Mel excitedly recognized.

"I know that place! It's a hotel."

"Why am I not surprised? Does that mean you've slept with all the desk agents and we should hide you lest they take a baseball bat to our windshield?" I asked.

Mel just talked over me. "I'll drive. We should be in and out in a few minutes."

"Merrin didn't have a room number," Chloe pointed out.

"And this address is downtown," I reminded him. "I doubt it'll be as small as the last place. I can't stand next to every room and see what I find through the doors; that'll take ages."

"I got it, don't worry." Mel opened the passenger side door for me, gesturing with a flourish. When I continued to stare in disbelief, he gestured again. "I *promise.*"

"Just get in," Chloe said, opening the back door and taking her own advice. I fought the urge to throw a little fit at Mel's lack of explanation but got in. Before long, we were on our way toward downtown Seattle, Mel humming along to some song on the radio that I didn't recognize. It reminded me of when we'd been driving to meet the Carlyles.

"Mel, do you remember what you were humming when I got all, you know." I flailed my hand, unsure how to describe it. "Melty."

"Ah." Mel made a thoughtful sound, took a second to think, and then nodded. "Yeah, I had Aqua stuck in my head, *Barbie Girl* specifically." I gaped at him, completely unable to decide if I was more flabbergasted that Mel liked such saccharine music or that my mood had been so warped that I'd not been able to recognize such a happy tune. "Why?"

"No reason," I said after a moment, deciding that, of all the things I'd learned about Mel that week, that was probably the least mortifying. Turning to Chloe, I looked her up and down. "You bring your guns?"

"Today, no. I don't really want them around the kids."

"But what if there's an ogre or a giant three-headed dog guarding them?"

"Then my tiny gun probably won't help."

"So what will? You're the expert all of a sudden. What do we do in the face of an angry, three-headed ogre?"

"We shove Mel at it and we run," Chloe suggested. Mel's whistle faltered for a beat. She grinned, jerking her thumb at the back of the car. "I got some stuff in the trunk that will help."

"What did Evadne charge you for it?"

"She didn't." Something about her inflection was odd, but she wasn't lying, so I just nodded.

"You think she will later?"

"I'm certain she won't."

Since my back was starting to hurt from the twisted position, I turned to face the front again. "I'm still going to maybe pray a little that there aren't any ogres in there."

Mel pushed ahead of us into the hotel, crossing the lobby quickly. When I attempted to match his speed, Chloe grabbed my wrist.

"Let him go. If he knows the women behind the desk, he'll probably have better luck charming them if you're not around. Actually, even if he doesn't know them."

"What's *that* mean?"

"You're not great with people." I frowned, but she pressed on before I could argue. "I know your empathy plays a factor, and I'm not saying you're just an asshole for no reason, but you've currently got chunks of a demon in your brain and you're stressed about saving these little kids. Let Mel do the schmoozing."

I grumbled but couldn't actually argue with the points she'd made. I'm good with my clients—with one arthritic exception—but out in the real world, it's a lot harder to be decent. Any simple, everyday activity that takes place outside my home can be like stepping into an emotional war zone. Just sitting at a traffic light that's too long can make me want to tear my hair out. Between the blood loss and the itching vampire bites, I was even crabbier than usual, and that was saying something.

Chloe and I stayed at the back of the lobby, watching Mel chat up the two women behind the desk. Even from where I was, I could feel how they were reacting to him and, to my surprise, it was all positive. Despite getting to know him over the past week, I wasn't sure I would ever get over my shock at seeing him be charming. He'd admitted to finding it funny that he can so easily ruin my day; why did these women not get the same treatment? Even with chunks of demon in my brain, I could feel their flattery and see the way they looked at him. It didn't seem right that the same man who made me feel like I was being swarmed by hornets could smooth-talk a counter full of desk agents.

Chloe and I watched him follow one of the women behind the desk and through a door into the back.

"You think he's paying for this information with a quickie in the copy room?"

Chloe chuckled but just shook her head. All in all, Mel was in the back for maybe fifteen minutes before he came to us armed with a bright yellow key card and a giddy smile.

"Apparently our ingenious kidnappers didn't think to make sure the place they brought the kids wouldn't have cameras. Lucy had checked Dirk in, so she knew who he was when we got to the part of the surveillance that showed them smuggling in the kids. She gave me a key to their room."

"Because you asked nicely?" I asked as Mel jerked his head toward the elevators and we all fell into step toward them.

"Because I'm a successful private detective with a trustworthy smile." Catching my look, he shrugged. "We have a history."

"Who *don't* you have a history with?"

"You," Mel pointed out.

"Oh, we have history. It's just vaguely reminiscent of one of the World Wars."

We made our way up to the tenth floor when it occurred to me how very strange and possibly illegal our actions were.

I elbowed Mel. "Hey, are the ladies downstairs gonna call the cops on Dirk and the demon?"

"No, I assured them I'd handle it."

"They were just cool with you taking on a possible kidnapper by yourself?"

"I didn't exactly tell them the whole truth, you know," Mel said. "I'm not an idiot." Noticing my disbelief, he scowled. "I'm not!"

We were quiet as we made our way down to the very end of the hall, but only because I was too scared to make fun of Mel within earshot of something that might want to eat me. As Mel stopped in front of the room, Chloe dug into the red backpack she'd pulled out of the trunk. She came out holding a rock.

"Is that to throw at the ogres?" I asked. Chloe smiled but didn't answer, holding the rock out and waving it in front of the door like a stud finder. Mel and I exchanged a look, though I wasn't sure his said the same thing as mine; he looked eager and intrigued.

"Nothing on the door," Chloe said, grabbing the key from Mel without asking. He let her and we both watched as she opened the door, pressed it back against the wall, and looked in. "Nothing set to jump out and eat our faces."

"We should send Mel in first, just to make sure."

Chloe ignored my comment, dropped the stone back into her bag, and stepped inside. I tried to control the worried tension singing through my muscles.

"I'm going to check it out, stay out here for a second," she said.

"Are you—"

"She's the one with the bag of goodies," Mel said, putting a hand on my arm. I didn't like it, but he had a point. I leaned as far toward the doorway as I dared without actually crossing the line of it and watched Chloe. The room was small, typical of every reasonably upscale hotel room I'd come across. Chloe walked it briskly, stopping at the end of the bed where the three children lay, asleep and still like the last time I'd seen them. My heart started pounding at the sight of them. They had no idea how close they were to being safe.

The memory of when I'd channeled Devon's panic wavered through my mind and I swallowed hard, tensing with the need to go to him, scoop him up, and rush him home. Chloe waved another item from her bag over the kids, but I couldn't see what it was with just the light from the doorway. When she turned to smile and beckon us in, I was the first over the threshold. Mel went straight to the kids, but I slid my hand along the wall until I found the switch and flipped it.

Immediately, all worry for the children disappeared from my mind and the only thing I could focus on was a fork on the dresser. It looked clean but out of place. Who would leave a fork just lying around? There was no plate to go along with it, no spoon or knife. It was just a metal fork alone in a hotel room with no kitchen, begging to be put away.

Naturally, in that moment I understood that the proper place to store a fork is in an electrical socket.

"What are you doing?" Chloe asked as I moved to the dresser, picked up the fork, and looked it over. Two of the four tines had been bent down, making it the perfect shape to fit where it belonged. "Gwen? Come help. Mel can't carry all three kids by himself, not in the puppy-weak state he's in."

I wasn't concerned with what she was saying or in Mel's bristly response. The kids were not a priority; putting away the fork was the priority. I knew just where it needed to go, too; there was an alcove above the sink at the back of the room, and while one of the outlets was taken up by a lighted mirror, the other was free and clear. It was the perfect height to just stride over and shove it in: no muss, no fuss.

"What are you doing?" Mel called from behind me. I couldn't see him anymore; I was too deep into the room. The closer I got to the light socket, the more content I felt. The very idea of shoving two of the tines into that shocked-looking plastic face made me almost weak in the knees. In that moment, I was in love with the idea. It was perfect in a way I could never be. Nothing could compare to the ecstasy I knew I would feel in just a few seconds.

"Would you put that—" Mel cut off, shock strangling his voice as I lifted my arm. The back of my jacket shot back, pulling the front with it, and I gagged as fabric cut off my air supply.

My feet left the floor but I barely had the self-awareness to reach back in an attempt to break my fall. My butt hit the carpet first, then my shoulders and my head. My left arm felt bruised, as it had briefly considered breaking my fall but not quite made it a reality. My right arm, however, still held the fork triumphantly in the air. Time passed as I tried to figure out what had happened, why I still held cutlery. Where had the outlet gone?

Was I lying on the floor? Unacceptable.

"Don't touch the fork," Chloe warned as Mel stepped into view. "It's got to be enchanted."

"What do I do?" he asked.

Hacking out a cough as my body realized what my brain didn't, I struggled around my heavy lungs and attempted to get back up. I had to work pretty hard to move my left arm properly. Finally, I made it to my feet, my breathing recovering as I started to feel steadier.

"We're gonna have to get her wet," Chloe said. There was a deliberate silence followed by, "Don't look at me like that. Running water. It helps."

Chloe put a hand on my back for all of a second before making a thoughtful sound. Realizing I could breathe normally, and therefore probably walk, I turned to face the socket again. Chloe took the fork out of my hand, moved ahead of me.

"What are you doing?" Mel asked. "I thought we couldn't touch—"

"I need that," I told her, a thread of panic coming loose in my belly. When she didn't turn around and give the fork back, I felt myself start to unravel. I shot my hand out, gripping her jacket as tightly as I could. "Excuse me!"

"Let go," Chloe said, trying to get free. I switched my grip to her wrist, reaching for the fork with my other hand. She stumbled slightly before turning to glare my way. "I said let go!" She started trying to pry my fingers off her arm.

"Are you *both* enchanted?" Mel demanded. "What the hell are you doing?"

"I need the fork!"

"It's *mine*," Chloe spat. She stopped trying to pry my fingers up and instead pressed against my wrist just right, shooting a line of pain up my arm. I let go without meaning to and she spun toward the outlet. "I've got this."

"Give it back!" The panic had spread to my limbs, lighting me up inside, making me desperate and shaky. Mel simply stepped between Chloe and the outlet, holding out his hand to stop her.

"What are you—Gwen!"

I threw myself bodily at Chloe. If I had to wrestle the fork out of her grip and stab her with it to keep her away, I would. She took my weight surprisingly well, barely stumbling before hunching and dumping me forward over her shoulder and onto the ground. I groaned at the impact, opened my eyes to find Mel staring down at me in shock.

"Chloe, what—"

"Get out of the way," she ordered. When she tried to get around him, he sidestepped, matching her. They danced around like that a few times, to the left, right, left again before she stopped, lifting her gaze to his. "Move."

"I won't. You're being—"

I got to my feet in time to see Chloe punch Mel in the stomach. When he doubled over, she pressed her hand into the back of his neck and shoved him to the floor. Without waiting to see if he was down for the count, she turned, held her arm out toward the outlet, and closed in.

Despite being slowed by whatever the demon had done to him, Mel got to his feet in a flash. Teeth bared in exasperation, he grabbed a bath towel from the bar mounted just inside the bathroom and tossed it over Chloe's head. I felt confusion scramble her brain as she went still, like a bird in a newly covered cage. I saw my chance to grab the fork, but before I could get to it, Mel repeated the maneuver with me. As the world went dark with terrycloth, I lost track of what I'd been doing.

There was… there was something I needed to get, right?

I felt Mel's hands on my waist, directing me to walk somewhere. It didn't take much maneuvering on his part, and the next thing I knew, the towel was gone from my head and a door was being closed in my face.

I took a step back to let my brain catch up to my situation. Phantom forks danced in front of my eyes and I rapped my knuckles on the door trying to grab one of them. When I tried to look down at my hands, I wondered why I was blind before figuring out Mel hadn't bothered to turn a light on when shuffling me into the bathroom. Realization dawned in an instant, though.

Chloe had my fork!

"Excuse me, please!" Fumbling, I searched for the doorknob. It took forever, but I found it, twisted it, pulled it. The door moved just enough to knock against my chest and I was briefly too ignorant to understand why I couldn't get out.

Pausing with the doorknob pressed against my belly, I wondered why Mel was so intent on keeping me from putting perfectly harmless utensils into perfectly harmless electrical sockets where they so clearly belonged.

It took me another eternity but I eventually understood that the door and my body could not occupy the same space. I stepped back, deliberately grabbed the knob once again, and tugged. Light followed the door into the tiny bathroom and I felt my eyes tear up as they adjusted. Once I could see, I turned to the left and my jaw dropped. Silver flashed in the light as Chloe tried to stab *my* fork into Mel's chest.

"That's not where it goes!" I insisted, offended that she had stolen my fork but didn't even know how to treat it properly. My feet carried me closer, seemingly independent of my mind as I took in the scene.

My cutlery nemesis was dangling off Mel's back, her forearm pressed against his throat. He was grunting, blocking her attacks as best he could. To my surprise, she jabbed him twice in the arm and didn't draw blood. When she got him in the neck, he let out a low, long growl and grabbed her wrist, fighting her as she used every bit of her strength to push the fork toward his face.

"I didn't want to do this," he warned, abruptly tipping forward. Chloe cried out as she flipped over his head, dropping onto her back on the floor. I watched the fork as she descended, seeing the perfect opportunity to get it back.

I scrabbled for the fork, leaning over her to grab for it, even as she let out a very human growl of her own and tried to hold it out of my reach. I pushed my hand against the side of her face but she let out a battle cry and knocked her thigh into the back of my knee to throw me off balance. A struggle ensued, Chloe dragging me down with her. We rolled along the carpet, kicking, biting, and slapping. Despite the fact that both of us were trying to get the fork and get away, all our shoving, clawing, and complaining couldn't separate us. She had the fork and wasn't willing to give it up, but I weigh more than she does and figured out pretty quickly how to use it to keep her down.

Luckily for me, she didn't try to stab me in the eye like she had Mel.

I'm not sure how long our tussle lasted, but it officially ended when Mel dumped an ice bucket full of water over us. My cry of, "I need it, please!" devolved into a sputtering coughing fit as Chloe paused with her free hand on my cheek, the fork held out at arm's length. Her wail of rage trailed off into a moan of confusion.

"Dammit," she said after a moment.

I did my best to wipe the water away from my face, flipped over to cough as much of it as I could manage out of my lungs. Chloe slapped my back and I looked over in time to see Mel gently lean down, slide the apparently disarmed fork carefully from her grip, and then stand up.

"You okay?" Chloe asked. I coughed again, silently cursed the water that had managed to make its way down into the cups of my bra, and nodded.

"I think so. What the hell happened?"

"That was almost fantasy material right there," Mel mused. "Too many clothes, of course."

Chloe got to her feet and reached down to pull me to my feet. Sure I was stable, Chloe turned to Mel and lifted her fist.

"I hit you once, I'll do it again."

Mel just laughed and tossed us each a towel.

Twenty-One

"If I never see another fork, it'll be too soon," I said once we were in the car and on our way back to Merrin's. I had Devon in my lap while Ashley and Felicity were strapped in the back seat next to me.

"How will you eat cake?" Chloe asked.

I scoffed. "With my hands. *Duh.*"

"Of course. I shouldn't have asked."

I was exhausted. The week had been the worst of my life. It even trumped the one that followed my cowardly decision to leave my ex-husband. I'd thought at the time that leaving the sweetest man on the planet would be the worst thing I ever experienced. Even considering that running away from my marriage had left me with ten years of bitterness and guilt, this was worse.

The kids were all asleep, still under whatever enchantment the demon had laid down. I could feel inconsistent emotions coming from them, so I knew their sleep wasn't genuine. Brushing my hand over Devon's hair, I looked up to Chloe.

"If Laurel and Hardy can't deal with the demon, what are we going to do with these little guys?"

"A specialist has been called in."

"That sounds ominous."

"It is," she said, though she shot me a small, encouraging smile. "I was promised he's the best, though—that once he's done with the demon, she won't cause trouble for anyone ever again."

"I was wrong; *that* sounds ominous."

Chloe chuckled. I fought off a yawn and spoke as she gave in to one as well. "Mel, how are you doing? You look distracted."

"I'm just thinking."

"About how Chloe stabbed you with a fork?"

Chloe threw me a look I didn't like. "Don't say that like you haven't

177

wanted to stab Mel yourself."

"Oh, don't get me wrong," I said, holding up a hand in defense. "I've never lacked for fantasies of jabbing Mel with something pointy, but it's one thing to fantasize and another entirely to actually try it."

Chloe hummed in agreement and looked to Mel. When he didn't speak, she poked his temple.

"What's going on in there?"

"Oh, nothing. I'm just fantasizing about jabbing Gwen with my—"

"Hey," I interrupted. "There are children present!"

Mel caught my eye in the rearview and smiled. Refusing to give in to the laugh in the back of my throat, I rubbed my hand over Devon's hair again and got back to PG topics. "So what's the verdict? Are you still weak as a kitten?"

"I'm a little sore where Chloe punched me and in all the places she stabbed me with a fork," he said after a moment. Chloe laughed. "And where she kicked me, but otherwise I'm fine."

"Fine like all better?" I asked.

"No, the specialist will need to work on him, too," Chloe said.

"Does the specialist have a name?"

Chloe was quiet for a moment. "That, you'll have to ask him."

She sure made it sound like a bad idea.

The atmosphere in Merrin's tiny apartment was uncomfortable, to say the least. Merrin was locked in her pantry with her cards again, evidently disinterested in meeting this specialist or seeing how everything ended. Laurel and Hardy were on demon duty, standing watch over the girl that had wreaked havoc on several lives during the last few weeks. She was bound and gagged on her back, motionless save for her head, which she kept lifted so she could watch the room.

Evadne was sitting on the couch, eying Laurel and Hardy with distaste, as if they were maggots she wished to squish under her stylish boots. Mel was keeping quiet, unwilling to risk Evadne's wrath in his state. I was tired, parked on the floor next to the children, wondering when the so-called expert would be arriving. The kids were still asleep, stretched out on the fluffy rug, a pillow tucked under each of their heads.

Chloe, however, looked completely relaxed, sitting in Merrin's desk chair, using her toe to spin it slightly left and right.

"Did he say he'd be so late?" Chloe asked Evadne. The fairy rolled her icy gaze to Chloe, watched her for a moment, and shook her head.

"He has not told me anything."

I jumped when someone knocked at the door.

"Better not be Girl Scouts," Chloe quipped, going to answer it. I turned to watch her, wondering why I felt nothing on the other side. In twenty-nine years, Hardy had been the only emotional void I'd ever come across. It didn't seem likely I'd come across a second so soon.

The man who stepped in looked human but most certainly wasn't. He looked tall, slim, and was dressed in a well-tailored charcoal suit. His skin was a soft brown, his hair black, his eyes the color of smooth, melted dark chocolate. Well-groomed and clean-shaven, he was casual as he entered the apartment, looking at everyone individually. He managed to make each quick look a heady connection, like we'd all made friends with him in an instant. Despite the fact that it had been raining outside, he was dry and carried no umbrella. His shoes looked as if they'd just been pulled from their box moments before.

"Evadne." He inclined his head slightly toward her, stopped just out of arm's reach of me. I suddenly felt very small sitting on the floor. Our visitor's eyes dropped to the children and the faintest trace of disappointment flickered over his face. "I see. And our problem child?"

Evadne simply looked to where the demon lay. When he turned to look at the girl, anger burst out of her, smacking against me like wet bread dough. I flinched, swiping at the slimy, thick feeling of it before my nerves caught up to the fact that nothing was really there. The man walked over slowly, lifted his hand lazily in the air, and flicked his fingers toward Laurel and Hardy twice.

"Off you go," he ordered calmly. Without waiting for them to obey, he dropped down into a crouch, meeting the demon's eyes. They scurried; Hardy even managed to make his retreat look small and terrified, despite his bulk. "I let you off your leash for one moment and this how you betray me."

The demon did her best to thrash but, like me just hours before—had it really only been hours?—she was paralyzed from the neck down. She did manage to smack her head on the wooden floor, but I'd bet that wasn't her intention. I wasn't entirely sure, since our visitor's emotions were so faint as to make me think I might be imagining them, but it seemed to me he found her rage funny. He watched her until she stopped struggling, saying nothing when she tried to speak through her gag.

When she stopped, however, he reached a hand out, grabbed her neck, and pushed to his feet in one smooth motion. It caused him no strain to lift her by her throat until she was on her feet.

"You've lost all the privileges I was so kind as to bestow upon you, Nysgrogh." He gave her name a very specific inflection and her eyes went wide.

I can't exactly say how I knew he was sucking the life out of her, but there was something there, under the obvious. Maybe it was the connection she'd created between us, or maybe it was just my lizard brain puzzling together what all my other faculties couldn't make sense of individually. Whatever it was, I *knew* what it meant.

Thanks to whatever the fairies had done to her, she couldn't really fight it. Because of the bruising grip the man had on her neck, she couldn't scream. When it was finished, when the last of the demon was gone and the girl's eyes closed, the man dropped her limp body to the floor.

I gasped at the heavy sound. I'd never been in the same room as a corpse before, let alone one that had been dropped like a bag of rotting oranges. I thought of Chloe's words earlier about the girl the demon had possessed. Supposedly she'd been lost long before, but that only made it worse. I stared at the ex-demon and wondered what would become of her. Did she have a family? People who missed her?

The man spun to face the rest of the room and flicked his gaze to Chloe. The question of what would happen to the dead girl died on my lips when he spoke.

"Who's next?"

"The kids," I said without thinking. My nerves couldn't outweigh the connection I still had to them. If their enchanted sleep was anything like the snotty nightmare I'd had over a tub of ice cream, I wanted it stopped as soon as possible. "They should get home soon."

The man was still, a faint smile on his full lips.

Chloe got to her feet. "The kids," she repeated.

"Very well." He moved forward, dropping to one knee in front of them. He was quick, merely placing a hand on each of their little foreheads for a beat before moving to the next. He stayed crouching as he finished, looking to me. I fought the urge to scoot away. "And you're the last."

"Am I that obvious?" I asked, trying for a casual laugh. It came out a squeak. He only smiled as he reached toward my jacket.

"Is this for me?" he asked. Puzzled, I looked down, flinching when he dipped his hand into my pocket to pull out a little pink square of paper. The candy thief had struck again.

"Just call me Pony Express," I sighed, gesturing for him to get on with it. The man smiled, read the paper over, and then lifted his gaze to mine.

"I take it you didn't know this was in there?"

"I've been a little busy lately."

"Would you like to read it?"

"Is it dirty?" I asked. He chuckled and twisted his elegant fingers in such a way that the note flipped in one move to face me.

It said simply, *You need shorter leashes, B.*

"Are you B?" I asked. He just watched me, his smile a wall between me and the answer. I tried for another. "Do you know who keeps leaving me these notes?"

Ignoring that question, too, he said, "I look forward to seeing you again." Then he pressed his fingertips to my forehead and I passed out.

I woke up on the couch in my office this time. It took me a bit to realize what was happening and my first instinct was to assume I'd just fallen asleep between appointments. When I heard Mel's voice in the waiting room, though, the week came flooding back to me and I propped myself up on my elbows. A second later, as the outer door opened and shut, Mel leaned tentatively through the doorway.

"Oh, you're awake."

"Where's Chloe? How'd we get here?"

Mel came in, dropped down in the chair across from me, and propped his ankle up on his knee. "She said she had some things to take care of and left me to make sure you got home safely. As to why we're here, Evadne kicked everyone out pretty fast after the suit finished up."

"The kids? They're safe?"

"As houses. Evadne took care of it."

"Can we trust her?"

"Normally I would say no, but this got out of hand. Generally speaking, upper fae don't care much about helping humans. As long as you're not a threat to them, they're not interested in you. This, however, went too far, got too close to their operation. They'll get the kids back to their families and set up some poor schmuck to take the fall."

"Just a random—" I realized I was still lying down and swung my legs around so I could sit up. The motion made me slightly dizzy but I pressed on. "They're going to just blame some random person?"

"They won't pick a priest out of a lineup and dump it on him, sweetheart. They'll probably pick someone who's pissed them off or made trouble for them. It won't be an innocent, don't worry."

I didn't feel any better about a frame job, but at least I could be sure the kids were getting home safe. That was the important part. I scrubbed my hands over my face. I wasn't sure of the last time I'd taken a shower, couldn't even remember what I'd eaten last. I gazed out the windows behind my desk before looking at Mel again.

"You look better."

"Than?"

"You did before." I grinned. "Chloe hit you pretty hard, and after getting kicked in the head by the demon, you looked a little green."

"I got my full power back." Mel grinned, waggling his brows as he leaned forward. "Who do you think carried you up here?"

I winced, not thrilled with the idea of Mel's hands on my unconscious body. To my surprise, though, I found I actually trusted him not to have gone too far. He hadn't taken advantage of me when I'd been drunk and that had been the least of the good-guy things he'd shown me he was capable of. If I could've super-glued the necklace to his chest for eternity, we might've been able to be friends.

"Chloe say how long her thing will take?" I asked after an awkward silence.

"She didn't. But I'm sure there's time for a quickie on the couch."

I wrinkled my nose in disgust. "You've been halfway decent this week but the answer will always be no. And, at this point, not only capital-N No, but also Ugh and Gross."

Mel only laughed, shaking his head in mock disbelief. I took a deep breath, got to my feet, and dragged my sore body toward the records room. I wasn't sure I felt well enough to eat solid food—for once in my life, I wasn't craving straight sugar—but tea sounded like a pretty good idea.

I was halfway there when the sudden appearance of Laurel and Hardy shocked me into a yelp and a stumble. Hardy remained a blank slate, his expression betraying no opinion on my embarrassing outburst. Laurel, however, was immediately irritated with me, squinting and turning his head as if he couldn't bear to look directly at me. Hand to my heart, I sighed out a breath, then turned to fully face them.

"What are you two doing here? I thought we were done with you."

"We have come to give thanks for your assistance." Hardy came over slowly, his head bowed slightly in respect. Laurel stayed back by the door, stiff and disapproving. I decided to ignore him, at least as well as I could with the cacophony of his emotions pounding at me. Mel stepped out into the waiting room, looked the two fairies over with the barest hint of interest. His presence seemed to outrage Laurel even more and I sighed, pointing at him.

"Hey, Skinny. You're kind of a pain in the ass to be near, you know that?"

He balked, gaping at me, horrified by my words. Hardy turned to him before he could speak, though, and whatever look they shared shut him up. When Hardy turned back to me, he bowed his head deeply.

"Our apologies, Gavel." His tone made the word seem like a formal title, though I had no idea why.

"Gav—"

Mel cut me off immediately, clearing his throat sharply. I flicked my gaze to him, but he wasn't watching me. In fact, he looked bored by the whole situation, his eyes roaming along the ceiling. Hardy continued as if I hadn't spoken.

"Please accept this payment. Your help exceeded our best expectations and we are humbled to be in your presence."

I blinked, flinching slightly when Hardy swung his arm around, held up his hand, and uncurled his massive fingers to reveal a tiny blue box in the center of his palm. I glanced to Mel for guidance and he nodded slightly. I took the box. It weighed nothing and didn't look all that dangerous with the little dark blue bow tied around it.

It made me nervous.

"Thank you," I said, scared of moving in case the box decided to open up and release a noxious gas or explode outward into a deadly shower of nails. "And this is—" Before I could finish my question, Mel cleared his throat again, catching my eye and twitching his brows over wide eyes in a way that clearly asked, "Are you nuts?" I shut up about the box.

When Hardy didn't move or say anything further, I squinted at him, at a loss for how to proceed. Since the payment was apparently a topic that was off limits, I moved on to another.

"You said my mistress sent you?"

Hardy's shoulders tensed slightly and Laurel sucked in a quick breath. I glanced at him, but he looked just as unpleasant as ever and I knew he wasn't going to be of any help.

"We still have not had the pleasure of speaking to her. We understand we are not worthy. Please tell her we meant no disrespect in asking for your help in such a trivial matter. If she should choose to punish us for wasting your time, she need only summon us."

"Hunh." I considered the fear in Hardy's voice and decided I was more than happy I wasn't who they thought I was. This mistress broad sounded like kind of an asshole. Before I could ask any more questions, Mel shifted, drawing my attention. He made an unsubtle gesture to indicate I should get rid of the fairies and I rolled my eyes. I don't know if Hardy saw Mel or just decided he was done with me, but he spoke, still bowing low.

"May we take our leave?"

Without hesitation, I nodded. "Please."

They were gone in an instant, leaving me standing as still as I could manage, staring at the box in my hand. Cautiously, I set it on the table.

"What do you think it is?"

"Payment," Mel said simply.

"Cash?"

"Doubtful," he replied. We both took a step back, still staring at the box. After a moment, I let out a nervous laugh.

"You think I should... I mean, will I be okay if I open it?"

"I have no idea. I don't have much experience with this. For all I know, their usual form of payment is a pet tarantula that likes the taste of empaths."

"Shut up," I said, glaring over at him. Mel was smiling but his gaze was on the box. Turning back to it myself, I let out a grunt of unhappiness. "I'd like to get out of here."

"Back to my place, then?" Mel asked.

I pretended he hadn't spoken. "Is Chloe coming back to meet us?" I didn't want to just leave the potentially deadly blue box for her to stumble on later.

"No, she said she'd probably be out for awhile, not to wait up."

"What the hell is she doing?"

"She wouldn't tell me."

"Well. All right. You can take me home, then." I pointed at him threateningly when he aimed twin finger-guns my way. "Where I will spend the night alone, without you. It's already going to take me ages to get the smell of your cheap cologne out of my guest sheets."

Mel paused on the way to the office door, turning to scoff at me. "My cologne is anything but cheap."

"Well, then you overpaid because it makes you smell like an old lady." I flipped the lights off, waited until he'd shut the door, and then leaned in to lock up. When I turned to Mel, he didn't look happy with me. Of course, I couldn't help but smile.

"Before your place, though, I'm supposed to show you something," he said as we approached the elevators.

"If you're planning on taking your pants off, I'll run screaming for the nearest cab."

Mel sniffed, looking offended. "With your attitude, I wouldn't show you that, anyway."

"Then I'm doing something better than every other woman in Seattle."

Twenty-Two

I was able to keep quiet for maybe five minutes before my curiosity reared its ugly head.

"Hey, so you said you don't have experience with this. How does that work?"

"Oh, I have plenty of experience with driving. I'm quite good at it, actually."

"Don't be a dick."

"What's that about my dick?"

"Probably syphilis. Answer the question."

Mel snorted, but didn't force me to keep up the banter. "I'm a werewolf, but that doesn't mean I spend time with fairies. We're close relatives of theirs—descendants, technically—and better regarded than humans like you, but still not terribly popular. As a general rule, we're ignored. I've come across the more powerful fairies here and there, even enjoyed the intimate company of a few, but mostly I prefer to pretend they don't exist."

"Because they give out boxes filled with empath-eating spiders?"

"Because they're a pain in the ass. And honestly, because I don't actually *have* to deal with them. With a few exceptions like Evadne, they don't live here, really."

"In Seattle."

"On this… planet." He paused to think. "I guess. I just know they can travel between here and their realm, but they usually don't bother."

"And their world is, what? Narnia?"

"You'd call it Fairy. It's not a really original name, but it's not the official name, either. Only they can even pronounce the actual name. I saw someone try once and it literally tied his tongue into knots." Instead of letting me stew on that unpleasant image, Mel gestured vaguely and continued. "If they can pass as human, some fairies or creatures of Fairy will hang around our realm, but generally they think people like you and werewolves like me aren't worth talking to."

"Well, joke's on them because I'm a delight."

Mel shot me a look I couldn't quite decipher but didn't like. I stuck my tongue out at him and continued with the interrogation.

"If you don't deal with them, how'd you know how to handle them back there?"

"Handle them?"

"Well, like, I was gonna ask about the blue box but your eyebrows told me to plead the Fifth."

"My eyebrows did what?" His tone threw me and could have meant confusion over my phrasing or self-consciousness over his brows.

I shook my head. "You did a wiggle thing with your face and I figured it meant I should shut up."

"It wouldn't be the first time you should have shut up," Mel said, and I couldn't argue. I do tend to run my mouth more often than is smart, but it had never bothered Mel before. In fact, half the reason I disliked him is that he'd occasionally make suggestions about what I could be doing with my mouth other than talking. "But the long and short of it is that it's never a good idea to appear ignorant in front of something that much more powerful than you are."

"Well, then, thanks for the wiggle."

"I'll give you a—"

"No."

Mel laughed at my instant refusal but didn't try again to seduce me. He was quiet for awhile as I went over the information he'd given me, wondering why, if I wasn't worth talking to, a pair of fairy scouts had shown up in my office thinking I worked for someone way above their pay grade. Come to think of it, why had Evadne been willing to help Chloe when she wouldn't help me?

"Hey!" I exclaimed as another realization shot like lightning through my mind. "You weren't freaked out by Chloe at all!"

"Should I be?" Mel asked, turning to lift a brow at me and check his blind spot before switching lanes.

"I mean, she had that funky stud-finder rock and she told you to get me wet, and then there was the phone call to Evadne, and she was pretty ballsy with the suit and you seem cool with it all."

Mel was quiet for a moment, making me think he might actually be considering my question. Instead, he smiled, his eyes still on the road. "Chloe told me to get you wet?"

"Oh jeez," I grumbled, crossing my arms petulantly over my chest. Then, reconsidering, I shot my hand out and whacked his elbow. Mel laughed, ignoring the assault. We drove in silence for another minute while I stared out the side window and tried not to give Mel any more openings.

When I realized the double entendre in even that, I hit him again.

Mel snorted and I wondered if he'd been reading my mind, or if he just found it funny any time I got mad at him, whether he knew the reason or not.

Before I could settle on an answer, we pulled up in front of a Craftsman-style home in Queen Anne. The yard was free of foliage, sporting a no-maintenance rock garden instead. The windows looked odd but I couldn't place why until we got closer: they had been boarded up inside with dark wood. There was no car in the driveway and the door sat back on a small porch.

"Did Chloe buy me a house?" I asked as Mel turned off the ignition.

"On the meager salary you pay her? Please."

"How do you know what I pay Chloe?"

Mel shrugged, turning to climb out of the car instead of answering. I grunted in annoyance and followed him out, hustling to catch up when he strode straight up the walk. I was halfway to the small porch when I slowed, trying to figure out what I was feeling.

"What is this?" I asked, stopping as my empathy registered a soft tingling along my skin. Even my arms started to prickle with goosebumps, despite my warm jacket. "What are you showing me?"

"Why?"

"What's here?" I demanded, spinning to face the streak of light that swished through my peripheral vision.

"Relax, you're safe. You probably just feel the sprites." Mel grabbed my wrist and yanked me toward the door. "They're harmless. Nature fairies."

"You swear? I've been attacked enough for one week. If I get smacked around again, I'm blaming you."

"Come on." Mel pulled me up onto the porch, parked me next to him, and then reached out to knock on the door. His knuckles made a sound like they'd hit solid steel and I raised my eyebrows. We stood in silence for over a minute but Mel didn't look bothered. I jolted when a voice finally rasped out of a nearby speaker.

"Come to gloat?"

"Let us in," Mel ordered. The voice didn't respond immediately and I wondered if Mel had dragged me to some secret underground gambling club. Was I about to enter a smoke-filled room where men sucked on cigars and women sashayed around in breast-boosting corsets, breakneck heels, and kitty ears?

"The fish flies at midnight," I mumbled, leaning close to the door as if it and I were in cahoots. Mel turned to me, his brows knit. "That not the password?"

He didn't answer, just turned forward as the heavy sound of a lock unlatching boomed. The door slid open slowly, as if auditioning for an old horror movie.

The inside of the house was blindingly bright. I squinted and let Mel go first, using his broad body to partially shield myself from what might have been halogen lights. Once inside, Mel stepped wide from the door and I did the same. The steel beast closed on its own, just as slothfully as it had opened.

My expectations about what the inside would look like could not have been further from reality. The house had been gutted, turning what once might have been a kitchen, living room, and dining room into one massive space. Other than support beams and the staircase, there was nothing but open, dark wood floors and plain white walls occasionally interrupted by the dark wood covering the windows. The upstairs was as bright as the downstairs and looked to be just as empty.

To the right was the only actual room I could see from my vantage point, left vulnerable through a doorway lacking a door. What once might have been the living room to my left held a metal bench and two metal folding chairs. At the back, from what I could see behind the staircase, sat an industrial kitchen dominated by a massive, shiny refrigerator making a low humming sound. I stepped further in, peering through the open doorway into what might have been a bedroom.

Not a single prancing waitress or fat mobster. What a disappointment.

A man stepped out from behind the staircase, moving toward us at a glacier's pace. He was above average height and probably would have been attractive had he not been so close to death. He was completely hairless, with sunken eyes and thin lips. He kind of reminded me of Mr. Burns but without the beak-like nose. In fact, he actually looked *less* healthy than his cartoon counterpart. He stared at me with intense brown eyes, scanning me slowly from head to foot. When his gaze got to my shoes, his eyes went a shade crazier and he pulled a travel-sized bottle out of the pocket of his green scrubs pants and tossed it to me. It was hand sanitizer.

"The least you can do is clean yourself," he rasped. I fumbled with the tiny bottle, squirting some into my hands. Tucking the bottle under my arm as I rubbed the alcoholic mixture into my skin, I glanced at Mel. He was hanging back, as close to the door as he could get, silent as a dead hooker. There was a small smile on his face and I had yet to figure out why.

Giving up on getting answers from him, I turned and held the bottle of sanitizer out toward the other man. He shied away, pointing spastically behind me. I found that I had failed to notice a metal trash bin tucked just to the right of the front door, full of barely used bottles just like the one in my hands. I rolled my gaze toward our host cynically and then dropped the bottle in with the others. He must have spent a fortune on the stuff and I wondered why he let anyone in at all.

"Why are you here?" he demanded. "What do you want?"

I shook my head, jerking a ninety-nine percent germ-free thumb at Mel. "This one dragged me here. I didn't even know where we were going."

"Liar." As the man whispered his denial at me, I found myself looking around the room again. He stood toward the middle of the cavernous bottom floor, glaring at me like I had invited a toddler into his china shop. Finally, I turned back to Mel.

"Would you please tell me what we're doing here? Why you brought me here to see this ..." I glanced back to the man, trying to figure out what he was. I could feel from the slow, syrupy glide of his emotions that he wasn't human, but that was as far as I could get. "Person."

"Look at him," Mel said. The other man breathed out, the sound a dry, angry wheeze. I really didn't want to do as Mel said, but I figured he probably wouldn't drive me home if I refused. Turning back, I did my best to really look at him, ignoring the fact that his emotions felt kind of like being felt up by Slimer in a dingy janitor's closet. I met his eyes and felt myself go still. Something in them was familiar, slithering down my throat and grabbing hold of my heart with a mouth full of sharp fangs. I took a step back, my eyes gone wide.

"You," I whispered. I was too distracted by the feel of his emotions to realize that he was advancing on me, that my step back had somehow resulted in him taking three steps forward. Whatever he was feeling oozed over my skin like a snail trying as viciously as it is able to mate with a rock; I couldn't name it but when it filled my chest, I felt sick with worry. I found that I was shaking my head, my eyes drawn to the fangs I hadn't previously noticed peeking out from under his lip.

"Dirk," Mel said, his voice a low warning. Dirk's gaze left me and moved to Mel. They squared off for a moment before Dirk peeled back his lips to reveal pale gums and gleaming fangs. I yelped, wasting no time in darting around behind Mel and using him to shield me.

"Get out," Dirk growled, his skeletal hands curled into claws.

I tugged on Mel's shirt. "Let's. Please."

"We'll go," Mel said, moving forward. I tried to hold him back, irrationally scared for his safety, but I might as well have been a leaf snagged on his sweater. He dragged me forward a step. "But if I hear you're cavorting with any more demons, I'll be back. And don't bother calling me for blood anymore."

Dirk hissed, turning as fast as his spent body would allow and moving back toward the staircase. His pace was slow, but he took the time to throw us three fang-filled growls as he went. Now, however, I found them as threatening as a sleeping puppy.

Mel looped his arm over my head and around the back of my shoulders, moving toward the door. It opened as slowly as it had before and Mel ducked us through as soon as the opening was big enough. We were at the end of the walkway when I stopped, moving away.

"What the hell?"

"Chloe suggested it."

"Harassing the angry vampire?"

"He can't really hurt you. That was the point."

I blinked at him, shaking my head. "What?" I demanded.

"She thought you might want to know that, without a demon in his pocket, he's harmless as a mosquito."

"Mosquitoes spread disease, kill entire villages!"

"You know what I mean."

"And what if he *does* hook up with another one? What if he decides to come after me for taunting him?"

"That's what the sprites are for." Mel moved toward the car, used his fob to unlock it, and opened the passenger door. "They're under orders to watch him, to make sure he doesn't gain any power he shouldn't have until it's his time."

"... his time? What does that mean? And what if he decides to come after me then?"

"Well, you'll be long dead by then, but we can tell your children to watch out. Or your great-grandchildren's kids, if I understand the whole thing right." Mel paused as I convulsed, swiping at the air when another sprite lit up my peripheral vision. "Get in, Grandma. I'll take you home."

A sprite came at me from my other side, making me yip. I could see them when I wasn't paying attention, but looking directly at them was impossible; they were nothing but a phantom glow at the edge of my vision. Lacking a better option, I darted forward and climbed into the car.

Once home, the first thing I did was check the locks on all the windows and doors. Then I showered, put on my most comfortable clothes, and checked all the locks again. Sonny perched on my shoulder working at a hunk of broccoli as I eyed the poetry-covered door of the fridge and wondered two things: what did I want to eat, and what the hell was I supposed to do about this prophetic candy thief?

He'd been pretty helpful, all things considered. But that didn't change the fact that I couldn't keep him out of my home, office, or Twinkies.

Sonny and I went into my office, where I dug around in my desk trying to find my pack of sticky notes. I found an old box of cheese crackers, a pair of socks, a half-eaten candy bar (only half-eaten? Had I taken a blow to the head I wasn't aware of?), and finally some purple sticky notes. Setting Sonny on his perch, I hunkered over the note as I finished off the candy bar, trying to decide what I wanted to say to the thief and if it should include a thank you or two for the help he'd given me.

"No," I told Sonny after a few moments. "That bastard's eaten enough of my sugar to thank him for a hundred helpful notes to hot-ass men in suits." Tapping the pencil on the desk twice, I sighed out an oath and scribbled the only thing that was really important.

Dear Candy Thief,
Are you sticking around? Do I need to start buying twice as many Twinkies?
—Gwen

Sonny and I headed back into the kitchen, where I stuck the note to the fridge and pulled out some of the food Chloe had made me. It was vegetables, but she'd saved my life; it seemed rude to let her food go to waste.

The next morning I headed into work early. I had missed too many appointments to count recently and I had a lot to catch up on. I was planning on calling each of my clients personally and offering them make-up appointments to help assuage my guilt. I was even willing to come in early or stay late where necessary. If Loraine wanted to see me four days this week, I would armor my empathy against her depression and give her all the tissue in the office. Chloe insisted that no one had been outraged when she'd canceled or rescheduled, but I still felt bad.

As I flipped on the kettle and stepped out of the records room, I realized that I'd never actually dealt with the payment that had been given to me by Laurel and Hardy. I eyed it suspiciously, wondering if Chloe, with her sudden wealth of preternatural knowledge, would know what it was or what I should do with it.

Deciding I was a little too nervous to risk opening the box and having my face eaten off—which would not have surprised me, considering recent events—I picked it up gingerly, carried it to my office, and locked it in my file cabinet. I stared down at the wooden drawer for what could probably be considered an unnecessarily paranoid amount of time before I let my breath out and decided I was safe.

I turned my computer on, leaned back, and waited for it to power up. My gaze fell on a pink sticky note on the side of my pen cup. I grabbed the square and read it over without hesitation.

You should definitely buy twice as many Twinkies! And you should memorize the fridge. I won't be around all the time, but the fridge has everything you need to know.

"The entire fridge?" I demanded, thinking of the hundreds of messages that had been left. Rolling my eyes, I mumbled, "Fat chance."

Crumpling up the paper, I went to toss it in my trashcan. Just as, I'm sure, the candy thief had meant it to happen, I noticed another message stuck to the side of the bin. I grabbed it, sighing at the note that said, *Don't roll your eyes. You'd be dead several times over if it weren't for me.*

I crumpled that paper up, too, tossed it in the can, and turned back to find that I hadn't previously noticed my top middle drawer was cracked open. There was a note there, too, and I had to pull the drawer open to read it. The entire thing had been filled with unwrapped Skittles, Tootsie Rolls, and a few wafer cookies. The scribbles on the note above said, *A bribe, then. Trust me on this. I can't be around all the time and you're going to need those insights.*

"Well, that's not ominous at all," I said with a gulp, glancing at the locked file cabinet in case the blue box got any ideas. When nothing happened, I turned to consider how dusty my drawer had been before buckets of loose sweets had taken up residence. Deciding I didn't care, I reached in and stuffed a handful of my free bounty into my mouth. I was on my third handful when the outer door opened and Chloe called my name.

"In here!" I said, barely audibly.

I got two more mouthfuls down before Chloe stepped in, noticed I was eating candy at seven in the morning, and sighed.

"Is that chocolate?"

"No," I said around a hunk of the same. Chloe rolled her eyes and I wished I hadn't crumpled the candy thief's second note. She made her way around my desk, her eyes going wide when she saw my haul.

"What's all this?"

Instead of answering, I handed her the third note with one hand and reached in to grab more candy with the other. Chloe slapped my reaching hand before she took the note, reading it over with a slight crinkle in her brow.

"The candy thief left you ... candy?"

"A bribe. He's good." When I reached for it again, she knocked my hands away and shut the drawer with her knee, leaning against the desk so I'd have to bump her leg to get at it again. I frowned down at the drawer, willing the candy to teleport to my tongue.

"So you have a guardian angel now?" Chloe asked. I shrugged, finished chewing, and swallowed the last of the candy before speaking.

"Maybe. I guess. I tried asking it why it kept bothering me and it gave me some nonsense about keeping me alive."

Chloe's eyes went wide. "You don't seem concerned."

"You didn't, either, remember? You wanted to feed it peanuts. Which, if it wanted peanuts instead of Twinkies, I'd be thrilled."

"Well—" Before she could get any further, I spun my chair slightly to face her, pointing up into her face.

"Speaking of being concerned, what the *hell*, Chloe? A few days ago you were squeaking in terror when Laurel and Hardy showed up and then you're pulling a gun on a demon and going Van Helsing on a vampire.

What happened?"

Discomfort rumbled like a storm, but her expression remained mild. After a few seconds, she shrugged, her gaze focused on the floor as if she'd spotted something worth considering. She reached to grab it before I could see what it was and tossed it in the trash. When she leaned back against the desk again, I couldn't help but notice she wasn't blocking me from my drawer full of candy anymore. I decided to play it cool, but I was itching to get back at the mixture. The thief really knew his candy pairings. If there was such a thing as a sugar sommelier, I was betting the thief was the best in the world.

"I grew up in Bremerton," Chloe said after a few seconds, as if that explained it all. I frowned when she didn't elaborate.

"And?"

"You know." She waved her hand and I shook my head.

"I never know anything. I can't even answer questions on *Celebrity Jeopardy*. Who do you think you're talking to here?" Despite the fact that I was convinced Chloe would stop me, I yanked open the drawer and reached in. Chloe blew out a breath, her eyes roaming to the window for a second before she shrugged and made a noncommittal sound.

"It's weird up there. Portland's got nothing on us. If you know where to look, that is. I went to school with several kids like you, actually."

"Empaths?" I managed. Chloe frowned at my garbled speech, plucked a tissue from the mini-box on my desk, and dabbed at my chin.

"You're drooling."

"Of course I am," I managed before swallowing. "This is delicious. I repeat: empaths?"

"Only in one case. There were two girls and one guy. Your kind seem to be mostly ladies, from what I've seen. Now, Daniel could sort of see sounds, even when they were well outside his hearing range. It was like synaesthesia." I opened my mouth to ask. "Google it," she said before continuing. I shut my mouth. "But it was more than that. We used to play this game where he'd write down three phrases in Morse code and we'd go to our classrooms and tap one of the phrases out. Even though we were all several classrooms away from him and we were just knocking gently, he could always pick it up."

"And then one day you needed to shoot him?"

"What? No!" Chloe shook her head, laughing fitfully as if she hadn't expected my comment to be funny. "I just knew from when I was a kid that there were other... things out there. It wasn't just them, either. I went to school with a werewolf and a troll, too. Half-troll, so she looked mostly normal, but still."

"A troll?" I demanded, my jaw dropping open. "Trolls exist?"

"Pretty sure all sorts of things exist."

"But—"

"Once I saw you were in danger," she interrupted just forcefully enough to shut me up, "I had to jump in. I had a gun, I used it. You know me." She waved her hand like it was no big deal. "When things go to shit, I really shine. I go into ass-kicking mode. How many insurance companies have tried to stiff you on a technicality?"

"But—" I tried again. Chloe pressed on.

"What are you expecting me to say, Gwen? That I'm covertly with the Secret Service and working for you is only a cover? You see me nearly every day. Have I ever touched my ear and said, 'The Eagle has landed' in a shifty whisper?" Chloe grinned, reaching down to shut the drawer before wagging her brows. "Enough of this, now; my childhood is boring. Let's talk something interesting, like how you're dating Mel."

"Ugh!" I spat, snarling at the very idea. Chloe dissolved into a fit of giggles.

"You two went on a date! You spent the night at his house! That's dating, my friend."

"We didn't date! It *wasn't a date!* We had some wine and we each made a pizza. His was better than mine, so I took it. You don't take someone's pizza if you're dating them."

"So you're saying he ate your pie?"

I scowled up at her, yanked the candy drawer out petulantly, and shoved at her with my other hand. "Get out. I have candy to eat. You have insurance companies to yell at."

"Well, call me if you need dating advice."

"I'll call you if I start to consider dating Mel so you can shoot me."

"Think of all the homemade pizza you could eat!" Chloe said, hopping to her feet. I swung out toward her like I'd hit her, but she dodged easily, giggling as she skirted the desk. "You have a nine-fifteen to start, but I'll let you know if I have to go save the president and can't stay that long."

"Get out!" I repeated, grabbing for more candy. Chloe winked and danced out the door, pulling it almost closed. I snarled after her, deciding that if she was dumb enough to think I could be into Mel, she was much too stupid to be hiding some big, secret life from me.

As I munched irately on my tangy, chocolaty, wafery bundle of deliciousness, I considered the last week, wherein I'd been hired by fairies, bewitched by a demon, nearly seduced by a werewolf, kidnapped by a vampire, and rescued by my gun-toting best friend. All things considered, sharing pizza and wine with Mel hadn't been the worst thing to happen, but I wasn't going to tell Chloe that.

About the Author

Olivia is a vegan thirty-something living in New Mexico with a clowder of cats and a stink of litter boxes. She enjoys vexing her kitties, cooking, watching action movies, and making up collective nouns for things that don't already have them (like a "stink of litter boxes"). You can find her and all information about her different series at OliviaRBurton.com.

OLIVIA R. BURTON

Gwen Arthur Novels

Visit OliviaRBurton.com for more information

www.ingramcontent.com/pod-product-compliance
Lightning Source LLC
Chambersburg PA
CBHW072104170626
46813CB00004B/1455